"Shall we remove your coat, my lord?"

Marcus shrugged out of his jacket and put the mud-crusted garment on the back of his chair, then extended his hand to Mrs. Prescott.

Lathering his hand, Alison was amazed at how strong it seemed. "Perhaps you might tell Miss Reed you know she was not responsible for the pigs getting out."

"Will you not allow me to enjoy a few moments' peace before I continue my role as guardian to such a calamity?"

Rinsing the soap from his hand, Alison then pulled clean linen strips from a box. The earl rose after Alison had wrapped his wound. She found herself looking into a pair of blue eyes which seemed to pull her ever closer to the man. His voice barely above a whisper, the earl said, "Mrs. Prescott, I do not know where to begin to thank you for all your kindness to me and Miss Reed."

"It has been a pleasure, sir." Alison spoke the words, but she could only think of how handsome he looked.

Marcus's hand came up and tilted Alison's chin just a bit higher. His mouth closed over hers and he was met with a willingness that made him forget every other consideration and draw her into the circle of his arms. Her answering response grew as did his own.

He knew he loved her and wanted to possess her . . .

from a WINTER COURTSHIP by Lynn Collum

ROMANCE FROM JANELLE TAYLOR

ANYTHING FOR LOVE	(0-8217-4992-7, $5.99)
DESTINY MINE	(0-8217-5185-9, $5.99)
CHASE THE WIND	(0-8217-4740-1, $5.99)
MIDNIGHT SECRETS	(0-8217-5280-4, $5.99)
MOONBEAMS AND MAGIC	(0-8217-0184-4, $5.99)
SWEET SAVAGE HEART	(0-8217-5276-6, $5.99)

Available wherever paperbacks are sold, or order direct from the Publisher. Send cover price plus 50¢ per copy for mailing and handling to Penguin USA, P.O. Box 999, c/o Dept. 17109, Bergenfield, NJ 07621. Residents of New York and Tennessee must include sales tax. DO NOT SEND CASH.

A WINTER KISS

Lynn Collum
Jo Ann Ferguson
Isobel Linton

Zebra Books
Kensington Publishing Corp.
http://www.zebrabooks.com

ZEBRA BOOKS are published by

Kensington Publishing Corp.
850 Third Avenue
New York, NY 10022

Copyright © 1996 by Kensington Publishing Corp.

"A Winter Courtship" copyright 1996 by Jerry Lynn Smith
"The Winter Heart" copyright 1996 by Jo Ann Ferguson
"The Winter Wager" copyright 1996 by Isobel Linton

All rights reserved. No part of this book may be reproduced in any form or by any means without the prior written consent of the Publisher, excepting brief quotes used in reviews.

If you purchased this book without a cover, you should be aware that this book is stolen property. It was reported as "unsold and destroyed" to the Publisher and neither the Author nor the Publisher has received any payment for this "stripped book."

Zebra and the Z logo Reg. U.S. Pat. & TM Off.

First Printing: November, 1996
10 9 8 7 6 5 4 3 2 1

Printed in the United States of America

CONTENTS

A WINTER COURTSHIP   7
by Lynn Collum

THE WINTER HEART   111
by Jo Ann Ferguson

THE WINTER WAGER   221
by Isobel Linton

A Winter Courtship

Lynn Collum

One

The chiming of the ormolu clock on the mantelpiece broke the silence in the elegant drawing room in Berkeley Square. Two fashionably clad gentlemen sat across a satinwood game table from each other, a study in opposites. The ten years which separated them, while evident to the eye of the observer, was not an obstacle to the friendship which had begun some six months earlier on the road from Dover.

Marcus Grey, the fifth Earl of Crandall, lifted his well-shaped hand over the marble and alabaster chessboard, pausing to ponder his strategy. His raven-black hair shone in the candlelight and dark blue eyes looked out from a handsome but weathered face. A superbly cut coat of black kerseymere framed his neat cravat which was a modest creation, unencumbered with jewelry. Twelve years of military service had taught him to stay with essentials.

Selecting a white knight, he moved the piece, then slumped back into the gold damask chair. "Check."

The younger gentleman, Sir Norton Stickley, leaned forward to survey the board. By contrast, he was the model of the Town Beau, with his russet coat and white waistcoat. Nestled into the folds of his intricately tied cravat, which even Beau Brummel had declared tolerable, was an amber stone. Cream-colored pantaloons and white silk hose with black pumps sporting large gold buckles completed his costume.

Frowning at what he saw, the baronet ran his fingers through his reddish-blond curls, mussing the artful disarray further. With a sigh, he tumbled his king to the board as a sign of his capitulation, then grumbled, "Damme, Marcus, I don't know why I allow you to talk me into playing chess. The boredom of winter in Town must be affecting my brain."

"After years of spending cold nights at the edge of a cook fire, I cannot complain of a quiet evening beside my own hearth." Lord Crandall gazed into the burning coals.

"That is because you have not sampled the joys of a Season in full. All the hostesses will be clamoring for you as the newest titled bachelor this spring, not to mention being a war hero. The time will come when you hate these long evenings with no amusements to attend." Stickley paused and stared at the door as noise in the front hall interrupted his discourse.

Lord Crandall tilted his head to listen to the arguing voices rising from below. Then he stood and asked, "Shall we see who has arrived to enliven our evening?"

Opening the door to the drawing room, the two men went to the landing and peered down. In the front hallway stood Banks, the butler, arms akimbo as he berated two footmen on their knees collecting a vast number of coins which were scattered on the marble floor.

Seated in a gilt chair was a female in a garish crimson pelisse with massive pink bows down the front. A matching bonnet with two large pink plumes bobbed each time the lady bowed her head to dab her eyes with a lace hand-

A WINTER COURTSHIP 11

kerchief. Her face was obscured by the hat's wide brim, leaving her identity a mystery.

"Hurry up and collect this female's blunt. Like I said, his lordship don't allow no doxies—"

The woman drew back her arm and smacked the butler with her reticule, which seemed to be empty due to a large tear in the bottom. "Don't call me that! I am a respectable female, you horrid man. I tell you I am an old friend."

"Madam, you can't show up here alone as bold as brass and expect me to announce you when—"

"Banks, is there a problem?" the earl asked with curiosity.

Before the butler could respond, the lady started up from her seat. "Major Grey, 'tis I, Pamela Reed, your old colonel's sister. Do you not remember me? This odious man refuses to announce me."

Lord Crandall could now see the beautiful oval face surrounded by golden curls peeking out from under the bonnet. Pale brown eyes shimmered with tears and a full, rosy mouth was drawn into a pout as she awaited his acknowledgment. He had not seen his late friend's sister since she was a veritable hoyden of fourteen. Clearly she had blossomed into a stunning beauty in the intervening years, but retained a flair for the dramatic.

"Miss Reed, what can have brought you to Town on such a night?" Crandall wondered what her guardian, the colonel's brother, was about to be allowing the young miss to roam around the country alone.

Standing beside him, Sir Norton murmured, "Must tell her 'tis not the thing to be calling on a gentleman unaccompanied."

The young lady advanced to the middle of the hall and

extended her hands in a theatrical manner. Her voice held a pleading note. "Augustus told me that if ever I had difficulties that I might apply to you for assistance. Oh, sir, I am in such a situation now."

Coming down the stairs, Lord Crandall feared Miss Reed might unburden herself further before the servants. He extended his arm to her even as he spoke. "Banks, have Mrs. Watson send some refreshments to the library."

"Very good, my lord," the butler replied through stiff lips. "But what about the . . . young lady's money?"

"My reticule burst from the weight of my coins. They are quite heavy when put into one bag," Miss Reed said, failing to explain what she was doing with such a quantity of change.

"Find another bag and have them sent to us when they are all collected." Lord Crandall closed his hand over Miss Reed's gloved one which rested on his arm. He was anxious to find out why the young lady had come and why she carried what appeared to be the remains of several quarterly allowances.

He ushered her across the hall to the library, signaling his friend to join them. When Sir Norton arrived, the earl closed the door against the curious eyes of the servants.

After removing her bonnet, the young lady settled into a chair near the fire. With a deep sigh, she assumed a tragic pose.

"Miss Reed, allow me to present Sir Norton Stickley. Stick, this is Miss Pamela Reed, sister of my late commander, Colonel Augustus Reed."

" 'Tis an honour, Miss Reed. Marcus has spoken of the heroism of your late brother."

"He was a valiant soldier, sir. I miss him greatly. He wrote me often of your own bravery, Major Grey." Miss

A WINTER COURTSHIP

Reed turned to stare into the coals in the fireplace briefly, then smiled up at the two men with such dazzling brilliance that Sir Norton uttered a small gasp.

Suddenly remembering himself, the baronet cleared his throat. "He is now the Earl of Crandall, Miss Reed."

"Forgive me, my lord. I heard you inherited your cousin's title recently, but somehow you will always be Major Grey to me."

Taking a seat behind his desk, the earl said, "I have difficulty remembering to answer to the name myself, my dear, so do not fret. Now, what is this urgent situation?"

"My Uncle Henry is trying to force me to marry his son, Cousin Tobias. So I gathered what money I could find, climbed out the window, and took the stage for London." The young lady's lip trembled as she ceased speaking.

"Why would Mr. Reed do such a thing, my dear?" Lord Crandall was unacquainted with Colonel Reed's brother, but he couldn't believe that wise soldier would leave his sister with an unscrupulous guardian. His memory of Miss Reed was of a child who very much liked attention. Was she merely trying to get her own way or was there any truth to this tale of a forced marriage?

"He wants to gain control of the fortune my maternal grandmother left me." As she saw the puzzled look in the earl's eyes, she added, "I am an heiress, you know."

Skeptically he asked, "And are you also a great reader of Gothic novels, Miss Reed?"

"Why, yes. Mrs. Radcliffe is my favorite."

Just then a knock sounded on the door and Mrs. Watson, the housekeeper, appeared. Hands folded primly in front of her black gown, it was clear Banks had informed the woman of his opinion of young ladies who called on gentlemen. Despite the butler's warning, her duty—or, more likely, curiosity—had sent her to the library. "Sir, I thought the young lady might like to refresh herself before tea is served."

"Oh, thank you. It was a very long coach ride from Hastings." Miss Reed stood up and followed the disapproving woman from the room.

No sooner had the door closed than Sir Norton said, "Marcus, you cannot doubt Miss Reed's tale. Why, it is the bravest thing I have ever heard. Imagine a young lady fleeing to London to escape the evil plans of her guardian."

"Good God, Stick, you could write those foolish novels yourself."

The baronet raised his head with wounded pride. "She said she was an heiress. There's many a man in the *ton* who would like to get his hands on a fortune *and* a beautiful lady at the same time."

"I know what the young lady professed. I have trouble believing Colonel Reed's brother a scoundrel." When Stick looked like he might protest, the earl added, "But I shall go and find the truth of the matter. The problem is I am in a devil of a coil with what to do with Miss Reed while I inquire into her tale, what with no female relatives with which to house her."

"Why, I can help you there, Marcus."

"If you are about to suggest your friend Miss Wingate and her mother, I think not." Lord Crandall had taken a decided dislike to the young lady who had captured Sir Norton's attention. She was beautiful, fashionable, and as cold as a fish in the earl's opinion. He was hoping the young man's infatuation with the reigning belle would soon pass.

A WINTER COURTSHIP

"No, for I do not think Miss Wingate would like to have a lady who would rival her beauty under her own roof. I was thinking of my older sister, Mrs. Prescott." The baronet frowned as if the thought that his flirt might be flawed offended him.

"You have a sister?" Lord Crandall was surprised. Stick's parents were dead and he had never mentioned any other relatives. "Why have I not met the lady?"

"Just arrived in Town this past week. Been living quietly in the country for the past year since her husband died. Told me to wait until she had her house in order before I paid a social call. I was going to take you over and make introductions then."

The earl sat quietly for a moment. If he read the flamboyant Miss Reed correctly, an older settled woman was just the thing for the chit while he went to Hastings to see her uncle. "Do you think she would be willing to take in a complete stranger until I can ascertain the truth of this escapade?"

"I am sure she would like it above all things," Stick replied with certainty.

A knock sounded and the butler entered, a pained expression on his face. "The young lady's money, my lord."

"Put it here." The earl gestured to the desk. "Have my carriage brought round in a quarter of an hour, Banks, for we are to take Miss Reed to Sir Norton's sister."

Just entering the room, the young lady brushed past the exiting butler. "I knew you would not be so unkind as to return me to Uncle Henry's evil clutches."

Lord Crandall, who'd stood when Miss Reed entered the room, came from behind the desk. "This does not mean you will be allowed to stay indefinitely, for legally I cannot keep you from your guardian should he demand your return. I must go to Hastings and see for myself just how matters stand. If what you say is true, then we will come up with a way to keep you safe from the gentleman and his son."

Miss Reed clasped her hands together, eyes glittering. "Augustus was correct. You are the best of fellows."

Embarrassed by the lady's praise, the earl changed the subject. "Banks has recovered your money. Perhaps you might explain why so many coins?"

" 'Twas all I had left after I bought this coat and bonnet with my allowance. But then I did not know I would need the money to flee. Is it not stunning?" Miss Reed twirled around to give them a better view of the coat.

"Your aunt selected that . . . style and colour?" Crandall asked doubtfully, looking at the oversized bows.

With a gay laugh, the young lady shook her head. "Heavens, no. Aunt Mary would have chosen a drab grey or blue. My friend from school, Eva Raulerson, said it was just the thing for catching a gentleman's eye. She grew up in London."

"Bull Raulerson's daughter?" Sir Norton exclaimed with horror. When the young lady nodded in the affirmative, the baronet could not contain himself. "You took fashion advice from a Cit's daughter? Why, Miss Reed, it just isn't—"

"She is my friend and I shall not hear a word to disparage her, sir." Miss Reed angrily marched forward to retrieve the bag of money from the desk. Yanking up the reticule, the edge caught on his lordship's inkstand, sending the container sailing to the floor. Ink flew out of the silver stand, landing in large blots on the Oriental rug.

Miss Reed burst into tears of apology while Sir Norton was offering his own for his loose tongue. Watching Stick extend his handkerchief to the sniffling chit, the earl hoped Mrs. Prescott was equal to the task of containing Miss Pamela Reed for a few days.

Alison Prescott looked up from her book. Her companion, Miss Grace Kimball, dozed nearby on a Grecian style sofa covered in rose damask. Her cap had slipped down over one eye, exposing frizzy grey curls and she snored with gusto. Alison, however, did not wish to wake her relative, for Miss Kimball talked incessantly.

The lady's favorite topic was her nephew, the Reverend Mr. Malcolm Hewitt, a gentleman with whom Alison was not acquainted nor did she wish to be. In truth, since employing her distant cousin, Alison had taken a decided dislike to the man and heartily wished never to hear about him again.

Returning to her book, she read on for several minutes. Then a smile came unbidden to Alison's lips and she glanced around the newly decorated chamber. She had selected nearly everything in the cozy room and was very satisfied with the result. It had been an exciting experience to have people listen to her opinion about fabrics and styles. Stuart had never allowed her a say in the smallest thing in five years of marriage. Having his life controlled by his grandfather, her husband had made it clear on their wedding night he would not listen to a mere woman. His voice filled with bitterness, he'd maliciously informed her he had been forced to marry to remain the old man's heir.

Alison had been devastated by her new husband's revelations. She'd been vulnerable after coming out of mourning for her mother and full of dreams of love and marriage.

Flattered by Stuart's pursuit of her when she'd arrived in Town, she'd accepted his hasty proposal. But whatever budding love she had imagined she felt died that night as he so cruelly informed her of his mercenary reasons for the marriage. He had duped her for his grandfather's money.

Pushing thoughts of her late husband from her mind, she went back to her novel, content with her new life. At six and twenty, she knew what she wanted without all the foolish dreams of a young girl. She was financially secure and could lead her own life unrestricted by the dictates of a tyrant.

A tap sounded at the drawing room door and the newly hired butler entered. "Sir Norton Stickley has arrived. Are you at home, madam?"

Resisting the urge to bound from the chair to greet her sibling, Alison said, "Of course, Gibson. Sir Norton is my brother."

"Very good, madam."

Several minutes later the baronet strolled into the room, looking very smart. He eyed the sleeping Miss Kimball and grimaced, then softly said, "Hope I have not come too late, Ally, but I need your assistance."

Coming out of her chair, Alison hurried forward and stretched to give her brother a kiss on his cold cheek. "Dear Norton, how glad I am to see you. What do you think of my little house?"

"Capital," Sir Norton said, surveying the room through his quizzing glass.

Lord Crandall, who stood quietly at the door beside Miss Reed, was struck dumb at the sight of Mrs. Prescott. This beautiful creature could not be Stick's older sister. She barely looked twenty with her auburn hair arranged into a cluster of curls around her ivory face and longer

A WINTER COURTSHIP 19

curls at the back, tied with a ribbon. Emerald green eyes twinkled up at her brother and her full pink mouth was spread in an appealing smile, revealing even white teeth.

" 'Tis so good to see you again after so long. As to your problem, there is nothing I would not do for you, my dearest brother."

"Told Marcus that, but I am forgetting my manners. My dear, may I present Miss Pamela Reed and my friend, Marcus Grey, the Earl of Crandall." The baronet then introduced Mrs. Prescott to his friends.

With a sudden start, Miss Kimball awoke. "What was I saying, my dear—" The lady straightened her cap, then eyed the guests with horror. "Dear Alison, why didn't you wake me?"

"They only just arrived, Grace." Introductions were made to Miss Kimball, then everyone was seated.

"Oh, Sir Norton," Miss Kimball began at once, " 'tis good to see you all grown up and quite the handsome gentleman. Why, I remember the last time I saw you— your late father's bailiff was lifting you out of the paddock after the sheep had trampled you when you opened the gate. We were afraid you would be scarred for life with all those little hoofprints—"

"Grace," Alison interrupted when she saw her brother's face flush red. "It is quite late and I believe the gentlemen have something they wish to ask. Now, what can I do to help you, Norton?"

"You can assist me by helping Marcus, Ally."

Alison turned to eye her brother's friend. He smiled at her and she felt her heart hammer in her chest. His crooked grin was endearingly boyish. But she was determined not to be fooled again by outward appearances, for Stuart had been able to charm the entire *ton* with his style and manners.

"I shall do whatever my brother wishes, my lord." Her tone was somewhat cool even to her own ears.

"In truth," the earl began, "I must ask a favor of you, Mrs. Prescott. Miss Reed has arrived in Town unexpectedly and, I fear, unchaperoned."

Miss Kimball gave a slight sniff and glared at the young woman who sat beside the earl. "My dear, once a reputation is lost it can never be retrieved."

Continuing as if there had been no interruption, Lord Crandall said, "Her uncle proposes—no, demands—a marriage to his son that is unacceptable to her. She has come to me, her late brother's friend, to aid her in stopping the event."

Alison glanced at the young girl, who sat quietly beside the earl. Even in the garish coat and hat, Miss Reed was striking; she looked very young and vulnerable, much as Alison had been when Stuart had married her. She'd spent five miserable years married to the rake and she would gladly try to protect anyone from such a marriage, even a stranger.

"Miss Reed, you are welcome to stay with me as long as necessary."

Sir Norton nodded his head. "Told you Ally was a great gun."

"Mrs. Prescott, you are too kind. I shall try not to be the least trouble," Miss Reed said politely.

Intercepting a strange smirk which passed between her brother and the earl, Alison wondered what secret they possessed about the young lady. Dismissing the look, she said, "I hope you will call me Alison, my dear. I am sure you will be quite comfortable here with Grace and me while the earl handles your affairs."

Turning to Lord Crandall, Miss Reed clutched at his arm. "What shall I do if you cannot get my uncle to give up his scheme?"

"I am sure that I shall be able to come up with a plan to keep you safe. Don't worry, my dear." The earl patted Miss Reed's hand. Then, looking up at Alison, he added, "We would appreciate any suggestion that you might offer, Mrs. Prescott."

Alison felt breathless as his gaze rested on her. "I-I shall give the matter some thought, Lord Crandall."

Miss Reed stifled a yawn.

"Why, you poor dear, you look exhausted. Grace, please go and inform Gibson to have a room prepared for Miss Reed."

After the frowning companion left, the gentlemen rose to take their leave. While Sir Norton said his goodbyes to Miss Reed at the drawing room door, Lord Crandall took Alison's hand in his own. She felt a slight tremor run through her at his warm touch.

"My dear lady, I can only say thank you for your help. I know what a great imposition this is that I, a stranger, ask. I hope you will allow me an opportunity to return the favor during the Season. Perhaps you and Miss Kimball would accompany me to a play?"

The theater had been one of the many reasons Alison had come to Town, but she realized this handsome gentleman might prove a danger to her heart and her hope for independence. "Thank you, my lord. But I do not plan to go about much in Society."

"Then I shall engage to change your mind, Mrs. Prescott."

Lord Crandall brushed a kiss on the bare skin of her hand and Alison felt a tingle all the way to her toes. Withdrawing her hand, she coldly informed his lordship, "I rarely waver from my decisions, sir."

"Ah, but you have not met an old campaigner like myself. I am not easily defeated. Shall I lay siege to your small house until you say yes? Think of me out in the cold street, night and day, getting weaker and weaker while waiting to hear you say yes to my simple request."

Seeing the twinkling amusement in his eyes, Alison relaxed and laughed. "You are being preposterous, my lord. We will discuss the matter when you return from visiting Miss Reed's uncle, hopefully with good news for the young lady."

"That is all an old soldier can ask, Mrs. Prescott." The earl bowed and joined Sir Norton.

Old soldier indeed, Alison thought. If he were truly old her heart would not behave in such an outlandish manner.

The gentlemen took their leave and the ladies retired to their rooms. As Alison lay in bed, she wondered how long it would take Lord Crandall to handle Pamela's situation. She knew she shouldn't but she was looking forward to seeing the dashing ex-soldier again. Pushing the thought of him from her mind, she reminded herself that that was no way for an independent lady to be thinking.

The large black coach rumbled through the nearly empty streets of Mayfair, returning the gentlemen home. Sir Norton was speaking about going to Hastings with his lordship. "That is, if you should like my company."

"I would not think of meeting Miss Reed's uncle without you, Stick. If for no other reason than to show you that the situation is probably not as dark as the young lady painted it." The earl pulled his cape tighter against the cold night air.

Peering through the dim light, Sir Norton tried to see the earl's expression. "Why are you so prone to doubt her tale?"

"Years of dealing with very green soldiers, my boy. The young often overreact to very small matters."

"Well, we shall have to wait and see. For now she is safely lodged with Ally."

At the mention of the baronet's sister, the earl smiled into the darkness. "Dashedly pretty woman, your sister."

"Do you think so?" Stick replied, as if the thought had never entered his mind.

"I intend to take her to the theater after we settle Miss Reed's problems."

The baronet frowned, then said, "She could use the entertainment after her long stay in Sheffield, but if she takes a notion into her head that she doesn't want to go there won't be any changing it. Been oddly stubborn since Beau Prescott died."

"She was married to the Beau?" the earl asked with surprise. He'd heard rumors about the man's womanizing even on the Peninsula.

No wonder the lady had been rather cool. She was judging him against one of the most notorious rakes of Society. But he was no rake, as the beautiful Mrs. Prescott would soon learn. After he had handled Miss Reed's problems, the widow would be the focus of his next campaign.

Two

"Good morning, Grace," Alison said as she entered the sunlit breakfast parlor. She eyed the large plateful of eggs and ham sitting before her companion, wondering how such a thin lady could consume such vast quantities of food, yet look so frail.

"There you are, my dear. I was hoping for an opportunity to speak with you before Miss Reed came down." Miss Kimball reluctantly laid down her knife and fork. "Do you think it wise to be hiding this young woman from her guardian?"

"Hiding! I would hardly call it that. We are merely acting as her chaperones while the earl goes . . ." Alison's voice trailed off. She was not certain what Lord Crandall was going to do to protect his friend's sister from this marriage. Remembering his large frame, she suspected he would be a formidable force.

Every time he came to mind she got a funny feeling in her chest. Pushing thoughts of the earl from her mind, she went to the mahogany sideboard and served herself.

"But, my dear, I am one who believes that young ladies are better advised to do as their guardians wish." Miss Kimball eyed her plate with longing while she spoke.

Alison brought her breakfast to the table and sat down. "Marriage is difficult enough when the pair enters it willingly, but to have Miss Reed forced into a union would be unthinkable."

"Oh, I wish my nephew were here. Malcolm would know just the thing to say to convince you of the folly of helping a ward defy her guardian."

Delighted that the oft-mentioned reverend was not present, Alison had no opportunity to respond, for Miss Reed entered the breakfast parlor. The young lady looked very demure in a blue sprig muslin morning gown, edged with white lace at the high neck and long sleeves. Alison was pleased that the garish pelisse of last evening was not her usual mode of dress.

Casting a warning glance at Grace to cease the subject, Alison rose, saying, "Good morning, Pamela. Did you sleep well?"

"The bed was most comfortable, but I was so worried about my uncle I do not think I closed my eyes all night," the young miss replied while she looked around the small apartment.

Noting the rosy cheeks and clear eyes of her guest, Alison merely smiled at this bit of nonsense. "I fear we are a small household, my dear, and I do not keep a footman on duty here. Would you allow me to serve you?"

Miss Reed lifted her hand in a staying gesture. "Please finish your own meal. I like things quite informal." She then proceeded to fill per plate with only slightly less than what Miss Kimball had taken.

Taking a seat at the table, she continued, "I do want to thank you for being so kind as to house a stranger. I know it cannot be quite comfortable for you and Miss Kimball to have me intruding upon you."

"Nonsense, Pamela." Alison reached out and covered the girl's hand. "Having my first guest in over a year is just the thing to enliven my spirits. Now, say no more on the matter and enjoy your buttered eggs or Cook will be quite out of sorts with us all."

The ladies ate in momentary silence until the butler entered the small parlor. "Cook sent the young miss a pot of hot chocolate, thinking she might not care for coffee."

Alison looked inquiringly at Pamela. The girl smiled, saying, "Thank you, Gibson, and thank Cook, for chocolate is my favorite thing in the morning."

The servant poured a cup of the dark, steaming liquid, then left. Pamela ate her meal with gusto while Miss Kimball chattered inanely about the weather, the fashions, and the coming Season. The subject appeared to interest Miss Reed a great deal for she asked numerous questions of the older lady who had always lived in London, albeit on the fringes of Society due to straightened circumstances.

"I take it, Miss Reed, that you have yet to sample the delights of a Season?" Miss Kimball inquired.

"I should have been brought out this March, but now . . ." Pamela slumped slightly. "If I am forced to marry Tobias Reed, he will most likely say London is a waste of time and money, for he is forever going on about crops and drainage and such." The young girl spoke for some time about her stormy relationship with her cousin.

Alison soon formed the picture of a very staid and autocratic young man who would have little patience with the lively and unpredictable Miss Reed. It was unfortunate the girl's uncle could see only the money and not the unsuitability of matching such a pair.

"Do not lose hope, my dear, for Lord Crandall seems determined to intervene in your affairs." Alison's curiosity about the gentleman got the better of her. "I take it the earl is an old friend of the family."

"Why, I have known him for years, only he was Major Grey then." The young lady spoke of her personal knowledge of the former soldier and of tales related through her brother's letters.

Miss Kimball took in Alison's rapt expression as her young guest chattered. Alarm filled the older woman. Had Alison formed a *tendre* for the earl? This would not do, for her own dear nephew, the reverend, was just the person for the widow.

Sinking into thought about just how to end Alison's fascination with the earl, Miss Kimball was brought back to the present when Miss Reed managed to spill an entire cup of chocolate on Alison's new linen cloth.

"Oh, my! I *am* dreadfully sorry." The girl rose and began to pat futilely at the spreading stain with her napkin.

"Don't give it a thought." Alison looked at her new tablecloth with regret, then rose and took the napkin from Miss Reed's hand. "The servants will take care of the stain, my dear. I would not want you to get chocolate on your lovely dress. Let us retire to the drawing room and make plans for the day."

"I shall remain behind, Alison. I know just the remedy to keep the stain from setting and shall advise Gibson on the method," Miss Kimball stated from her chair.

"Why, thank you, Grace. Come, Pamela, and don't fret over the occasional accident."

As the door closed behind the departing pair, Miss Kimball's mouth puckered in thought. She must come up with a plan or her dear Malcolm would lose to the earl. She had done her best to sing the praises of the young vicar, but Lord Crandall might ruin all her plans with his handsome good looks and easy manners.

The lady was so deep in thought that when the butler came to remove the dishes and the soiled tablecloth, he never received the important remedy for removing the chocolate stain.

Lord Crandall leaned back in his chair and surveyed the crowded public rooms at The Swan. He always stopped at this posting inn for the excellent food and service, but a mill to be held nearby this afternoon had the large hostelry overflowing with fashionable bucks shouting for service. There being no private parlors to be had, the earl was seated near the doorway to the hall.

Having just finished a hearty meal, he sat drinking The Swan's excellent ale as he waited for Sir Norton to return from his conversation with an old acquaintance. About to take a drink from his tankard, Crandall paused as two men came and stood behind him in the hallway and conversed in hushed tones. Their position made it impossible for the earl to avoid their private dialogue.

"Father, there was no need to accompany me in this search for Cousin Pamela. We have little doubt that she has gone to London to her friend, Miss Raulerson, or Major Grey. I shall be able to find her and bring her home before she creates a scandal in Society." The man sounded irritated.

"Little I care what Society does or says. I am coming so that I might give that . . . hoyden a raking-down that she will not long forget," the older man snapped.

The earl turned to eye the pair. Father and son were much alike. Brown hair, eyes, and clothing did nothing

A WINTER COURTSHIP 29

to distinguish either man. Clearly, he was looking at Miss Reed's relatives and what he was hearing did not bode well for that young lady's future.

"And well the ungrateful chit will deserve such a trimming, but the weather will only aggravate your gout, sir. Allow me to recover the wicked child and you will have time by a warm fire to determine the punishment for this trick she has played."

"I have already decided the penalty. The chit shall be locked in her room for two weeks. Then she might listen to me or her aunt better. You will have all that time to finish your plans for your wedding as well as have the banns read. No sense in allowing my niece to ruin all our plans."

The earl's eyes narrowed as he watched the Reeds. This was not a man who would be swayed by talk of honour and fairness or even threats of exposure. He was clearly determined to get his hands on Miss Reed's fortune. She must be quite an heiress if the looks of determination on these men's faces were any indication.

Just then the landlord came and ushered the gentlemen to a table near the fireplace. They settled down to warm themselves and partake of a meal, heads still together discussing the situation.

Lord Crandall came to a sudden decision and signaled his friend. Tossing coins on the table, he donned his greatcoat as Sir Norton arrived.

"I apologize for staying so long, but Bartworth had the most amusing tale about Caro Lamb." Pulling his coat on, the baronet asked, "How long until we reach Hastings, Marcus?"

"There has been a change in our plans, Stick." The

earl led the way out of the inn, setting his beaver hat at a rakish angle over his black hair.

"But what about seeing Miss Reed's uncle?" Sir Norton hurried behind, putting on his own hat.

"I have just *seen* that dubious individual and I am now convinced that he is quite unscrupulous and determined to have Miss Reed's fortune for his son."

Frowning, the baronet came alongside the earl as he made his way to his phaeton. "Then what are your intentions, Marcus?"

"At the moment I have not a clue, but I feel certain I shall be able to rely on the good sense of your kind sister once we return to London. Together we shall find a way out of this fix. Unfortunately, Mr. Reed will be coming to my residence in Town, for they suspect that is where she has gone." The earl climbed up on the seat of his sleek vehicle and took the reins from the post boy.

"Then the only solution is to remove Miss Reed from London," Sir Norton replied, scrambling up beside the earl just as that gentleman cracked his whip above the horses' heads.

Alison eyed Miss Reed across the top of her tambour while she pushed the needle through the fabric. The young girl sat staring into the fire, a melancholy look on her lovely face. "Are you sure you would not like something to read, my dear?"

Pamela looked up at the clock on the mantelpiece. "I am not a great reader of the classics. Do you think the earl will be back tonight?"

"Not likely, for I am certain it took much of the day to reach your home. Hastings, was it not?"

A WINTER COURTSHIP

Pamela nodded. "I was merely hoping to know my fate before retiring."

"Know your fate, child?" Miss Kimball said, looking up from the letter she was writing to her nephew at the small secretary. "Very few of us are blessed with such knowledge. One is usually best guided by their elders on matters of the future."

Alison could sense a lecture coming on and interrupted. "Perhaps you would ring the bell for our tea, my dear. It is getting late and I am sure you will soon be for your bed. I would not want you to go unfed."

Pamela rose and did as she was bid. Moments later, Gibson entered with a large silver tray and placed it beside his mistress. In honour of their guest, Cook had outdone herself. There was a variety of cakes and tartlets to tempt their appetites.

Pouring the tea for Miss Kimball, Alison hesitated a moment before giving the cup and saucer to Pamela to take to the lady. Surely the incident this morning had been only a freak accident, she told herself.

To Alison's relief the girl successfully delivered the brew to Miss Kimball along with a plate filled with treats and returned to accept her own. They chatted idly while they had their tea.

"I have books besides the classics, Pamela. Do you not like novels?"

A glimmer of interest appeared in the young lady's brown eyes. *"You* read novels? Why, Tobias said that anyone who aspired to gentility read only improving works."

Alison laughed. For all Stuart's faults, he had not begrudged her such entertainments. "I believe that novels are quite popular with the *ton*. There is a selection in the top of the secretary on the left side. Go and see if there is something which might pique your interest."

Returning her empty cup to the tray, Pamela went to the Hepplewhite bookcase, making sure not to disturb Miss Kimball, who had resumed her writing. Rows of books were visible through the glass door. She pulled it open and removed several novels from the shelf without reading the titles so as not to disturb the older lady. Seated once again, she regarded the choices she had made.

"Why, you have *Castle Rackrent* by Maria Edgeworth. I adore her writing. Do you perchance have any of the volumes of *Tales of Fashionable Life?*"

"They are on the second shelf." Alison was pleased to finally find something besides her own plight to occupy the girl's thoughts.

With the eagerness of youth, Miss Reed put the books she had chosen on the table beside her. In doing so, her hand accidentally knocked the handpainted vase full of hothouse flowers to the floor. The porcelain shattered into large pieces and the water made a dark stain on the rug.

"Oh, I am so clumsy!" Pamela wailed, then burst into tears.

Putting her stitchery aside, Alison rose to comfort the distraught miss. "My dear, you must not cry so. After all, it was not a very pretty vase. I believe some distant cousin sent it to me and I am heartily glad to be rid of it."

"Truly?" the girl asked, sniffling into the handkerchief that she'd pulled from a pocket.

"You may ask Grace."

Miss Kimball took this as an invitation to assist her mistress. She put the finished letter into her pocket and came to console the bumbling young lady. "Why, I cannot tell you the number of times since decorating the house she has threatened to get rid of it. The colours are not quite right for the room."

"I am glad to hear it, but I shall not feel right unless you allow me to purchase another as a replacement."

Seeing the look of determination on the girl's face, Alison agreed to the purchase of a new vase at some future time. "Now, Grace, why don't you take Pamela upstairs and get her settled in for the night. On the way, please tell Gibson that we have had an accident."

After their good nights, Miss Kimball led the girl out of the room, leaving the door open. Alison could hear her companion telling the story of when she broke her mother's favorite tureen as a child.

She stood eyeing the clutter of flowers and bits of porcelain on her new rug. The water would most likely dry without leaving a stain but if it did, she would move a chair to cover the mark.

A deep masculine voice sounded from near the open door, causing Alison to jump.

"I see Miss Reed has been up to her usual tricks," the earl drawled.

Sir Norton stepped around his larger friend and surveyed the carpet. "Told the footman on duty not to announce us. Ally, best tote up the damage done by the chit and give Marcus a bill. Although in fairness, if you claim more than a halfpenny for that hideous vase, it would be robbery."

"Don't be silly, Norton, as if I would ask for money from his lordship over a few trifles."

"How few?" The earl arched an eyebrow.

"Never mind. Will you gentlemen not be seated and pray tell me why you are returned so quickly?"

As the earl and Sir Norton moved to take a seat, Gibson

arrived with a broom and bin and quickly cleared away the mess. "Shall I bring fresh tea, madam?"

Alison shot a questioning look at her brother.

Sir Norton, now casually stretched out in a chair near the fire, winked at her. "Something warm would do nicely if you have a spot of brandy to add to the brew."

"Very good, sir." The butler nodded and left, returning some minutes later with a footman who removed the old silver tray. Gibson replaced it with one which held a fresh pot of tea and a decanter of brandy.

After the gentlemen were served, Alison again asked about their early return.

The earl looked down at his dust-coated Hessians. "Mrs. Prescott, we did not make it all the way to Miss Reed's home. In truth, I had a chance encounter with her uncle and cousin, who had set out to search for the girl. We had all stopped to dine at an inn just south of East Grinstead."

"And was the meeting all that dear Pamela would wish?" Alison averted her eyes from the earl's long expanse of manly limbs.

"After inadvertently overhearing the gentlemen's conversation, I decided not to broach Mr. Reed on the matter of his niece. I fear that Miss Reed's account of his intent is correct. Worse, he is on his way to my residence to inquire about his relative, for I am one of the few she was acquainted with in Town."

Sir Norton, who was pouring a liberal amount of the brandy into his tea, added, "I suggested we remove her from London, but am at a standstill as to where."

The earl watched as a frown appeared above the lady's lovely green eyes. Her simple cream silk evening gown trimmed with Brussels lace showed her enticing figure to perfection, making it difficult for him to concentrate on matters concerning Miss Reed.

"So you did not actually speak with Mr. Henry Reed?"

"I overheard information that was damming for that gentleman and decided the wiser course would be to return to Town. I wish to solicit your advice about what best to do to protect the young lady from her grasping relatives."

"I believe that I must agree with my brother. She should be removed from Town at once. But she can no longer remain under your care and protection if they are wise to her movements. You must lodge her somewhere with no obvious ties to you or your family."

The earl watched the lady rise and move gracefully toward the curtained window. She seemed to be giving the problem considerable thought as she stood quietly gazing out into the darkness, giving him a tantalizing view of her slender white neck.

The baronet, having helped himself to an apple tart, startled his sister from her musing. "What about taking her to Grandmother Wilkinson? The old tartar is forever saying she would like a companion in that drafty old manor."

"Tartar! Why she is the sweetest natured woman on earth." Alison turned to chastise her brother for his unfair characterization of their maternal grandmother.

"She has snarled at me for ages."

"And can you blame her after you sneaked your new colt up to your room on your eighth birthday, causing her to have to replace the carpeting *and* some of the flooring?"

The earl gave a shout of laughter. "You must tell me some time about your adventures as a young man. Between sheep and horses you seemed to have had your contretemps with animals."

Sir Norton smiled. "She simply did not understand that Ramses was my first thoroughbred. At the advanced age of eight, I was convinced her ham-handed groom might let him get trampled by my late grandfather's stallion."

"Perfectly logical thinking to me," the earl said.

"So, Lord Crandall," Alison asked, mouth twitching, "just how many horses do *you* have stabled in your upper bedchambers?"

"Thankfully, all my grooms are quite capable and I have been spared that necessity."

As the trio laughed, Alison came back and took her seat opposite her brother. "My grandmother's home would be an excellent place to take Pamela, for the lady resides just outside of Edinburgh." Turning to her brother, she added, "I should like to visit the dear lady myself and I am sure she has quite forgiven you for your childhood trick."

"I suppose you are suggesting that I accompany you there." When Alison nodded in the affirmative, the baronet said, "Might as well go, with Town so devilishly flat."

"Then we are agreed. We leave . . . shall we say at nine on the morrow? That will give us time to pack."

Realizing he must soon take his leave from the beautiful widow, the earl prolonged the moment. "Scotland is an excellent place for Miss Reed to remain until she is of age or her uncle relents. Are you certain your grandmother will not mind having a young lady about?"

"I fear it is not my grandmother who will not like the scheme but our Miss Reed. It can be rather bleak there during the winter despite the fact that the neighborhood is quite social." Alison failed to mention her own worries about how much damage the clumsy child might do to her relative's estate.

"Have no concerns on that point. I shall have a conversation with her should she prove reluctant before we leave tomorrow." The earl rose, knowing it was time for them to take their leave.

"*We,* my Lord? Do you plan to accompany us to Edinburgh?" Alison's heart began to pound at the thought of the long journey north in his lordship's company.

"Why, of course, Mrs. Prescott. She is a virtual stranger to you and Stick. I would not leave you to handle arrangements on your own. Besides, it shall give me all the time I need to convince you to go to the theater with me once we are back in Town." The earl gave her a smile that sent her pulses racing.

Alison covered her confusion by escorting her brother and the earl to the door, a warm feeling inside her that he still wished to accompany her to a play. After the gentlemen were gone, she informed a disgruntled Grace about their journey and then made her way up the stairs to her own room.

Taking down her auburn curls, she reminded herself that marriage had not suited her and was to be no part of her future. She had often argued bitterly with Stuart during the first years, but soon came to realize she wasted her breath. After his grandfather died, he took fiendish delight in being cruel to her before the servants and his closest friends. Her only defense was not to allow him to see her pain and humiliation. His own death had released her from that terrible existence and she would never again give a man that much power over her life.

Just before she blew out her candle, she thought she must keep the earl at a polite distance for the sake of her vulnerable heart.

Three

"Scotland!" Pamela Reed whispered with dismay as she sat slumped in the window seat of her bedroom, her *portmanteau* packed and ready. She paid scant attention to the lovely scene beyond the pane where the morning sun glinted off the frost on the roof of the neighboring house, creating a jewel-like glitter of colour. What filled her mind was the fading dream of her much longed for London Season, clearly an event now destined never to occur.

A scratching sounded at her door, interrupting her melancholy thoughts. Then Miss Kimball entered with a maid. "I see you are all ready to go, Miss Reed."

"I did not wish to inconvenience Mrs. Prescott's servants any further since I knew both you and she must be packed. I only have this small piece."

"Most thoughtful of you, my dear." The older lady turned to the maid. "Lucy, take this down with the others."

With a curtsey, the servant took the bag and left Pamela was surprised when Miss Kimball, instead of following the maid, came to the window with the obvious intention of conversing. From her frequent barbed comments, Pamela believed the older woman disapproved of her.

Miss Kimball cleared her throat. "I hope you don't

mind my saying so, but you don't appear pleased about this journey to Mrs. Prescott's grandmother."

Straightening, Pamela forced a sad smile to her lips. "Pray, do not think I am unaware of what everyone is doing on my behalf. I should not be so ungrateful. 'Tis only that I have longed to be in London for the past year and now I am off for the country again within a day of arriving."

Miss Kimball took a seat in a yellow silk wing chair near the window. The lady had spent a disturbed night after the widow informed her of the decision to take the girl to Scotland. But somewhere near dawn a plan formed which might keep dear Alison from becoming further enamored with the earl and this innocent miss would be her unwitting partner. "Ah, I suspect that a Season is the thing which all young ladies long for most."

"I must not think about the event any longer, for it shall not be. I must go bravely to Edinburgh and not be the least bit of trouble to his lordship."

Pamela sounded so martyred that Miss Kimball would have laughed at her dramatics if the matter were not of such importance to her plans. She merely watched the girl strike one tragic pose after another, issuing great sighs all the while. "To be sure, dear child."

Pamela's brown eyes brightened and she suddenly brought a delicate hand up to her cheek as if struck by a thought. "Perhaps when I am one and twenty and no longer under my uncle's guardianship I shall have an opportunity to come to London. I am an heiress, you know. Oh, but at that age I shall be the veriest ape leader. I suppose by then it would be quite useless to dance at Almack's and visit the King's Theater or even get presented at court. What gentleman would look at me then?"

"My dear," Miss Kimball said as if speaking to someone who lacked wits, "you could have all that at once if you were a married lady, and much more freedom as well."

Pamela's lips pursed as if she'd tasted a lime. Then she said, "Not married to Tobias."

"You are not seeing the obvious, dear child. Your cousin is not the only marriageable gentleman. A marriage of convenience would solve your problems. Why, if you entered wedlock with someone like your brother's old friend, that would give you all you wished and more. You could stay in Town with all the delights of the Season, *and* you would be a countess."

"Marry Lord Crandall!" Pamela's eyes grew round. "But . . . but he is so old."

"You are being terribly missish for one in your situation, child. Why, the earl can scarcely be five and thirty—just the right age, in my opinion, to make an excellent husband. I can tell you that he will be quite the eligible bachelor this spring. The ladies in Town adore war heroes, especially handsome ones. If you dally very long, some female shall come along and whisk him away." Miss Kimball watched the changing emotions move over the girl's face.

"If I were ever to think of a marriage of convenience, would not Sir Norton be a more suitable husband? He is quite handsome as well and the right age for me." Pamela looked out the window as she pondered the two gentlemen who were helping her. She had not failed to note that Sir Norton's fashionable attire far outshone the earl's simple elegance.

"True, the young man is quite the Town Beau. But one cannot compare a baronet with an earl, my dear. Besides, there are rumors that the gentleman is about to make an offer for some lady of the *ton*." Miss Kimball felt that this simple falsehood would do no harm to anyone. "On the other hand, I can see that the earl is quite unentangled and a very dashing fellow. Just give the idea some thought."

Miss Kimball, having planted the seed, rose and exited the bedchamber, urging the child to hurry and get her bonnet and pelisse as the gentlemen would soon arrive. She left Pamela with her thoughts more disturbed than ever.

"Good God, Marcus. We shall be quite a spectacle leaving Town like a military parade." Sir Norton eyed the three carriages pulled up in front of his sister's house.

Lord Crandall, pausing at the front door, watched the footmen load a trunk onto the first coach, which would carry the servants. "The ladies must be transported with the greatest of comfort. Mrs. Prescott and Miss Kimball are traveling on my account and I would not want them to suffer for any reason."

"Well, I hope you encouraged Ally to bring two maids—one to take care of the ladies and one to pick up the pieces behind Miss Reed."

The earl chuckled. "Have pity on little Pamela, Stick. Accident prone people are very often the ones who suffer most. I had a lieutenant once who in the course of six months managed to fall from his horse, sit upon his saber, and shoot himself in the leg. We finally persuaded him to give up his weapon and assist the doctor for he was more a danger to himself and us than any ten French soldiers."

"Then I suggest for our own safety we keep Miss Reed completely unarmed as well."

Gibson opened the door to the gentlemen and escorted them into the drawing room. Alison Prescott was seated at the Hepplewhite secretary making a list of directions for the servants. She rose and greeted her brother warmly, and the earl with polite reserve.

Dressed in a spruce green traveling gown with gold military style frogging down the front, Alison was undeniably pleased to see the look of admiration in the earl's eyes. She gestured for them to be seated. "As soon as the trunks are loaded, I believe we are ready."

Lord Crandall arched one eyebrow. "And how has Miss Reed taken the news? Do I need to lend my voice to encouraging her of the wisdom of her leaving Town?"

"She is, of course, disappointed at the outcome of your journey. But she accepted your decision. I believe her desire not to marry her cousin far outweighed other considerations," Alison replied, noticing that the earl looked very handsome in his tan buckskins and blue coat.

The earl nodded, but was forestalled from making further comment when Miss Kimball arrived bearing the message that all was ready for them to depart. They exited the parlor to find Pamela Reed standing on the stairs, again dressed in her startling red pelisse and bonnet, the towering pink plumes making her appear very tall. She eyed the earl with a speculative gaze. "Good day, my lord, Sir Norton."

The baronet stepped forward and offered his arm. "May I escort you to your carriage, Miss Reed?"

The young lady hesitated a moment, then turned a blinding smile on the earl. "Can I not ride in your phaeton, Lord Crandall? I have just traveled all the way from

Hastings in a stagecoach. I am certain you would not object, Sir Norton. It will give you a chance to converse with your sister."

Both men looked slightly chagrined. The earl did not wish to be saddled with a chattering miss and Sir Norton, as an aspiring Corinthian, detested travel in a closed coach.

Bravely, the baronet replied, "Whatever you wish, Miss Reed, but I fear Marcus brought his curricle, deeming the phaeton a waste while traveling at the modest pace which will keep you ladies most comfortable."

Alison felt a strange feeling in the pit of her stomach at the thought of Pamela and the earl rolling along together in his curricle. The girl was his responsibility for now, so what did it matter that they traveled together?

The earl turned to Alison, interrupting her troubled thoughts. "Do you think it wise for Miss Reed to be riding openly out of Town with me, Mrs. Prescott?"

"A very good point, my lord." Alison was pleased with the earl's astuteness. "Pamela, your uncle may already be in London searching for you. You cannot risk being seen. I am sure the earl will gladly take you up with him on one of the days of our journey."

"But I shall do nothing to attract attention to myself," Pamela pleaded, pouting prettily.

Sir Norton lifted his quizzing glass to eye the bright pelisse. "Miss Reed, I must assure you that your attire cries out for one to notice its . . . design and hue."

An angry flush appeared on Pamela's cheeks. Alison deemed it time to intervene between the youthful pair. "My dear, you are simply too dashing in that coat for anyone to ignore."

Appeased by this bit of flummery, Pamela stepped

down and took the baronet's arm as if she were bestowing a great favor upon him. "Then I shall ride in the carriage with you, dear Alison, for I would not want all your efforts on my behalf to be for naught."

Alison saw the earl silently mouth the words "thank you" over the top of Miss Reed's head as Sir Norton led her out to the carriage. She felt a foolish rush of pleasure at the simple gesture.

Lord Crandall came up and offered his arm while she nervously tied the ribbon on her matching green bonnet. His close proximity made her knees feel quite weak. "My lord, I apologize for Norton's loose tongue around Miss Reed. I have never seen his manners so sadly lacking."

"Can't say I blame him. That coat and bonnet make her look like a Bird of Paradise."

"Nonsense. They are somewhat . . . inappropriate for her age, but no one would mistake her for anything but a gently bred miss with that innocent face. Besides, I have added a simple blue pelisse and matching bonnet to my trunk which I hope to coax her into wearing before we are very long on the road."

"That should prove easy. Just give the chit a cup of chocolate while she is dressed in that cursed costume and your problems are solved."

Alison shook her head as she placed her hand on his extended arm, attempting to suppress a smile. "You are quite bad, you know."

Lord Crandall liked the way a dimple appeared in the lady's cheek as she struggled not to smile at him. "True, I must find some lady who is willing to redeem me."

A shuttered look came into the widow's face as she looked away from him. "I am sure there are any number of young misses who would be willing to take the role."

Leading Mrs. Prescott out to the carriage, the earl wondered why she seemed to withdraw each time he tried to flirt. Was her marriage to the Beau such a misery that she now judged all men by him? He would discreetly inquire of Stick about his sister, but first they must get safely out of London, unseen by Miss Reed's relatives.

The carriages traveled north at a steady pace and by one of the clock they were deep into the country. His lordship, having sent the servants ahead to make arrangements for nuncheon, was glad when he spied the lead coach parked at a quaint inn with a weathered sign proclaiming The Blue Boar.

Sir Norton grumbled, "Damme, Marcus, we must speak to that coachman for waiting so long to stop for nuncheon. I could eat an entire . . ." As words failed him he looked at the sign and said, *"Boar,* I am so sharp set."

"You must tell me how blue boar tastes, for I have no stomach for such a delicacy. But I fear you must complain to me for I told Pratt that since the ladies had a basket of refreshments with them, to travel until one. I wanted as many miles as possible between us and London before Miss Reed and her red coat and pink plumes were seen. You must admit that she would be remembered if someone were asking."

The baronet, who was appalled by the garish costume, was struck by the wisdom of this. "I had not given the matter a thought except to wish Miss Reed would burn the rig."

Handing the reins to the post boy, his lordship jumped to the ground and watched the large traveling coach containing the ladies enter the yard. He had questioned Stick carefully about his sister, but his friend would say little but that Ally had had a tough go of it with Prescott.

The earl's batman exited the inn and came to his side. "My lord, we have arranged a light meal for the ladies in a private parlor."

"Excellent, Atwood. Make certain all the servants are fed before you set out again. You know what I wish for lodgings for the night."

Eyeing their cavalcade of coaches, the servant grinned. " 'Tis a might different from our travel on the Peninsula, sir."

"Just so," the earl said distractedly. He was patiently waiting for Mrs. Prescott to step down from the carriage. When he saw her alight, he hurried forward to escort her into the inn. His man was left with a surprised expression on his face.

"Ah, so that's how the wind be blowin'," Atwood muttered to himself as he walked back to speak with the coachman of the first carriage.

Unfortunately for Lord Crandall, Miss Kimball saw his advancing figure. "Dear Alison, allow me to take your arm. I fear I feel a bit dizzy after so long in that swaying vehicle."

Concerned for her companion, Alison paid little attention to his lordship's advance. She took the lady's arm to assist her to the inn.

Miss Kimball saw an opportunity and said, "My, how nice Pamela looks on the earl's arm. They make quite a couple, do they not?"

Alison felt a tightening in her chest when she glanced back as the earl bent down to say something to Miss Reed, which brought a laugh to the lovely girl's lips. She almost denied that they made a nice couple to her companion,

A WINTER COURTSHIP 47

then pressed her lips closed and escorted the lady into the inn. What was it to her anyway?

His lordship, having seen the widow aiding her older cousin, was left to escort Pamela to the inn. The chit had been too long with the talkative Miss Kimball, he thought, for after she'd answered his query about the comfort of her journey, she chattered away about the scenery of the countryside through which they had passed.

Miss Kimball felt pleased with her little ruse. She even managed to keep Alison by her side until all had freshened up and the meal was served.

Sir Norton sat on the other side of his sister. His lordship was forced to be seated beside Pamela Reed. This was clearly going to be a wearing trip, Grace decided, but dear Malcolm would thank her when he won the widow's hand, not to mention her fortune.

Atwood had arranged a sumptuous meal for the group and soon Alison's worries about Miss Kimball were relieved as she watched the lady consume vast quantities of roast duck, sliced ham, braised potatoes, and creamed peas. Later she finished her meal with poppyseed cake and lemon tarts.

For her own part, Alison ate lightly, often finding the earl's disturbing gaze on her during the meal.

"Is everything to your liking?" he asked with a gentle smile.

"You have seen to every comfort, my lord." She looked back to the green peas floating in cream sauce, feeling uncomfortable by the effect his deep blue eyes had on her emotions. She was foolishly bereft of conversation as he continued to watch her.

Pamela unwittingly covered Alison's pause. "Sir, my brother could not have done a better job of seeing to our needs. I want to thank you sincerely for what you and Mrs. Prescott are doing for me."

"Marcus is no end a good fellow. We are all delighted to be helping you, Miss Reed," Sir Norton interjected to remind the young miss that he, too, was assisting her. Then he proceeded to tell the tale of his meeting with the earl on the road from Dover.

Miss Reed, still smarting from the baronet's criticism of her coat, directed much of her dialogue during the meal to Lord Crandall, much to Miss Kimball's delight and the earl's frustration. Each time he tried to engage the widow in conversation, Pamela immediately offered some comment.

Lord Crandall achieved some measure of success at speaking to the widow alone after the meal was completed, for he came upon her as she stood outside waiting for the other ladies to exit. Sir Norton was off busily inspecting the horses before they resumed their journey and the lady stood donning her gloves beside the carriage.

"Shall I order something warm for you ladies to drink in the coach? It looks as if the weather means to turn cold and rainy." The earl eyed the grey clouds covering the sky.

"You were perhaps thinking of chocolate, my lord?" The lady's green eyes twinkled up at him.

Lord Crandall laughed. "No, I would not be so cruel as to wish all three of you to have to don new apparel. In truth, I find you quite beautiful in green and Miss Kimball . . . very suited to grey. I simply meant that Atwood has a way with making a hot pot that is quite the thing when it's cold."

Alison ignored the compliment. "Hot pot, sir? Whatever is that?"

"I believe it is some type of spiced ale and brandy boiled together. Regardless of the ingredients, 'tis quite warming on a cold winter's day."

"I do not think it a wise choice. We still have wine in our basket should any of us wish some refreshment." Alison softly laughed as a sudden vision of them arriving at some posting inn for the night and the clumsy Pamela being terribly foxed as well.

At that moment, the others joined them and Pamela at once renewed her request to ride with his lordship. "We are well away from Town now, sir."

"Not yet, my dear," the earl said, quickly pointing to the darkening sky. "I would not wish you to be soaked, for it looks like a downpour is coming."

Pamela eyed the threatening clouds doubtfully. Fortunately for the earl, at that moment a particularly biting wind swirled around them, which convinced her that she did not wish to be wet on such a day. "Very well, my lord. But I should like to ride in your carriage one day during the trip."

Lord Crandall wished he could ask Mrs. Prescott to join him, but having refused Miss Reed he could not now offer to take the widow up with him. "I promise that each of you ladies shall take a turn in the curricle with me before we reach our destination."

Before Alison could protest, the earl hurried the ladies into the coach and ordered the coachman to have a care with the coming bad weather.

Joining his friend, who was already seated in the curricle, the earl invited Stick to take the ribbons. Sir Norton was pleased that a whip of Marcus's ability trusted him enough to drive.

They had been on the road for nearly an hour, during

which time the baronet had finally exhausted the subject of his lordship's excellent bays. Having been quiet for several miles, Lord Crandall was surprised by his friend's question.

"I say, Marcus, don't you think Miss Reed seems rather taken with you?"

"Don't be absurd, Stick. She is merely more comfortable with me because I am an old acquaintance and her brother's friend." He thought the chit a mere child, especially when she stood beside the poised Mrs. Prescott. Now there was a woman to warm a man's blood.

Sir Norton again lapsed into silence for several minutes as if pondering the earl's explanation. "I think there is more than just friendship in the young lady's tone. She never speaks to me with quite the same intensity."

"And that means she is attracted to me! No, my boy, I believe she is merely punishing you for calling into question her taste in apparel. What amazes me is that you have any success at all with the ladies, with that loose tongue of yours."

"The thing is, Marcus, I have never uttered such things before. I suppose I feel this brotherly instinct to guide her since she is now alone. I promise not to say another word on the subject."

The earl made no comment to this. He seriously doubted there was anything brotherly about Stick's feeling for the pretty Miss Reed, but he did not say so. The thought of such a stickler for appearances as his friend and the accident prone Pamela being in love made him wince. Marcus merely changed the subject.

The weather grew steadily worse as they went north. Near three of the clock, the men stopped and raised the hood on the curricle, for a fine mist began to fall. Marcus became concerned that the weather would hinder their journey. But he reminded himself that Henry Reed would be equally impeded if by some misfortune he were to learn of their whereabouts.

As the light gave way to the early darkness of the storm, the two vehicles pulled into the yard of the large inn chosen by Atwood. When the three ladies and two gentlemen were all finally in the warmth and light of The Crown's taproom, Lord Crandall was startled to see two gentlemen of his acquaintance standing near the large fire.

Dressed in Hussar's uniforms, the travelers created a blaze of colour in the muted surroundings of the inn. The younger of the two turned and spied the earl. "By George, if it ain't Marcus Grey."

Turning to greet his old friend, a red-haired man wearing the rank of a colonel called, "Marcus, well met. Why, the last time I saw you, you were covered in mud and chasing Frenchies over the horizon at Waterloo."

Lord Crandall laughed. "Unfortunately, the victory had barely been declared when I learned my uncle and his son had both died in a carriage accident, ending my military career by a stroke of ill luck. I was required to return to England and take on my responsibilities. 'Tis good to see you both managed to come home unscathed."

The earl presented Major Thomas Wallingham and Colonel James Owens to his friends. The gentlemen were at once delighted to meet the late Augustus Reed's sister, but no one questioned her being with Lord Crandall. It was soon agreed that the soldiers would dine with them in the private parlor.

As the ladies removed their coats, Pamela nervously fidgeted with the buttons on her red pelisse. "What if these gentlemen should accidentally meet my uncle when they return to London? They might tell him where I am, not knowing him to be a blackguard."

Alison took the girl's hands. "They did not say they are going to Town, but I am sure his lordship will do what he deems necessary to keep the gentlemen from carrying tales, even inadvertently."

"You are right—I know I can always depend on Lord Crandall to protect me." Pamela's eyes glittered with dawning realization.

The ladies made their way down to dine. Due to Miss Kimball's managing of the seating arrangement, Alison found herself flanked by the two soldiers at the table.

"Colonel Owens, are you in the neighborhood visiting family?" Alison inquired politely.

"Thomas and I are both from a small village near the border. We often take leave together to visit home. We are now returning to our unit, which is garrisoned near Brighton."

"Do you plan to make a stay in Town on your way back?"

"Merely for the night, I fear. We have delayed so long in returning that we shall be unable to sample the delights of London. What brings you to this inn?" The colonel smiled at her with interest.

Alison was relieved that the men would not be long in Town, but she was still concerned. "We are going to visit relatives."

"And, if I am not being to presumptive, is Marcus here to accompany you or Miss Reed?"

Looking up at the earl, Alison saw his gaze was riveted on her and Colonel Owens. She attributed his interest to worry that she would tell her companion too much about

A WINTER COURTSHIP

their circumstances. She was not so foolish. "Why, he is merely escorting his late colonel's sister. Since he is my brother's friend, I offered to chaperone the young lady. I am only recently acquainted with his lordship."

"Excellent, for I should dislike setting up a flirt with an old friend's intended." Colonel Owens raised his glass to her.

"Is that what you are doing, sir?" Alison smiled at the soldier. While she liked the colonel, she did not feel that same attraction she had felt upon meeting Lord Crandall. That left her quite willing to engage in some harmless banter.

At the opposite end of the table, Lord Crandall was being subjected to a catalogue of the virtues of Miss Kimball's nephew. The earl, assuming an expression of interest, was instead watching his old friend flirt with Mrs. Prescott. Feeling a strong desire to call the man to task for his marked attention to the beautiful widow, he restrained the impulse and wished the meal were over.

What rankled the earl the most was that Mrs. Prescott did not seem to be the least put out by the soldier's flirting. Why then did she always seem to draw back each time he attempted to draw her out? Not that he got much opportunity to speak with her. Between Pamela and Miss Kimball, he often found himself exactly where he did not wish to be, across the room from the object of his interest.

He was brought back to the present when Pamela Reed overturned Norton's glass of wine, effectively ending the meal. The ladies rose to retire since they planned an early start.

As they were saying their good nights, Marcus got an opportunity to speak with Alison. "Did you enjoy the evening?"

"Your friends are very pleasant, my lord. Do you think it advisable to suggest that they not mention their meeting with Miss Reed to anyone?"

"An excellent suggestion, my dear. I shall address the matter before they leave in the morning. I do not know what I should do without your excellent advice."

"I am certain an 'old soldier' like yourself would be helpless as a newborn," Alison teased.

Marcus grinned. "Have I been such a managing fellow?"

"Not in the least. I would say you have been very receptive to my suggestions regarding Pamela, my lord." Alison was actually surprised to realize the truth of this. Here was a man who valued a woman's opinion.

"You seem surprised, Mrs. Prescott. Did you not realize that soldiers are the most compliant of gentlemen? After years of taking orders how else could it be?"

"How else, indeed?" Alison smiled as she followed the other ladies up the stairs.

The gentlemen stayed to share a round of brandy and recount old tales from the war. Slowly, one by one, they each retired until at last Marcus found himself alone in the large room, making plans for their journey. On the morrow he would try to spend some time alone with Alison Prescott. He'd enjoyed their brief exchange. If it required that he had to lock Miss Kimball and Pamela in the carriage, then so be it. With thoughts of the widow at the front of his mind, he went up to his room for the night.

Four

Early the following morning, Alison arrived in the private parlor to find that the two soldiers, having already breakfasted, were about to take their leave. Colonel Owens sent Wallingham to see to the carriage, then lingered to place a kiss on her hand as he said his farewells. "I hope to see you in Town during the Season, Mrs. Prescott. Your lovely smile has given me the incentive to come to London frequently."

"I should be delighted to see you there, Colonel."

"Perhaps you would consider allowing me to escort you to some function." The soldier held her hand longer than was truly correct.

"Miss Kimball and I would welcome a visit from both you and Major Wallingham." Alison gently removed her hand, not wanting to foster false hopes.

"Then we shall look forward to the occasion. Will Miss Reed be staying with you in Town?"

Alison hesitated. "Not that—"

Relief filled her when the earl arrived in the parlor at that moment, sparing her the necessity of answering.

"Off so early, Jamie?"

"Thought we ought to get moving with so far to go. The rain might come again from the looks of it."

Peering out the window into the morning darkness, Alison asked, "How can you tell that before daybreak, sir?"

"No stars, madam. A soldier must know all the tricks about predicting the weather."

Alison turned to the earl. "That means Pamela will not be able to ride in your carriage again, my lord. She will be quite crushed."

The earl shook his head. "No, I shall take her up with me until it starts to rain to spare you her complaints. Jamie, might we have a word alone outside?"

The soldier bowed and the earl followed him out. Alison suspected he meant to tell his friend the circumstances about Pamela and request his silence.

She drifted to the window to look out, but could barely see the two men in the faint dawn light as they walked over to a curricle where Major Wallingham was already seated. They stood speaking earnestly for several moments.

Pamela entered the parlor, red pelisse and bonnet in hand. "Where are the gentlemen?"

"I believe Norton is not yet down and Lord Crandall is saying his goodbyes to the colonel and the major in the yard."

"The soldiers are leaving? I wished to bid them a safe journey for luck. I always did so with my brother except on his final leave, for I was away at school." The girl dropped her bonnet to the table and quickly went to the door, pulling on her coat.

"They are only going to London, my dear, not into battle," Alison called, but found herself speaking to an empty room.

Looking out the window, she saw Pamela dash across the nearly empty yard, weaving her way through the ruts

A WINTER COURTSHIP

of pooled water left from the rain. As the girl's luck would have it, she slipped on the mud and went sprawling into a particularly large puddle.

Intent on helping the hapless child, Alison ran to the door and straight into her brother as he was about to enter the private room. "I do apologize, Norton. You are not hurt?"

"Not a bit, but what is the matter, Ally?"

"I shall be back. There has been an accident."

Sir Norton stepped aside. *"What* a surprise! Is Miss Reed unharmed and may I be of help?"

"Perhaps you could find the innkeeper and have them provide hot water and a bath." Alison started towards the inn door, but halted when it opened. The colonel and the earl escorted a very muddy young lady inside.

"My dear Miss Reed," the soldier said, clutching her arm, heedless of the mud staining his gloves. "Is there anything I can do to help you?"

"You are most kind, Colonel, but I would not wish you to delay your journey. I shall be fine once I am clean. I bid you a safe and pleasant trip," Pamela said bravely.

The earl smiled at his friend. "You may be assured that we shall take care of Miss Reed. I know you must be back at your regiment soon so you may go with an easy mind."

"Miss Reed, 'twas a pleasure meeting both you and Mrs. Prescott. I hope to see you all in Town during the Season." With that, the colonel bowed and left.

Pamela, chin trembling, tried to smile at Alison. "Do you think my coat can be cleaned? 'Twas so very dashing."

Alison looked at the earl, but could only detect the slightest sparkle in his blue eyes. "Come, child, we must get you out of those wet things. We shall worry about the garment later." Glancing at her brother, she noticed he had drawn back in distaste at Pamela's condition, fearful of ruining his own splendid attire. Hoping the muddy girl would not note his reaction, Alison called, "Norton, pray do as I asked."

At once, the baronet disappeared into the rear hallway which led to the kitchens. He could be heard shouting for hot water and a great deal of it.

Marcus kindly tried to soothe the girl's sensibilities. "Miss Reed, I shall see that breakfast is awaiting you when you come down."

Taking the young lady by the elbow, Alison led her up the stairs. She called over her shoulder, "Might you have my trunk unloaded, again, my lord? I have just the thing for Pamela to change into for her ride in your curricle."

"I shall be allowed to ride with his lordship today?" Pamela halted her inspection of the muddy coat. Looking back at the earl, she gave a grateful smile. "Thank you, my lord. I am looking forward to the journey." Then she allowed herself to be led upstairs.

Nearly an hour later, Alison and Pamela joined Sir Norton, Miss Kimball, and the earl in the parlor where a large breakfast was laid. The young lady, now dressed in a white gown with a blue dot and blue ribbons, looked as if she'd regained her high spirits.

"Can you believe it, my lord? Dear Alison and I are the same size. She has kindly offered me this lovely gown *and* a new pelisse and bonnet of the latest fashion."

Sir Norton, who'd risen as the ladies entered, attempted to make up for his former gaffes. "Miss Reed, you would attract notice no matter what you wear."

Pamela smiled, then looked at the earl in anticipation of a compliment, but he merely nodded in agreement.

Alison was surprised by her brother's compliments and wondered if he was being merely kind or if he was interested in Pamela. Despite the child's awkwardness she liked her quite well, and if Norton felt drawn in that direction, she would not object to his marrying even if she would never again enter that holy state.

Miss Kimball cleared her throat impatiently. "Is it not time to eat? I am feeling faint from this delay."

Some thirty minutes later after a large meal, the two coaches set off to follow the servants' conveyance, which had left as soon as Alison's trunk had been reloaded. The earl handed Pamela, looking lovely in her borrowed blue pelisse and bonnet, into his curricle and covered her comfortably with a blanket. The baronet joined his sister and Miss Kimball in the closed carriage if not with enthusiasm, at least with some semblance of complacency.

Just as the carriage moved forward, Alison heard Pamela utter a loud giggle at something the earl said. With a sigh, she settled down to wonder about what his lordship would say to Pamela.

Miss Kimball, who could not stand silence, began to regale Sir Norton with the tale of her last trip to the Reverend Mr. Malcolm Hewitt's home in Devonshire. She knew endless facts about his household.

By the time the party stopped to dine at one of the clock, the baronet was nearly glassy-eyed. Pulling his sister aside after the older lady had left the vehicle, he said, "Ally, who is this cursed vicar? If I hear one more word about the excellence of Hewitt's manners, his house, his dog, and his servants, I shall throw myself under the wheels of a passing carriage. I tell you now, if Miss Reed rides with Marcus after we have eaten, I am riding on the box with the coachman."

Alison laughed, then pointed out the large drops of rain which were beginning to fall. "I believe that Pamela will gladly give you the honour of riding in an open carriage during the rain. Despite a hood, one always gets so damp."

His face brightening, Sir Norton uttered, "Thank God. I have never been so happy to see the coming of a storm."

After the meal, the earl again changed traveling companions and rode with a grateful Sir Norton. The coaches traveled steadily north as the rain came down. The wind whipped occasional bursts of mist onto the men, but neither complained about being cold or damp.

Alison watched the drops roll down the window of the carriage while the other two ladies slept. Her thoughts were of the two gentlemen in the curricle. Smiling, she wondered if Norton was as comfortable now after several hours in the cold and rain as he had been while here in the moderate warmth of the traveling coach. The earl, being a former soldier, probably paid scant attention to the conditions. Little seemed to affect his calm and controlled demeanor, and she liked that in a man.

In truth, she had found nothing that did not intrigue her about his lordship, but she would not allow herself to be drawn in by her fascination. She had found that a man might be everything polite until he got a wedding ring upon his bride's hand. Stuart had easily charmed her into thinking him the perfect gentleman. Only after they wed had his true nature been revealed. No, she would never again risk the miseries of marriage. Closing her eyes, she tried to push thoughts of Lord Crandall from her mind.

Just before dark, the carriages arrived at the White Hart

Inn. Alison was surprised to find that she had been able to sleep. She inquired about the gentlemen's comfort during the trip, but they did not complain. However, each gladly accepted the steaming hot tankards of liquid containing Atwood's secret recipe.

After an excellent meal, the ladies decided to retire for the evening. His lordship delayed them momentarily, saying, "I have good news. The innkeeper tells me we are within half a day's drive of the border."

There was a general murmur of approval, then Sir Norton said, "We are making good speed despite the weather. I say we shall be at my grandmother's in two days' time."

"We must thank you, my lord," Alison said to Lord Crandall. "You have made the journey as comfortable as any trip I have ever traveled."

Miss Kimball, not liking the look which passed between the widow and the earl, frowned. "Let us retire ladies, for we shall have an early start in the morning."

The earl countered, "There is no need to rise before eight. We are making good time and I know how fatiguing travel can be."

Miss Kimball ushered the two younger women out of the parlor. She made certain that Alison had no opportunity for private discourse with the earl.

Pamela, who had remained quiet during the discussion of the journey, went glumly to bed. She knew she had little time to prevail upon the earl to enter a marriage of convenience, although she still was uncertain that was what she wished. But if she did, she had but two days to get the Earl of Crandall to ask for her hand in marriage. Oh, what a dilemma!

***

A sharp knock sounded on the ladies' bedroom door at six of the clock the following morning. Alison, startled from a light sleep, rose from the bed, pulling a pale peach wrapper over her night rail. Somewhere deep inside her, she knew there was something wrong as she lit a candle.

She opened the door to find the earl fully dressed in tan buckskins and dark green coat, a worried frown on his handsome face. Alison felt her cheeks warm as his gaze swept over her attire. "Is there something amiss, my lord?"

Marcus felt suddenly speechless as Mrs. Prescott stood before him, auburn hair tumbled about her shoulders, night clothes doing little to conceal her feminine curves. He longed to reach out and draw her into his arms, then he gave himself a mental shake. Things had taken a serious turn. "I fear I have bad news. Atwood awoke me to say that Stick is ill with a fever. I think getting wet yesterday did not agree with him."

Alison felt a tremor of fear. Norton was rarely ill, but their father had been taken off with a fever. "I shall get dressed and go to him immediately."

Closing the door, she discovered both Miss Kimball and Pamela sitting up in their beds, the latter on a trundle. The young girl tossed back the covers. "Sir Norton is ill?" When Alison said he was, Pamela continued, "I hope you will allow me to share the nursing with you. I was quite good at it when I was at school and I know the recipe for several excellent possets."

Unused to dealing with the sick, Miss Kimball added her tepid offer of help as well.

Alison agreed to accept their assistance, but knew she must be careful when allowing the clumsy child in Norton's room. Perhaps she would send Pamela down to make some harmless posset.

The trio quickly dressed and Alison went at once to her brother's room. The door was opened by his man, Baldwin.

" 'Tis a fever, ma'am. Not like Sir Norton to be sickly. Can't recollect his ever bein' so before." The grey-haired servant gestured for her to enter.

She came in and found her brother coughing and complaining about staying in bed. His face was flushed and he sat listlessly slumped against a stack of pillows.

"You do not look at all well, my dear."

"We cannot delay our trip because I have come down with a trifling cold, Ally. I shall be fine. Just need a good breakfast and—" The baronet was unable to finish as he sneezed three times.

"Nonsense," the earl said, entering the room. "We shall send for a doctor. We cannot set forth unless he says you are well enough to travel inside the closed coach."

The earl's tone brooked no argument. "Damme, Marcus. If Miss Reed were to end up married to that cousin of hers because of me, I should never forgive myself."

"I doubt her uncle has the slightest inkling of where the child has gone. We are well away from London and can afford a day or so for you to recover, can we not, Mrs. Prescott?"

Alison smiled gratefully at the earl for his kindness. "Lord Crandall is right, my dear. You cannot go out in the winter weather with a fever."

"Then leave me and go North. I shall be—" Sir Norton sat up to argue his point.

"There will be no discussion until a doctor has rendered his opinion," the earl interrupted.

The baronet slumped back on his pillows. "Don't think you can be ordering me about like your troops, Marcus."

Alison smiled, but decided that she would put an end to Norton's protests. "His lordship is only doing what I want by sending for the doctor, so do be quiet and rest until the gentleman arrives."

The earl then went to give orders to the innkeeper and the local doctor was duly summoned. While the aged medic was with her brother, Alison searched out the earl in the public rooms. "I want to thank you, Lord Crandall, for being so understanding about this delay. I would not wish to leave Norton alone with just his valet, even though I know Baldwin would take excellent care of him."

The earl frowned. "Did you think I would ask you to leave him in his condition? I fear you do not hold my gender in very high esteem, Mrs. Prescott, if you thought such."

Alison blushed. "I-I did not mean . . . that is to say . . . I apologize if you think I was impugning your honour, my lord. It was only that I thought you might have felt some urgency to continue, not knowing if Miss Reed's uncle was following." She turned and walked to the window, looking out at the dreary weather and people's comings and goings. "I fear I have had little reason of late to think that gentlemen are prone to consider anyone's desires but their own."

Marcus felt a rush of anger at Beau Prescott that he could have treated his wife such. He moved to stand beside her, gazing down at her lovely profile as she continued to watch the early morning traffic entering and leaving the inn yard. "I did not take offense, madam. But my honour would not allow me to disregard a lady's wishes, especially knowing how you must feel about your brother. Do not confuse me with your late husband."

Alison's gaze flew up to his face. How did he know about Stuart? Had tales reached as far as the continent? "Did you know . . . the Beau?"

The earl watched the colour drain from her beautiful face. "No, my dear. I simply guessed from what little Stick told me about your former circumstances. I shall wish you better luck when you marry again. You deserve someone who will cherish you the way a wife should be."

"Marriage, sir, is something I shall never risk again. If you will excuse me, I must see to my brother." Alison left the room feeling the earl's gaze upon her. How had they gotten on the subject of her former life?

Marcus watched Mrs. Prescott go back up the stairs, her head high and her back rigid. Her avowal never to marry made him long to go after her and kiss her into soft compliance—make her wish to be his wife, but he knew he must go slowly. There was still this damnable business with Pamela and her family to be resolved before he could pursue his interest in the widow uninterrupted.

Settling into a chair, he order a tankard of ale and waited for the doctor and Mrs. Prescott to come down. He hoped Stick was not seriously ill, for his sister's sake.

The earl's patience was rewarded when Alison accompanied the doctor downstairs. She seemed to have regained her composure as they listened to the doctor confirm that the baronet had caught a simple cold. In his learned judgment, it was not serious, but he would advise them not to travel until the fever was gone.

Leaving a set of instructions and a potion that Stick pronounced vile, the doctor abandoned the young man to the ministrations of the ladies and admonished the cranky fellow to follow their advice.

After the gentleman left, the earl turned to Alison. "Can I not coax you into eating breakfast, Mrs. Prescott? You will need all your strength for your nursing."

"Thank you, but I shall have Mrs. Martin send a tray up. Kindly entertain Miss Reed, for I think she shall be quite bored with this delay."

"I shall do whatever you wish, madam." The earl bowed and watched the widow hurry up the stairs. Did she wish to avoid him or was it mere concern for her brother? With a shrug of his shoulders he went to search out Miss Reed and see what damage she was wreaking.

"Milord," the innkeeper's son called as he entered the stables. "Ye best get to the kitchens afore me ma takes a wooden spoon to the young lady."

"A wooden spoon?" The earl came out of the stall where one of his two bays was stabled, closing the gate behind him.

"Aye, Ma whacks me and me brothers with her cook spoon when we're in trouble."

With a sigh, Marcus asked, "What has Miss Reed been about? She was reading quietly when I left her half an hour ago."

The red-haired urchin shook his head. "Don't know what the lass was a-fixin' to do, but her done broke me ma's favorite bowl and spilt molasses all over the place."

"What is your name, my boy?"

"I be Luke, milord, after me da."

"Well, Luke, show me the quickest way to the scene of the disaster."

The lad ran out of the stables and around behind the inn. The earl could hear the bitter complaining of Mrs. Martin, the innkeeper's wife, before Luke even opened the door.

"The kitchens ain't no place for a lady of quality and I'll brook no one intrudin' where they don't belong. Look at this mess and me with the stagecoach due in less than two hours. And the bowl my Lucas brought me all the way from Sheffield ruint. I tell you—" The plump woman halted her tirade as she spied the earl entering the back door.

Marcus could see Pamela's handiwork clearly. She stood at the end of a large table. At her feet was a bowl broken into several pieces, its contents spilled down the front of the girl's borrowed dress and splashed in a growing circle on the floor. "Well, my dear, I see you have been busy. Did you decide to take up cooking to fill your time?"

"Sir, I was trying to mix a recipe for curing colds that my Aunt Mary uses, but . . . the molasses got sticky and when I tried to wipe my hand, I dropped the bowl by accident."

The innkeeper's wife, hands on hips, demanded, "And I'm wantin' to know what this child is doin' in here and who'll pay for my bowl."

"I am not a child and I am perfectly capable of mixing a posset. Well, if only the bowl had not been quite so big. I shall pay for the bowl, for I am an heiress, you know."

"I shall pay for the bowl, Mrs. Martin. You, Miss Reed, might want to let Mrs. Prescott take care of her brother. You need only worry about yourself."

Pamela looked down at the dark stain on her dress and

tears began to pool in her eyes. "I shall have nothing to wear at this rate."

Alison and Miss Kimball arrived at that moment to see what the ruckus was. Upon hearing Pamela's lament and seeing the state she was in, Alison thought she would be the one with nothing to wear if they did not keep the child out of trouble.

Pushing the worry from her mind, she set about trying to appease the innkeeper's wife while Miss Kimball went to comfort Pamela. "I fear this was my fault, Mrs. Martin. Pamela came up trying to help and I sent her down to make her posset when she offered her services. We shall have it cleaned up in a trice."

The plump woman seemed to realize how she was speaking to a guest. Her tone suddenly softened, "No, no, madam. I shall put Luke here to cleanin' it up. He is a good boy and will help. I was just upset about my bowl and such. You take the young lady upstairs and we'll take care of the cleanin'. Annie here will put some water to boil."

"Pray, go to our room, dear Pamela. Grace and I shall bring water." Alison urged the girl to leave the scene before she began to cry in earnest.

Miss Reed turned with a slight sniffle and disappeared in the direction of her room. Alison drew the earl away as Mrs. Martin and her servant went back to work, and Luke started to clean the mess. Miss Kimball came close to overhear the conversation.

Alison bit lightly at her lip before saying, "I guess I should have known better, but she was so intent on doing something to help. I thought it safer to have her out of Norton's room.

The earl smiled. "You had better go after her now. I

have come to fear leaving Miss Reed to her own devices at all."

Miss Kimball's eyes took on a cunning look. "Yes, my lord. I would say what the young lady needs is a husband to look after her."

Lord Crandall's eyebrows rose at the notion. "But she is just a child."

Taking Alison by the arm to lead her away from the earl, the companion said, "Why, she is the perfect age for marrying. Young enough to mold to the ways of a gentleman without the least resistance. Shall we go up and pick out a dress for Miss Reed to wear, dear Alison?"

Marcus followed the ladies into the hall, then watched them go up the stairs. He could almost wish Miss Reed would fall in love and marry. The obligation he felt to her brother would be supplanted by her husband's right to look out for her. And he would be free to convince Mrs. Prescott to consider him as a suitor. But he must be patient. They were nearly at their destination and he must take care to settle the child's affairs before he worried about his own.

Five

". . . And Mr. Raulerson even bought Eva an Irish thoroughbred. She is a wonderful rider," Pamela said, chattering to Alison about her former school life. The girl eyed Sir Norton, who lay in bed across the room listening, and she airily added, "I am not so high in the instep as to think of Miss Raulerson as a Cit despite the fact that her father is in trade. She was the liveliest of my school friends."

After a cough, the baronet replied, "I am sure she is very nice, Miss Reed, but I would not recommend you air your views on Cits to the *ton*. Society people are rather proud and hold themselves above such common citizens."

Alison, sensing the pair might argue, said, "Norton, you should be resting. Are we disturbing you with our conversation?"

"In truth, Ally, I do not feel but a little ill. I think it foolish to be delaying our trip for—"

"We are all perfectly happy to stay until your fever subsides." Alison rose and went to her brother. Laying her hand upon his forehead, she could feel only the slightest warmth. "I think that by night your fever should be gone."

A brief knock sounded on the door, then the earl entered the room carrying a portable secretary. "How are you feeling, Stick?"

"More restless than ill."

"A good sign that your malady is not serious in nature." Seeing Alison beside the bed, he inquired, "Is he still feverish, Mrs. Prescott?"

"Only a little, my lord." Alison began to straighten her brother's covers to distract herself from Lord Crandall. Why could she not simply ignore his blue eyes and winning smile?

"Miss Reed," the earl said, advancing toward the young lady, "I have come with a task for you. Miss Kimball made the suggestion to me, and I quite agreed."

"I shall do whatever you wish, my lord."

"I think you should write a letter to your aunt, explaining that you are safe and have found employment as a companion."

Pamela started to her feet. "But, sir, how will you get the letter to them without them knowing where I am?"

"Never worry about that, my dear. I shall have it delivered by messenger. They shall never know who helped you. Holding your aunt in some affection, I thought you might want to ease her mind."

The young girl sagged back in the seat. "Yes, I do."

The earl placed the small wooden secretary on the table by the window. "You will need a candle, for I fear the light is not bright enough here for writing."

"Allow me, Pamela," Alison offered, while the earl moved a chair to the table. She brought one of the two candles which were burning on either side of Norton's bed due to the greyness of the day.

As Pamela dipped her pen into the inkstand, Alison walked to the opposite side of her brother's bed to put some distance between her and Lord Crandall. To her dismay, he followed her.

"Miss Kimball suggested that I take the child out for a walk after her letter is written and I was hoping to convince you to join us."

About to protest, Alison was interrupted by the baronet, whose voice sounded hoarse. "Yes, Ally, I insist you go with them, if only to make certain Miss Reed stays clean and dry."

Looking at Pamela, who was fidgeting with the quill, all the while dropping spots of ink on the paper, Alison smiled. "I should be delighted to join you, my lord."

Over at the table, Pamela was having a difficult time thinking what to say to her aunt. Seeing several blots of ink on the sheet on which she'd written "Dear Aunt Mary," she put the pen down and crumpled up the paper. Retrieving the pen, she inspected the point for sharpness, then hunched down on the table to think.

Suddenly remembering the candle, she sat up and moved it closer to the window so she would not end up with tallow in her hair. Then she leaned forward, putting her chin upon her hands to think. She would simply write that she did not want to worry her aunt and that she would be quite safe with the family who now employed her, remembering to send her love as well. Satisfied with this, she sat up to remove a clean sheet from the secretary, but her elbow bumped the brass holder. The candle toppled into the curtain, which ignited with frightening speed.

Pamela jumped to her feet, backing away from the spreading flames. "Oh, no! Oh, no!" was all she could utter in her fright as her trembling hands covered her mouth.

The trio across the room dashed into action. The earl

A WINTER COURTSHIP

and Alison ran to the blaze. He pulled the entire rod down to the floor, then she opened the window to let the smoke escape. Both began to stomp out the flames.

Sir Norton, despite wearing only his night shirt, left the bed and immediately took the frightened girl in his arms and uttered comforting words.

Pamela found herself staring breathlessly into a pair of kind green eyes. Her heart fluttered at the feel of the gentleman's strong arms encircling her. She felt safe and yet trembled at the same time.

Hearing Lord Crandall call a warning to Alison to be careful, Pamela was suddenly aware she must help. Reluctantly backing away from Sir Norton, she spied the bowl of lavender water Mrs. Martin had sent up to bathe the baronet's fevered brow. She quickly picked it up, flinging the contents at the burning curtains.

Lord Crandall, having finished extinguishing the fire, turned to see how Miss Reed fared and received a bowl full of water down the front of his coat, buckskins, and Hessians.

Pamela, realizing her efforts to help were merely another mistake, threw down the bowl and rushed to the door. She hurled the portal open and discovered Miss Kimball about to knock.

The older woman at once saw the young lady was greatly distressed. "Whatever is the matter, child?"

The anguished miss was so overcome with emotion, she merely shook her head and dashed from the room with a muffled sob.

The only thing Miss Kimball could see of the room from where she stood in the hall was the baronet standing beside his bed, legs exposed to view. "Sir Norton, have you no decency? To be exposing an innocent girl to such an indecorous view of your unsightly bare limbs is unthinkable. For shame, sir!" Putting her nose in the air, she followed the distraught Miss Reed.

Scrambling back into bed, the young man said, "Unsightly! I was always wont to think that my limbs were quite fine."

Alison ignored her brother's grumbling and struggled to suppress a smile as she turned to the earl. "Perhaps, sir, you should change. Then we might raise Miss Reed's spirits with that walk you spoke of."

"Ah, but who is going to raise mine, dear lady? I've come to think we shall not make it to your grandmother's in one piece," the earl said half teasingly.

"Nonsense! Pamela's accidents are usually quite harmless and she has our constant companionship to prevent anything serious. I am certain she will outgrow these mishaps."

"I say, Marcus, do you think my limbs unsightly?" Sir Norton asked, still offended by Miss Kimball's cutting remark.

"Oh, stubble it, Stick. No one gives a thought to your limbs with Miss Reed about wreaking havoc. I shall send Mrs. Martin up to clean this mess." So saying, the earl left to change his clothes.

Alison smiled. Even the earl was losing patience with Pamela and her 'accidents.' Going to the window, she closed it since the smoke was gone and the cold air now made the room chilly. Perhaps this walk would recover the gentleman's good humor as well as Pamela's. But she could not fault him, for even she was finding the young lady wearing. In truth, one of the things she quite liked about his lordship was his humor.

A WINTER COURTSHIP

Sir Norton interrupted his sister's thoughts. "Unsightly limbs. Whatever shall I do, Ally?"

Alison looked back at her brother. "Stop worrying about Miss Kimball's thoughtless remark and get some rest. I am going to accompany Lord Crandall and Miss Reed on a walk."

"But how can I sleep, knowing that everyone thinks my limbs—"

"Norton! Do stop being ridiculous. If you are so worried about such, simply do not attend parties in your nightshirt." So saying, Alison left the room.

"Attend parties—why," Sir Norton suddenly laughed. Alison was right. He was being absurd. Then he remembered the way Miss Reed had gazed at him when he held her during the excitement. A dashed pretty girl, that one. He liked the way she felt in his arms. She needed someone to watch out for her, and he was not adverse to being the one. With that thought, he settled into the covers to sleep.

Miss Reed's thoughts were equally turned to Sir Norton as she sat in the room she shared with the other ladies. What did he think of her and her stupid accidents? But it mattered not the least, for Miss Kimball said he was almost betrothed to another, she thought with a sigh.

The chamber door opened and Miss Kimball entered their room. That lady knew she needed a moment alone with the chit to impel her in the right direction. "Are you quite all right, my dear?"

"Just feeling foolish for my clumsiness."

The older lady sat on the bed with a cunning glint in her eye. "Did you decide against my suggestion of marrying Lord Crandall, my dear?"

Pamela stood and glumly looked in the mirror to see

if she had suffered any smoke damage. "Well, I guess it would be preferable to living as a companion in Scotland. But, why would he want to put up with such an awkward—nay, dangerous—miss?"

"Don't be silly, child, men love nothing more than to feel needed. Pray, who needs protecting more than someone like yourself? But you must spark the earl's interest. Flirt with him, flatter him, let him know you like him. If that does not work, hint that such a marriage would not be abhorrent to you. You must make things happen."

Patting her mussed blond curls into place, Pamela frowned. "It will seem so strange to be doing such with my brother's friend." But, she mused, not so strange with Sir Norton.

"Stop thinking about him as merely a family acquaintance and remember he is a handsome hero of which most girls dream." Really, the child was quite uncooperative.

Alison entered the room. "Are you quite recovered, Pamela?"

"I do so apologize. I don't know how these things happen."

"Never mind, child. Get your hat and pelisse, for the earl is taking us for a walk."

Miss Kimball immediately tried to stop Alison. "My dear, who shall sit with dear Sir Norton if you are off with the earl?"

"It was my brother who insisted I go, Grace. If you are so worried about him, why do you not take a turn in the sickroom?"

"No, no, if you think he will be fine alone, I shall stay in here and read."

"Come, Pamela, we do not want to keep the earl waiting." Alison found herself eager to join the earl on a walk, but reasoned it was because she had been cooped up in her brother's room all day.

The wind blew in occasional gusts, swirling dried leaves and straw around the threesome who ambled down the road out of the small village. The earl couldn't figure out how he had managed to get only Miss Reed to take his arm. He glanced ahead at Mrs. Prescott, who walked some ten feet in front. She looked exceptionally pretty in a dark purple pelisse with matching bonnet. Her lavender gloved hands were tucked inside a large white fur muff, her excuse for not taking his arm.

Miss Reed interrupted his thoughts.

"I do hope you have forgiven me, my lord. To have thrown water on you—"

"Think no more about it, dear girl." He had never realized how tiring young ladies could be with their constant chatter about first one bit of nonsense and then another. Now Miss Reed had taken to uttering the most foolish compliments about his horses, his carriage, even of his so-called bravery during the war.

Looking at the widow, who had stopped to inspect the stone carving atop a gate post, the earl admired her quiet composure. She merely enjoyed her surroundings without feeling the need to converse. This was what he wanted in a woman, but he would honour his commitment to Miss Reed's problems first. He just wished Mrs. Prescott would give him some encouragement. With no particular reason other than to hear her pleasant voice, he called, "Are you too cold, madam? We can turn back at any time."

"I find the air quite refreshing." Alison turned to go

further up the road. She found she very much disliked Pamela's flirting with his lordship. Or was the chit merely trying to make amends for the accident? Glancing back at the pair, the girl simpered and fluttered like a practiced coquette.

Looking away, Alison puzzled over Pamela's strange behavior. Her musings were interrupted when a large grey dog of questionable parentage but with decidedly kind eyes entered the road from a break in the tall stone fence.

"Why, hello, just who do you belong to?" she asked playfully. She bent to pet the animal, whose tail wagged with glee at the attention.

Miss Reed clutched the earl's arm as they advanced on the widow and her new companion. "Sir, do you think Alison should be touching a strange animal?"

"He appears quite friendly. I often think animals sense a great deal about people." The earl envied the attention the widow lavished on the stray dog.

A sharp whistle sounded on the breeze, then a boy's voice called, "Boney, Boney, where are ye?" Moments later a lad exited the woods from the same hole in the fence as the dog and stopped in his tracks. "Milord, didn't think to see ye out here, what with the weather bein' so uncertain." Seeing the trio around his dog, he added, "Boney's not botherin' ye, is he?"

"Not in the least. Ladies, allow me to present the innkeeper's son, Luke."

The boy, who looked to be ten years of age, pulled a felt hat from his head, exposing tousled red hair as he bowed to the ladies. His arrival on the scene caused Boney to dance about with excitement.

Pamela clung to Lord Crandall and drew back as the mutt came up to sniff at her skirts. Luke's eyebrows rose at the lady's reaction. "Be ye afeared of dogs, miss? Boney's not a bit mean."

"No, I-I simply prefer cats." Loosening her grip, she bravely reached down and gave the dog a single pat, then quickly clamped her hand on the earl's arm again.

"Cats! Why you're agoin' toward the Canes' cottage and Mrs. Cane's got a new litter of kittens in the barn. If you'd like, I'll take ye to seen 'um."

Pamela smiled up at the earl. "Could we, my lord? For I adore kittens above all other animals."

"What say you, Mrs. Prescott?" the earl inquired agreeably.

"I am enjoying the walk, sir. If Pamela longs to see kittens, I have no objection. Lead the way, Luke."

They followed the lad and his dog down the road. Alison was glad for a distraction, for it might lessen Pamela's rather forward behavior. Not that she could blame the girl for finding the handsome earl attractive, she thought, as she glanced at him through her lashes.

Luke drew Alison's attention with a shout. He'd slowly widened the gap from the others but now stood waiting at a gate and gesturing for them to enter. Beyond the fence was a small cottage and a stone barn with four covered pens in the rear.

A man exiting the barn called to the lad, "Luke, what brings ye to us?"

Scrambling over the wall, the boy ran to the man. "I've brung some guests from the inn what want to see the new kittens."

The farmer eyed the trio curiously. "Well, they be welcome."

Marcus opened the gate for the ladies and they entered the farm yard. Tipping his hat to the man, the earl said,

"I hope we do not inconvenience you, sir. I am the Earl of Crandall and this is Mrs. Prescott and Miss Reed. I must compliment you on an excellent looking farm."

The farmer beamed, tugging at his hat in respect to the ladies. "My lord, we're honoured. I'm proud to say that we raise the finest pigs in three counties at Cane Cottage."

The earl fell into conversation with the farmer about his methods. Pamela, not the least interested in the subject nudged Luke. "Can you take me to the kittens?"

The lad nodded, and bounded off toward the large stone barn, his dog trailing behind.

Pamela turned to Alison. "Come, do you not want to see the little darlings?"

Shaking her head in the negative, Alison gestured for the girl to go with the innkeeper's son. "I fear cats make me sneeze. Stay with Luke and try not to get into trouble, my dear."

The earl watched Pamela disappear into the barn. He would seize the opportunity to spend time alone with the widow. "Well, sir, do not let me keep you from your work. Mrs. Prescott and I shall take a turn around the yard while we wait for Miss Reed's return."

"Very good, my lord, and know that the young lady be welcome to come see the cats anytime her likes." So saying, the farmer disappeared behind the barn.

Marcus smiled at Alison. "Do you think it safe to allow Miss Reed in the barn by herself?"

"Why, Luke is with her. He seems a sensible young lad and surely will keep her from harm."

"Let us hope. Will you join me, for I should like to inspect Mr. Cane's excellent pens. I am new to being a

A WINTER COURTSHIP

landlord and would know all I can to provide better for my people."

"I should be delighted, my lord." Alison had no doubt that the earl would excel at caring for his tenants as he had at being a soldier.

Laying her hand upon his arm, she froze as a multitude of high-pitched squeals emanated from the barn. Involuntarily she clutched the muscular limb where her hand rested. She felt the earl place a reassuring hand over her own, filling her with a sense of well-being despite what she felt would be another of Pamela's 'accidents."

"Shall we see what Miss Reed has done now?" The earl gave a soft sigh of resignation.

They started toward the open door, but halted when a veritable sea of small, squealing pigs came pouring from the open barn door. With one fluid movement, his lordship swept Alison into his arms as the army of baby swine rushed headlong at them.

The din of the fleeing animals barely penetrated Alison's awareness. Her thoughts were centered on how strong Lord Crandall's arms were and how hard was the chest upon which she was cradled. Looking up, she was transfixed by his blue eyes, which gazed at her with strong emotion.

Marcus stood staring into a pair of bewitching green eyes as he held the desirable woman to him, hoping to protect her shoes and gown. Feeling the small pigs bumping against his boots, he smiled and his eyes traveled to her full pink lips.

Alison was brought to her senses when she realized the earl was about to kiss her. Fearing her will to resist was not strong despite her thoughts on marriage, she stammered, "My lord . . . this is Farmer Cane's livelihood running loose and Miss Reed was surely responsible."

"Are you unharmed, madam?"

"Quite," was all that Alison could utter, so confused were her emotions as the earl set her feet on the ground.

Turning to see the small curled tails disappearing into the farmer's woods with an excited Boney in pursuit, he shouted, "Luke!"

The lad appeared in the open doorway, eyes wide with fear. "Here, sir."

"Make certain the ladies get safely back to the inn."

Pamela came hesitantly past the lad. Seeing the look on his lordship's face, she called, "I did not cause the gate to fly open, no matter what you think, sir."

"Go back to the inn and please try to stay out of mischief until I return. Mrs. Prescott, I shall rely upon you." Without further comment, the earl disappeared behind the barn in search of the farmer to alert him about the events.

Pamela's chin struck a stubborn line. "I tell you, Alison, it was not my fault. The strap holding the gate was worn through and it broke when Mrs. Cane's cat jumped upon it to get away from Boney."

Taking the girl's arm, she lead her to the closed gate. "It does not matter now, my dear. The earl will handle the problem."

Alison gave little thought to the pigs as she led Pamela back to the inn. In her mind she kept going over the moment when the earl had swept her up from the onslaught of animals and held her close. Despite all her best intentions, she found that she vastly enjoyed the moment. Whatever was she to do about her growing attraction to Lord Crandall? She would have to simply put thoughts of him from her mind, for she was determined not to wed again. Was she not?

Marcus stepped into the warmth of the inn. He could not ever remember being so tired or so dirty. He hoped never to see another pig and wished he did not have to see Miss Reed, either. The bumbling chit was hopeless.

He spied Mrs. Prescott at the foot of the stairs in conversation with Atwood.

"Sir, you are back," the valet said, interrupting whatever the lady had been saying.

The earl was gratified by the look of delight which filled the lady's eyes. "My lord, I have been so worried. It has been dark for hours and we had no word of you."

Atwood advanced to remove the earl's muddy greatcoat. "I told madam that you have faced many dangers in battle, so she should not worry so about a few swine."

"Atwood, if Bonaparte's army had been comprised of pigs, we would have lost at Waterloo. I daresay they are the fleetest and slipperiest creatures on earth. If not for Cane's five sons we would still be chasing them. I hope never to have to deal with one again."

Alison laughed. "But sir, why did you not simply pay Mr. Cane for his pigs instead of helping him catch them?" She could imagine no other gentleman bothering to get himself dirty for a mere farmer.

"In truth, I had not the stomach for leaving the little things to freeze in the woods overnight." The earl gave Alison a wry grin. "Foolish considering their fate, I know."

She did not think it foolish in the least. It said much about Lord Crandall's kind character.

As she watched the valet remove the earl's coat, Alison's eyes widened when she noticed a bloody cloth wrapped about his hand. "Sir, you have hurt yourself."

The servant folded the coat over one arm, saying, "I shall get the medical kit, my lord."

Atwood disappeared up the stairs, and Alison led the earl into the private parlor.

"Where is our dangerous Miss Reed?" Marcus really had no wish to see the girl until his exasperation had passed, but was curious about her absence.

"I have set her to reading to Norton, and Grace is there for propriety's sake. I felt certain that between them they could prevent Pamela from bringing down the inn."

"How is Stick?" The earl slumped down into a chair at the table, making certain to choose the one closest to the fire.

"His fever is gone and he is determined to travel in the morning."

Marcus was surprised at how much the thought of getting Miss Reed to her destination pleased him. "The doctor said he might when he was feeling more in curl. I say we wait and see what the morning will bring."

Atwood returned at that moment with a large wooden box and a bowl of water. He set them upon the table. "Sir, if Mrs. Prescott might handle your wound, I could make you something special to warm you."

The earl raised one questioning eyebrow, gazing at her. Alison felt the blood rush in her ears at the thought of touching him. "I-I shall take care of his lordship. I suspect he is in great need of one of your drinks, Atwood."

"Very good, madam." The valet left Alison to the task.

"Shall we remove your coat, my lord?"

Marcus shrugged out of his jacket and put the mud-crusted garment on the back of his chair, then extended his hand to Mrs. Prescott. She appeared nervous as she took a bar of soap from the box then gently removed the soiled cloth and drew his hand over the bowl.

Hoping to eliminate her uneasiness, he asked, "Shall I strangle Miss Reed before I dine or after?"

Alison's gaze flew to his face. Seeing the teasing twinkle in his eyes, she smiled. "Did you know that both she and Luke declare that 'twas the cat which caused the gate to open?"

Shaking his head, the earl laughed. "What, an accident in which our Miss Reed was present and not the culprit? Then I must ride for Canterbury to inform the Bishop that a true miracle has occurred."

Lathering his hand, Alison was amazed at how strong, even relaxed, it seemed in hers. "Perhaps, you might tell her you know she was not responsible for the pigs getting out. She has been fretting and fuming since we returned."

"Will you not allow me to enjoy a few moments' peace before I continue my role as guardian to such a calamity?"

Rinsing the soap from his hand, Alison bent over it to see the wound. "You may have your rest, sir."

"Is it deep?" The earl's husky voice sounded next to Alison's ear, making her heart hammer loudly.

Straightening, she pulled clean linen strips from the box to cover her discomposure. "I do not believe it to be very serious, my lord."

The earl rose after she wrapped the wound. She found herself looking up into a pair of blue eyes which seemed to pull her ever closer to the man. His voice barely above a whisper, the earl said, "Mrs. Prescott, I do not know where to begin to thank you for all your kindness to me and Miss Reed."

"It has been a pleasure, sir." Alison spoke the words, but she could only think of how handsome he looked.

Marcus's hand came up and tilted the lady's chin just a bit higher. His mouth closed over hers and he was met with a willingness that made him forget every other consideration and draw her into the circle of his arms. Her answering response grew as did his own. He knew he loved her and wanted to possess her.

Hearing Miss Reed and Miss Kimball's voices in the hallway, he reluctantly released Alison. She gazed up at him as if the kiss had brought about some revelation. He hoped she was as shaken by the embrace as he had been.

Alison's knees trembled and her face flushed while she stared up at the earl. To her dismay, she felt a burning desire for another kiss. What was she thinking? This was not the behavior of a woman determined never to be under the control of another man. She heard the door open and the ladies entered. In a daze, she moved away from this man who seemed to draw her resolve right out of her.

Oblivious to Alison's blush, Pamela eyed the earl closely for signs of temper, but could see none. "There you are, my lord. We had grown quite worried."

"I am safely back and very sharp set." Marcus moved away from Alison, who was busy putting away the medical supplies.

"Were you injured, Lord Crandall?" Miss Kimball asked, staring at the box.

"Just a scratch. Have you ladies dined?"

"Yes. Alison insisted we not wait, but we shall keep you company while you enjoy your meal." Pamela was delighted that the earl was not angry with her.

Miss Kimball, however, took note of the blush on Alison's face. What had the pair been about here alone? She was going to have to step up her plans. "Alison, dear, you might want to go up and say good night to Sir Norton. I believe he is about to retire. I shall go with you, for I am rather fatigued myself."

Alison was still in such confusion after the kiss that she allowed Grace to lead her from the room after saying good night. As the earl came to bid her a pleasant sleep, his eyes seemed to send her a special message that warmed her heart.

She paid her brother a brief visit, then went to her own room. He did seem better, and they would continue their journey tomorrow.

Meanwhile, Grace Kimball lay in wait with a new plan aimed at her mistress. The older woman remained quiet until the maid had prepared the widow to retire and left.

"I had a long talk with Pamela after you returned today. She was quite distressed that the earl blamed her for the release of all those animals."

Alison crawled into bed, paying little attention to Grace's chattering, her mind still dwelling on the earl's kiss. "Well, as you saw he was not in the boughs over the incident."

"Just as I told her it would be. But you know how a young lady in love can be." Miss Kimball saw a sudden tightening of Alison's hand on her blanket.

"In love?" Alison could scarcely say the words.

"Yes, my dear, she has fallen for dear Lord Crandall and a better match I cannot imagine. She, who especially needs someone to look after her, will have an excellent person to care for her and keep her safe from her uncle and even herself."

Alison could find nothing to say, so stunned was she by the news. Pamela in love with the earl? An ache started in her heart as she lay under the covers, for Alison realized the girl had a prior claim and a need for Lord Crandall. What did it matter to her, she thought, for she had planned never to marry again. Had she not?

Some time later Alison heard Pamela quietly enter the room and retire to her trundle. Above her, Alison still lay awake, a heaviness centered in her chest, for while she did not long for marriage, she knew that the earl had touched her heart as no other had. With such painful memories of her marriage still fresh, she must never again allow a man to get so close as she had Lord Crandall.

Six

Sir Norton rose from the table as Alison and Pamela entered the private parlor. "Ladies, you look especially lovely this morning. Why, the pair of you are like spring flowers on this cold winter day." His admiring gaze lingered over Pamela, who wore a pink sprig muslin gown with white lace at her neckline and cuffs.

Alison noted he briefly glanced at her emerald green check with green velvet sleeves and bodice, before returning to gaze at the lady in pink. Seeing the besotted look in her brother's eyes, she suddenly realized he was likely to be hurt by Pamela's attraction to the earl. She pushed the thought aside, knowing there was little she could do to protect him. "How are you feeling this morning, my dear?"

"I am only a little out of frame, Ally. The fever has not returned and I shall do for the trip."

The door to the room opened and Lord Crandall ushered Miss Kimball into the room, having encountered her on the stairs. "Good morning. You are looking more fit, Stick."

"Yes, I was just telling Ally I was ready to travel. I say, Marcus, how did you injure your hand? Are you going to be able to drive today?" Sir Norton eyed the bandage curiously.

"'Tis a mere scratch from a jagged stone, my boy. I shall be able to tool my carriage as usual, so don't be getting any ideas that you are not to ride with the ladies." The earl smiled and followed Miss Kimball to the table.

The baronet shook his head. "I had no intention of offering *my* services as driver. I am not fool enough to be riding in the open in this weather with a cold, for I declare this is the dreariest morning yet. I was going to offer Ally's talents. Taught her to handle the ribbons myself."

Miss Kimball immediately protested. "Sir Norton, how could you suggest that your own sister take a seat out in the cold? I am certain his lordship is quite capable of driving his own carriage. We shall manage quite well with four in the coach."

With no thought but to defend her brother, Alison said, "Nonsense, Grace. I should be delighted to drive Lord Crandall should he wish it, regardless of the weather. You know you will be more comfortable with only three."

Alison eyed Pamela to see if she were upset to have her place usurped. But the girl seemed perfectly content to ride inside as she leaned close to Norton and whispered something. Then the pair laughed.

The maid arrived with breakfast and all appeared settled with traveling arrangements as the party sat down to eat. Later, however, the earl approached Alison about riding with him. "My dear Mrs. Prescott, I should be delighted to have you accompany me, but there is no need for you to drive."

"Do you fear that I shall overturn us, sir?"

"No, for I am certain Stick would not have suggested you take the ribbons were you the merest whipster."

The earl's crooked smile made Alison think she should

ride in the closed carriage for her heart's sake, but she would not be so craven. "Then I shall be your coachman this morning."

When they were seated in Lord Crandall's curricle, Alison felt a nervous tremor rush through her at the thought of driving for the earl. It had been years since she'd driven a spirited team. Except for the pony cart on the Prescott estate, Stuart had not allowed her to drive, belittling her skills unseen. But as soon as the ostler released their heads, the horses responded with well-matched ease to her commands.

The earl sat quietly as she maneuvered the coach out of the yard and onto the road. With a skillful crack of the whip, she set the curricle at a steady pace. She found driving his lordship's vehicle an exhilarating experience. Despite the bone chilling cold, the threatening skies, and the earl's disturbing presence beside her, Alison enjoyed her turn with the ribbons immensely.

"I must compliment Stick on being an excellent teacher," the earl said after observing her driving for several miles.

"Yes, Norton is the best of brothers." Alison was suddenly reminded that the earl was about to unknowingly hurt her sibling should he marry Pamela.

"I shall suggest that he give Miss Reed lessons in Edinburgh when he is more himself."

"That might not be for the best, my lord. I fear that Norton's growing attachment to dear Pamela is doomed to disappointment."

Marcus frowned. He, too, had seen the look in Stick's eyes when they rested on the chit. But why should his suit not prosper? Thinking that the baronet's sister was being merely protective, he teased, "Do you worry that our Miss Reed will break Stick's heart like she does most other objects she touches?"

"Sir, I do not find this a matter for laughing about. Pamela might well have her heart set in another direction completely." It seemed clear to Alison that the earl was unaware of Pamela's new feelings for him.

"I beg your pardon, madam. I fear that an excess of levity is one of my greatest faults. But I would not worry so about Stick for if he sets his mind to it, I am sure he could win any woman's affections."

"Oh, dear," Alison said distractedly.

"What is the matter?"

"Look, sir, it is beginning to snow."

The earl reluctantly drew his gaze from the lovely profile of Mrs. Prescott to see a few tiny flakes drift past the carriage. More ominous was the white haze of snow in the distance which nearly obscured a farm sitting beside the road.

"I fear we are in for a very bad storm. We shall be lucky to get half a day's travel."

They continued northward into the ever-increasing storm. As the number as well as the size of the flakes multiplied, Alison realized the earl was correct. She began to have difficulty seeing the road as snow quickly accumulated on the frozen ground.

She was about to surrender the reins to his lordship in defeat when they entered a small village with an inn at which sat the lead coach of their party. Pratt, the coachman, stood near the road signaling them to enter the yard.

"Sir, I can't see to drive no more. Atwood says he reckons this here storm is here for the day and we ought to get rooms afore we get stranded on some moor."

"I think Atwood made an excellent suggestion. See to

this carriage." The earl jumped down and helped Alison. "Go and find a warm fire—you must be quite frozen. I shall assist the ladies when their vehicle arrives."

Hurrying into the inn, Alison was greeted by the earl's batman. "I've arranged rooms with Mr. MacTaggart. There's tea awaitin' you in the private room, Mrs. Prescott."

Thanking the man, Alison entered the low-beamed chamber, going straight to the fire. Some minutes later, she was joined by the rest of her traveling companions.

"Oh, Ally, are you quite frozen?" Sir Norton came to hold his sister's still-gloved hands.

"I am fine. How are you feeling?" Alison thought his cheeks a little flushed, but hoped it was nothing but the result of the cold wind.

"I think perhaps I might retire to my room and rest a bit. I am more tired than I would have thought after so short a trip."

Pamela laid a hand on the young man's arm, eyes filled with concern. "You must take care of yourself, Sir Norton. A cold is nothing to trifle with. We insist you go to bed and rest for I heard the coachman say we would travel no more today."

Miss Kimball sneezed. " 'Tis as I feared. *I* am coming down with a cold as well. I knew I should not be near anyone who was ailing for my health is so often indifferent."

The earl made no comment, but went to the door and called Atwood. "See if the landlord can arrange a private room for Miss Kimball, for she is becoming ill and needs rest."

"Why, that is most kind of you, my lord." Miss Kimball felt a twinge of guilt for her conspiracy against the earl, but did not soften her resolve one bit.

Alison took charge. "Come let us put our unwell travelers to bed."

The earl held the door as the group exited the parlor. It looked as if they would be here for the duration of the storm. Perhaps he ought to have a word with MacTaggart about paying for any items of broken crockery or singed curtains. He strode from the room in search of the innkeeper and to find Atwood, for a hot drink was just the thing Marcus needed.

Upstairs, Sir Norton was given into the care of Baldwin with strict instructions for him to go to bed. Then Pamela and Alison made certain that the maid, Lucy, would stay with Miss Kimball after she fetched the ailing lady's tea.

Finally shown to the room which she would share with Pamela, Alison began to remove her bonnet and coat. She still felt frozen from the ride, but did not regret her time with Lord Crandall. She knew in her heart she would miss him when their journey together ended.

The sounds of other carriages entering the yard reached their ears. Alison rubbed her hands together to get the warmth back into them. "By nightfall this inn will most likely be filled to overflowing with stranded travelers."

Pamela, who'd quickly removed her outer apparel, walked to the window to look down at the newest arrivals. A low, moaning sound began to emanate from her. The girl reached out and clutched the curtains with frustration.

"Are you all right, my dear?" Alison asked from the fireplace where she stood, hands extended to the heat.

"No, no, it cannot all have been for naught." Pamela shook her head, never taking her gaze from the scene below.

"What has been for naught?"

"Our coming north, for Uncle Henry and Cousin Tobias just arrived at this inn."

With a sinking feeling, Alison went to the window and looked down to see two rather plump gentlemen having an animated conversation with Pratt. How had they found them after so many days?

Pamela flounced away from the window and threw herself on the bed. "My life is ruined. I have to accept that. I must marry Tobias or Lord Crandall and I shall never get to do what *I* want or wed who I want."

Alison was bewildered. She was not surprised that Pamela did not want to marry Tobias, but why was she saying such about the earl? "My dear, I thought you were . . . in love with his lordship."

"I do love him—like a brother. But Miss Kimball thinks I should enter a marriage of convenience with the earl to save myself from Tobias." The girl sat up and dabbed at her eyes with a handkerchief she'd pulled from a pocket.

Suddenly feeling lighthearted, Alison joined Pamela on the bed, wondering why Grace had been encouraging the child on such a path. "My dear, you do not need to marry Lord Crandall, if you do not choose. I shall do all in my power to protect you from your uncle and I am certain the earl will do the same. You will see—I am determined that should you decide to marry it will be for love."

"Truly?" The girl looked at Alison with hope.

Wishing to brighten the child's spirits, she teased, "Yes, even if I have to have your uncle sent to the gaol."

Pamela giggled through her tears.

"Now, you remain here and I shall go down to confront your uncle at Lord Crandall's side. Together, we shall see you through." Giving the girl's hand a squeeze of encouragement, Alison rose and marched out of the room, a light glowing in her green eyes. She did not dwell on her relief that Pamela would not wed Lord Crandall, merely on stopping Mr. Reed from marrying the chit to anyone she did not love.

The earl tapped the log with the heel of his Hessian, causing a shower of sparks as it shifted and began to burn more intensely. He settled into a nearby chair in the public room to drink the hot spiced brandy Atwood had provided, wondering when Alison would be down.

He was finding himself thinking more and more of the enchanting widow. He enjoyed flirting with her and teasing her, but he knew her wounded heart must be slowly allowed to heal. He could not rush his fences with the lady, but it was not easy, for every instinct made him long to take her in his arms.

The sounds of arriving travelers disturbed his thoughts. It was fortunate they had ended their journey early, for The Lion would be filled to overflowing as the storm worsened.

Suddenly the door to the inn flew open as if caught by a strong gust of wind. The innkeeper's protests could be heard. "Sir, 'tis true his lordship be here but ye cannot—"

"I shall speak to Major Grey or Lord Crandall or whatever the blackguard deems to call himself!" Henry Reed shouted, striding into the room as if he owned it. His son followed closely behind, looking very much like a brown fighting cock ready to do battle.

The earl rose and faced the men with a sense of relief that the matter of Pamela Reed would at last be resolved and he might get on with his own pursuits, especially of Mrs. Prescott. Placing the half-finished drink on the mantelpiece, he bowed. "Gentlemen. I am surprised to see you."

The innkeeper scurried behind the bar where he kept a cudgel for his more rowdy patrons, convinced that the old gentleman and his son meant to cause mischief. A maid joined him, whispering questions as they watched the new arrivals glare at the Earl of Crandall.

Alison arrived in the hallway unseen, but she heard Mr. Reed roar, "No doubt, sir. It took my groom two nights of drinking Blue Ruin with your underfootman to learn of your whereabouts."

"Two nights? I would have hoped the fellow was made of sterner stuff." The earl took a sudden interest in his signet ring.

"Is that all you have to say, Lord Crandall?" Henry Reed snapped. "No explanation of why you have betrayed your friendship with Augustus by eloping with his sister?"

Marcus laughed. Why, the very notion of him wanting to marry such a chit was ridiculous. "Sir, you are harboring a false impression. There was never any question of a runaway marriage."

The old man's face took on a rather purple hue. "So, you simply meant to ruin her. Well, sir, I demand satisfaction."

Marcus's gaze shot to the gentleman's round face, the amusement gone from his eyes. "Sir, I have no intention of exchanging shots with you over a mere misunderstanding which can be easily cleared."

Mr. Reed stamped his cane upon the floor. "Shan't meet me, eh? Then, I demand you summon a vicar at once. Tobias brought a special license and we shall have this 'misunderstanding,' as you say, corrected."

The innkeeper, MacTaggart, nervously intruded into the conversation. "But, sir, you're now in Scotland, you don't need—"

"Silence, man. Do not interrupt your betters." Tobias Reed glared at the man.

Marcus stared at Pamela's uncle in silence. Why was he suddenly trying to marry the little madcap to him? That would cut his son out of the chit's fortune.

Alison, who'd stood quietly by, realized that the earl seemed unfazed by Mr. Reed's bellowing. Why, he was demanding the earl marry Pamela or he meant to draw blood. Thoughts of Lord Crandall lying wounded sent tremors of fear surging through her.

At once an idea came to Alison that would stop the old man's demands and keep them from fighting. Steeling herself, she entered the room with a nonchalance she was far from feeling. "Well, sir, I should like to know why you are making such a public spectacle by shouting at my husband in a taproom."

Alison was vaguely aware that the maid and innkeeper suddenly began to whisper to one another. They knew she was professing a falsehood by calling the earl her spouse, for Atwood had called her Mrs. Prescott on her arrival. She ardently hoped they would not contradict her.

"Husband?" Mr. Reed seemed suddenly to deflate. "You are already married, Crandall?"

The earl realized immediately what Alison was trying to do and while he could handle Henry Reed with no assistance, he was elated that she'd come to his rescue. Drawing her into the circle of his arm, he said, "Yes, sir, allow me to present you to my wife, Lady Crandall. My dear, this is Mr. Henry Reed and, I believe, his son, Tobias Reed, Pamela's relatives."

A WINTER COURTSHIP

The younger man, placing his fists at either side of his waist in frustration, said, "Then why the devil have you brought the annoying chit to Scotland without so much as a by-your-leave to my mother or father? I wager you have had to cross a lot of palms to cover the damage along the way."

Enjoying the heady scent of the lady's perfume, the earl laughed. "My *wife* and I were taking Miss Reed to Edinburgh. Lady Crandall's grandmother resides there and wishes a companion, a post which your niece says is more desirable than marrying a cousin."

Mr. Reed looked at his son with puzzlement. "What cousin? She has no cousin but you."

Tobias Reed shrugged his shoulders. "I think, sir, you have been taken in by some fanciful notion of Pamela's. She has quite a creative imagination."

Alison and Marcus exchanged a baffled glance. The earl, looking back at the two men skeptically, asked, "Do you, Mr. Tobias Reed, not intend to marry your cousin?"

There was such a look of horror on the young man's face there could be little doubt about his feeling. "Why, I should remain a bachelor all my days before I would marry that . . . that headstrong catastrophe."

The father added, "My son is already betrothed to Miss Harriet Amberson, sir. Wherever did you get—oh, so Pamela got some wild idea the marriage being planned was for her and Toby." A deep chuckle escaped the old man. "Why, sir, you might as well try to mix chalk and cheese. She must have overheard my talking about my foolish hopes of uniting them when they were little. Believe me, since they are now grown, I have come to realize that none of us would have a moment's peace with these two at one another continually."

Alison, amazed at the mix-up that had sent them on a journey to Scotland, spied Pamela quietly slipping down the stairs. Before the others saw the chit, Alison inquired, "What were you going to do with your niece after Mr. Reed married his fiancée?"

"Planned to hire a companion like her father wanted. Gel must have a Season or there will be no hearing the end of it." The old man shook his head.

Upon hearing her guardian's words, Pamela's face brightened. Dashing down the remaining stairs towards her uncle, she threw herself at the stout man, almost making him fall but for the assistance of his cane. "Do you mean it, Uncle Henry?"

"If you can manage to stay out of trouble until March, child." Returning her hug, Henry Reed seemed genuinely glad to see the girl, despite the trouble he had been put to.

"Oh, I promise I shall be good."

At that moment the loud clatter of boots on the stairs sounded the arrival of Sir Norton, looking anything but his usually immaculate self. His waistcoat was unbuttoned, his cravat hanging loose at his neck, and Baldwin was following behind trying to help him into his coat as he rushed into the room.

Oblivious to all in the taproom but the girl, he went straight to Pamela and stepped in between her and her uncle, a belligerent set to his jaw. "You cannot force her to marry against her will. I shall not allow her to be so mistreated, sir."

Seeing the darkening of Uncle Henry's countenance, Pamela took the baronet by the arm. "Sir Norton, 'twas all a misunderstanding. Tobias is betrothed to another. Uncle has said I might have a Season."

The young man suddenly realized his mistake. His face

flushed red and he looked at Alison, who nodded agreement, then gave him a smile of encouragement. "But I . . . I mean, sir . . ." Straightening, he pulled his coat closed. "Mr. Reed, I most humbly apologize."

Henry Reed frowned. "And just who are you, young man?"

"I am Sir Norton Stickley, sir, at your service and . . . and I should like your permission to pay my addresses to your niece," the baronet finished in a rush, then smiled down at Pamela. "If that is agreeable to you, my dear?"

The young lady clasped her hands to her heart. "I should like that above all else."

A look close to relief appeared on Henry Reed's face. "A baronet, eh? Come, is there somewhere we might get to know one another, my boy? Cannot be handing over my niece to just any pup who applies for her hand."

The earl, not surprised by the turn of events, suggested, "Sir, you are welcome to use the private parlor I have engaged. You may interview Stick in less public surroundings."

The old man eyed the innkeeper and maid who had been witness to the earlier scene. "Thank you, my lord, and may I offer an apology for my behavior?"

"Sir, you acted as any concerned relative would have under such false impressions. Do not give the matter any further thought for I shall not."

Pamela's uncle and cousin bowed, then led the glowing couple into the parlor. As the door closed, they could hear Mr. Reed saying, "Now, Sir Norton, I would know your circumstances . . ." The rest of the inquiry was lost to those in the taproom as the portal clicked shut.

Pleased that her brother had declared himself, Alison was more aware that the earl still held her close. The feeling of his hand on her arm sent exciting shivers through her. Seeing the innkeeper watching them curiously, she moved away from the disturbing gentleman.

Marcus bowed playfully. "Thank you, my beautiful wife, for coming to my rescue."

Calling her his 'beautiful wife' suddenly caused the image of her dead husband to surface in her mind. Only Stuart had called her that, but in a voice filled with sarcasm in front of his latest mistress. Forcing the painful memory down, she said, "My lord, now that Norton and Pamela are about to be betrothed, we must inform Mr. Reed that we are not truly married."

MacTaggart cleared his throat and came from behind the counter. "But my lady, you *are* married to Lord Crandall. As I tried to tell the other gent, you don't need no special license. You're in Scotland, madam, and by declarin' yourself his lordship's wife and him doin' so, too, that is all the ceremony you needs."

Married! Alison was filled with a flood of horrible memories. She began to back away from the earl and the innkeeper. She felt suffocated at the idea she had lost her freedom again because she had merely misspoken.

Married! The word kept echoing in her mind. Only fresh air would clear her befuddled thoughts.

Marcus watched the emotions evident on Alison's face. He knew his own elation at the news was not matched and the thought filled him with fear. Reaching out for her, he said, "My dearest Alison—"

She put up her hand in a staying gesture, then suddenly turned and dashed out of the inn without a bonnet, coat, or gloves. She nearly stumbled as she swerved to avoid another group of stranded travelers who were about to enter.

A WINTER COURTSHIP

Startled by his wife's sudden exit, Marcus knew he must go after her, but he wanted to be assured of the facts. While he went to get his riding cape which he'd tossed over the back of a chair, he asked, "You are certain of this? We are truly and legally wed?"

"As certain as my name is MacTaggart, my lord."

So, Marcus thought, he had won the lady's hand, but could he win her heart? He tossed the cape over his arm and went to do that very thing.

Alison ran through the blinding snow until the cold air made her chest hurt. Slowly coming to a halt, she could feel the large flakes brush past her lashes, with one occasionally landing in the curls about her face. There was only cold and silence around her, but her thoughts were on fire.

She was married to the earl. All her plans of controlling her own destiny were gone. She was again at the beck and call of a husband. Suddenly the gentle kiss they shared at The White Hart flashed in her mind. It had been like being truly kissed for the first time. Was that how *real* love felt?

"Alison." The earl spoke her name gently as he came out of the swirling whiteness. "You will freeze with no coat, love."

She stood staring up into his blue eyes while he draped his driving cape about her shivering shoulders. Snowflakes began to gather in his black hair and on the shoulders of his grey coat.

At that moment she was struck by how he'd ignored his own needs for her. At no time had Stuart ever thought of her first. But then there was little about the earl that was like her late husband. Why did she keep thinking about the two men as if they were one? Because she was afraid. Afraid to repeat the same mistake.

Seeing the concern and caring on the handsome face staring down at her, Alison knew she could trust this man. He was of a completely different ilk than Stuart.

A warm feeling began to fill her. Here was a man who cared what she thought and felt. He had demonstrated it again and again, but she was so blinded by her fears that she'd denied what was before her. She had foolishly refused to accept her feelings. She loved him.

As Alison stared at him, Marcus took heart. Her eyes were no longer staring in horror, but looking soft and hopeful. Encouraged, he poured out his feelings. "I think I fell in love with you at our first meeting, dearest wife. Dare I hope that one day you might return that regard? I know that your first marriage was unhappy, but I promise to cherish you until the day I die."

"I do love you." She was surprised at her own vehemence. All her fears faded into the distance as Marcus took her in his arms and tenderly covered her lips with his. The kiss soon burned with the long suppressed passion of each for the other.

"My lord, my lord." Atwood's voice sounded quite near.

Reluctantly lifting his head the earl looked at his new wife's green eyes, which were filled with such love he felt overjoyed. "Over here, Atwood!" To her, he asked, "What do you think? Has she set her uncle's coat on fire or poured a cup of chocolate over her cousin's head?"

Laughing, Alison settled into the warm curve of her husband's arm. "Simply be grateful that it is no longer your worry now that Norton wishes to marry her."

"True, there is only one lady with whom I need concern myself and she is beside me safe and unharmed."

"Sir," Atwood said upon finding his master. "May I wish you happy?"

"Surely you did not come out in the snow to congratulate me on my good fortune in marrying this beautiful lady."

"No, sir. I came because that maid what was present in the public rooms was chattering to all the servants about you getting married. The news reached Miss Kimball and she is in hysterics, madam. Keeps babbling about plans she had for you and some nephew, a vicar. Lucy thought you might want to come calm the lady."

Alison laughed. "Good heavens, is that why she has been praising Reverend Hewitt's virtues to me?" She fell silent for a moment. "Why, that must have been the reason she made that foolish suggestion to Pamela that she should marry you. She wanted to distract you, for she already had plans for me."

Marcus made a face of mock horror. "Miss Kimball is far more fanciful than Pamela if she thought I could be lured into marrying the chit once I set eyes upon you, dearest."

Alison felt blissfully happy.

"Atwood, go make the lady a strong drink and tell Lucy my wife will be there shortly."

"Very good, my lord." The batman disappeared into the storm.

Marcus felt a shiver of cold run through Alison. "Come, my love, I must get you to a warm fire. We already have two ill—I could not bear having you succumb as well."

"What shall we do about Grace? I do not think she will wish to remain with us, since we foiled all her plans."

"Stay with us?" Marcus's tone was one of shock. "Never, dear heart. Why not send her to this vicar of hers? Then I shall have you all to myself."

"You forget that my brother, Pamela, and her relatives are still here." Alison felt a rush of excitement at the look her husband gave her at that last statement. She glanced away, embarrassed by the turn her thoughts had taken, and spied the inn through the curtain of white flakes.

The earl stopped her in front of The Golden Lion, ignoring the curious post boys on duty. "My darling Ally, do you not realize that Pamela and Stick are barely aware there are other people here but themselves? I think when Mr. Reed takes her back south, Stick will follow."

"Only Norton? Do we not leave as well?" She felt breathless as he drew her into his arms.

"I have developed a fondness for this country inn. 'Twas here I got my fondest wish. I am not ready to leave just yet. Can I not coax you to grant my wish to be alone here for a few days with you, dearest love?"

Leaning down to kiss his new bride, the earl paused when the sound of glass breaking interrupted him and Pamela's voice full of apologies sounded through the broken pane. Soon the babble of Henry and Tobias Reed could be heard lamenting the chit and Sir Norton defending his future wife.

A momentary frown appeared on Marcus's face. "Promise you will not offer to present the chit this Season, should she and Stick delay the date of their marriage."

Alison smiled. "I promise. Being alone with you is the thing I long for most." She then surrendered to her husband's kiss, which ignited such a smoldering fire in her that she gave no thought to anything but being in the arms of the man she loved.

About the Author

Lynn Collum lives with her family in DeLand, Florida. Her first Zebra regency romance, A GAME OF CHANCE, is available at bookstores everywhere. Lynn is currently working on her next Zebra regency romance, to be published in July 1997. Lynn loves hearing from her readers and you may write to her c/o Zebra Books. Please include a self-addressed, stamped envelope if you wish a response.

The Winter Heart

Jo Ann Ferguson

One

"And it is not as if you have anything else to do, Joyce dear."

Joyce Stuart knew she should have devised a reason not to give her great-aunt a look-in this afternoon, even though Lady Eloise Anthony would accept no excuse not to respond to one of her invitations, which bordered on commands. Every call to this room with its gold wallcovering that Joyce had made on her great-aunt in the past six months had been aimed at easing Lady Eloise's on-going vexation with everything Joyce did. From the moment Joyce had first met her great-aunt, Lady Eloise had made no secret of the fact that she was disappointed that the younger daughter of the late Reverend Mr. Stuart had failed to make an excellent match during the past Season. Not even Joyce's sister Charity's happy marriage to an earl had eased the old woman's dissatisfaction.

So many times Joyce had come to call on her greataunt in this cluttered sitting room with its collection of portraits of the family currently in Lady Eloise's good favor. The others had been banished to the upper hall. Books and pieces of art were scattered across every table. Lady Eloise liked to have all her lovely things around her, and, even now, when she was preparing to return to the country, nothing had yet been packed.

Lady Eloise was always determined to be the first one to arrive in Town at the beginning of the Season and the last to leave. That way, she would miss nothing—none of the gossip, none of the intrigue, and none of the betrothal announcements.

All the things that Joyce Stuart would happily hear nothing of for the rest of her days.

Joyce forced a smile as her great-aunt regarded her coolly. This would not be an easy visit. The Season and the Little Season were solely memories, and Joyce remained unmarried, unbetrothed, and, worst of all, without a single prospect of changing her marital state. She could not have found a way to irritate her great-aunt more.

But apparently Lady Eloise had discovered a way to complicate Joyce's life.

"Lady Eloise," she said, stretching to put her hand on the old woman's gnarled fingers, "I normally would not deny you any favor you asked, but taking care of a twelve-year-old boy?"

"Charles Everett is family, albeit a most distant connection. I know how willing you are to do what you must for family."

Joyce hoped she was not flushing as she did each time Lady Eloise—or anyone else—mentioned the ignoble events that had plagued Joyce's first Season. Yes, she would do anything to make sure her older sister did not come to ruin, but assuming the responsibility for a child was a different matter entirely.

"I have no experience with boys of that age," she said, hoping her great-aunt would acquiesce to common sense. "Surely someone else would do a better job taking care of young Charles."

"You must have worked with youngsters at your father's church."

Joyce sighed. She truly had affection and respect for this cantankerous old woman who wished only the best for her grandnieces, but Lady Eloise was a continual trial. "Charity spent more time with the children than I did."

"Your sister is not in Town, and you are. Poor Charles cannot stay here on Grosvenor Square alone, and there would be nothing to keep him entertained at Graystone Manor. That is why, now that I am leaving for grassville, I thought you would be the best one to tend to him until his parents return from their sojourn in France in a fortnight or two."

"But, my lady—"

"Now, now, Joyce, this is no time to show that unattractively stubborn streak of yours. I have made my plans to go to the country, and I see no reason to change them when you will be able to handle the situation so admirably."

"I would suspect," Joyce said quietly, "there are more things to interest a lad in daisyville than here in Town when the *ton* has taken its leave. A boy of that age will wish for all kinds of adventures to keep him entertained."

"Adventures? Bah!" Lady Eloise raised her quizzing glass to her nose. "You know what so-called adventures can bring. Ruin of reputation and self. I thought you had learned your lesson."

"I have!" she averred. "That is why I am not the proper one to oversee the lad. If—"

When footfalls came toward the sitting room, Joyce looked over her shoulder. A lanky lad stood in the doorway that was flanked by tables topped with art and bric-a-brac. His blond hair fell forward into his eyes as he tugged at his coat and high collar with the discomfort of a lad accustomed to neither. She nearly recoiled when she saw the fury in the boy's eyes, which warned her he was no happier with Lady Eloise's machinations than she was.

"Ah, here is the dear boy now," said the old woman. "Come in, Charles, and greet Miss Stuart. Joyce, this is Charles Everett."

"Good afternoon, Miss Stuart," the lad mumbled.

Joyce guessed men had faced the hangman with more warmth than Charles expressed as he entered the room. "Good afternoon, Charles."

Before Joyce could add more, Lady Eloise said, "Miss Stuart has agreed to welcome you into her home." Her smile faltered. "I should say, as lief, into her sister's home. You will enjoy Berkeley Square. Don't you think so?"

Joyce never did discover what Charles thought on that or any other subject. Lady Eloise gave neither of them a chance to say more than "Yes, my lady" or "Of course, my lady." With quick efficiency, Charles's bags were stored in the boot of Joyce's carriage, and they were sent on their way from Grosvenor Square so Lady Eloise could turn to the task of overseeing the packing of her household for their return to the country.

Charles did no more than mumble in response to her polite questions during the short ride, so Joyce could not resist breathing a sigh of relief when the carriage slowed in front of the simple doorway at the far end of Berkeley Square. She peered out of the carriage through the winter darkness, which had swallowed the Square. Few lights broke the ebony fog clinging to the walkway, for many of the denizens had already left for the country. Smoke hung close to the ground, captured by the cold.

She drew back into the carriage as wind swirled beneath her wide-brimmed bonnet. Pulling her wool cloak closer, she shivered against her berry red spencer. She guessed her nose and cheeks would be nearly as scarlet.

If she had the sense of a goose, she would have left Town along with the rest of the *ton*. She had told herself that, after five years of living near the shore, she could endure the icy breezes off the Thames. Mayhap that was so, but she had not counted on it being as cold this winter as it had been during the previous one.

She had heard her abigail Hélène complaining just this morning to the butler, Marshall, that if the winters continued like this in England, now that the war with Napoleon was over, she intended to return to southern France. "Where the weather is humane," the abigail had mumbled as she hurried closer to a fireplace.

Joyce agreed wholeheartedly as she waited for the tiger to open the carriage door. Trying to keep her smile from quivering with cold, she said, "Here we are, Charles."

He remained hunched in his coat and gave her no answer. She sighed. This might be even more of a mistake than she had feared at Lady Eloise's house.

"Thank you," she said, as the tiger handed her out. Pulling her cloak more closely to her chin, she waited for Charles to jump down to the walkway.

"Miss Stuart," murmured the coachman's assistant, "were you expecting a caller?"

She looked past the chubby tiger to discover a man standing on the steps by the front door. In the dim light from the lantern on the carriage, she could not see his face. Who would be calling at this hour on such a wintry evening? She was not at home today.

The tiger whispered, "Miss Stuart, no need for you to greet this man. Let me go and find Marshall. He will take care of the blackguard loitering on the steps."

"Thank you, but I do not believe it is necessary to send for the butler," she answered as Charles stepped down from the carriage.

The man on the steps made no motion toward leaving. She wondered what he wanted.

Softly she added, "Do stay near until I am certain he is no trouble."

"Of course, miss. We always wait until you are safe within the house."

Joyce was tempted to offer the tiger an apology, for he was clearly vexed at her failure to notice his attention to his job. Apologizing would only make the situation more uncomfortable. And, in the wake of the call on her irascible great-aunt and assuming responsibility for Charles, she wanted only to get inside, kick off her damp slippers, curl up beneath a coverlet, and sip a cup of hot chocolate.

"Why are we standing here on the walkway?" asked Charles, irritation radiating from him as he folded his arms tightly in front of him. "It is beginning to snow."

Indeed it was, Joyce noticed. Lingering here in the midst of a snow shower was absurd. This weather had been threatening for days, but, until now, they had endured no more than a chilly rain.

"Bring the bags in and have them brought to the guest room," she ordered quietly and motioned for Charles to come with her.

The man on the steps turned as she came up to the iron railing at the bottom of the trio of risers. A thick cloak draped him in shadows, but the brim of his tall beaver was sprinkled with snowflakes.

"Lady Blackburn?" he asked, his words rumbling through the night.

"No."

"Are you of this household?"

"Yes."

The man blinked at her curt replies, but his voice remained serene. "Would you give me the courtesy of your name?"

Glad that Charles stood nearby, but unsure of how much help the boy would be, she said quietly, "I am Joyce Stuart. Who are you?"

"Geoffrey Wilcox, Lord Dartmouth at your service, Miss Stuart." He took her gloved hand and bowed over it.

She started to draw her hand back as he raised his head, but she froze as surely as if the icy wind had grown even more frigid. Yet it was not the evening's chill that held her, but Lord Dartmouth's regard. There was nothing chilly about the sparkle in his shadowed eyes; still she could not move.

As he stared at her, a slow smile tilting his lips, she appraised him as candidly. He was swathed within that black wool cloak and a greatcoat, but she suspected the breadth of his shoulders was no illusion. When he drew her up to stand beside him, his eyes were less than a finger's width above hers. Light brown hair twisted across his forehead. Even in the sparse light drifting from the windows on either side of the door, she saw his nose had been broken at least once. She could, with ease, imagine him facing another pugilist in a battle of fives.

Her nose wrinkled at a most peculiar aroma. It was as

if he had loitered too long too close to the kitchen hearth. No ashes cluttered his cloak, so she could not guess why he carried such a scent with him through the winter evening.

"Miss Stuart, I—" A strident sound interrupted him.

"What is that?" she gasped.

"That is this." Lord Dartmouth picked up a cloth-covered case that had been hidden behind his thick cloak. He lifted one side of the paisley shawl and peeked into it. "Look quickly. I don't want him taking a chill."

"Him?" Joyce's eyes widened as she saw a brightly plumed bird within an ornate cage. The bird, which was the length of her forearm, gave her a malevolent glare and screeched again.

When Charles spoke, Joyce glanced over her shoulder. She had forgotten the boy.

"What is it?" he asked.

Lord Dartmouth raised the shawl again and let the lad look inside. The bird squawked indignantly before the cloth dropped over the cage.

"This is Napoleon," Lord Dartmouth said.

"Napoleon?" Charles grinned, surprising Joyce, for she had not seen him smile. He should do so more often, she thought, for he already had a smile sure to break young misses' hearts in a dozen years. "Why Napoleon?"

He chuckled. "I am afraid you will discover for yourself once he has warmed himself up. He makes noise endlessly and never says anything worth listening to." Pointing at the carton, he added, "And the cat in there is Josephine."

"Because she wishes to get closer to Napoleon?" Joyce asked.

"Very good, Miss Stuart." He shivered. "Can I ask that

I might be allowed to continue this conversation with you and your young friend in the house? If Napoleon gets zneezy on this chilly night, he might never recover."

"I fear I do not know you, my lord. Will you tell me why you are calling?"

"From your grim expression, I am certain I could persuade you that I am a most dangerous man. Mayhap, even as we speak, dozens of Bow Street Runners are planning to enhance their reputations by taking this despicable thief." He inched closer to her.

She put up her hands to keep him away. Her arm was grasped, and she was tugged back toward the walkway.

"Stay away from her!" Charles shouted.

Not sure if she was more astonished at Charles's abrupt gallantry or Lord Dartmouth's lack of it, she grasped the railing to steady herself. When broad fingers covered hers, pinning them in place so she would not fall, she grabbed Lord Dartmouth's arm with her other hand.

She began, "Charles, there is nothing to—"

The boy erupted between them, knocking away Lord Dartmouth's hand and careening into her. Lord Dartmouth shouted. Charles shouted. She had no time to answer either of them as they all tumbled into a heap on the walkway.

Two

Pain thrust through Joyce's hip and her elbow as she hit the walkway.

"Miss Stuart! Are you hurt?" asked a deep voice.

"Miss Stuart! I cannot breathe!" exclaimed a lighter one.

The voices rang through her, one from beneath her and one from over her aching head. Fire seared her face. If any of the residents of Berkeley Square discovered her in this most ignoble position, she would never hear the end of it from Lady Eloise. Of course, her sister Charity would simply laugh and remind her that pride goeth before a fall. Not that Joyce had been overly proud of how she was handling the encounter with Lord Dartmouth... Dear God, she was prattling in her head!

"Miss Stuart? Can you move? I cannot breathe."

Someone wiggled beneath her. Before she could move, strong arms scooped her up as if she weighed no more than one of the snowflakes. She gasped and gripped the scratchy wool of a greatcoat. Pulled up against a sturdy chest, she flinched when a resonant laugh caressed her. She looked up at Lord Dartmouth's smile.

"The poor lad is rewarded with an impromptu embrace for his chivalry," he said, chuckling again. "Are you uninjured, my boy?"

"I am fine." The petulant tone returned to Charles's voice. "Put Miss Stuart down!"

The tiger rushed over from the carriage. "Miss Stuart, do you wish me to hail a Charley?"

Joyce wanted to tell all of them to calm themselves. Before she could, Lord Dartmouth's laugh rumbled through him to stroke her far too intimately.

"Miss Stuart," he said, "please reassure your champions that I have no wicked intentions toward you and that there is no need to call for one of those worthless Charleys when, if I understood you correctly, we have a Charlie right here." He grinned at the boy and got a scowl in return.

"Put Miss Stuart down!" Charles jammed his fists into his hips, thrusting forth his chin in a threatening pose.

"I shall be glad to if you promise not to be such a valiant hero." Lord Dartmouth gently set Joyce onto her feet, wiping snow from her bonnet. "I ask you again, Miss Stuart, may we continue this within? You may trust me to be a complete gentleman. If you remain concerned about my intentions and my credentials as a gentleman, you need only open the door and allow me in while you send for Oliver. He will give us a proper introduction."

He continued to brush snow off her, his hands flitting from her bonnet to her shoulders and down her sleeves. The motion was as innocent as anything Charles might have done, but sweet warmth sifted through her spencer and along her skin with each touch. She edged away, not wanting to be tempted by sensations that she had not expected to feel with this jobbernowl man. She must have hit her head quite hard to be bothered by a mindstorm like this.

Lord Dartmouth's eyes widened, then narrowed into

shadowed slits. She had insulted him. She was sure of that when he said coolly, "Please send for Oliver."

"He is not—"

Napoleon let out a fearsome sound.

"Miss Stuart, may we argue about this within the house?"

Joyce nodded. Keeping the man standing on the front steps in the midst of a brangle endangered not only the bird's health. She didn't want Charles to take a chill, and, despite his brave assertion, she suspected he had had the breath knocked out of him. "Do come in, my lord, before your creatures are worse for the weather."

The footman at the door stared, wide-eyed, as Joyce led the parade into the house. Sending him for the butler, she turned to see Charles staring at the walls of the round foyer with its staircase that curved up to the gilded ceiling three floors above.

She understood his amazement, for she had never seen another house with its foyer decorated with a mural of sailing ships conquering the waves sweeping from one section of the wall to the next.

Smiling, she loosened the buttons on her snow-and-dirt-speckled spencer. "It is unique, isn't it?"

"Is the rest of the house like this?" the boy asked.

"Oliver is wildly proud of the ships of the Blackburn Line," Lord Dartmouth answered as he set the birdcage and the carton on the floor by the stairs. Straightening, he added, "Unless his new wife has redecorated, you will, young man, see signs of the family's shipping business displayed in every room."

Joyce realized the darkness had not misled her. Lord Dartmouth's roughly sculptured face would never be deemed handsome, but something about it drew her gaze.

His smile? Mayhap, for it possessed a warmth and a sincerity she could not doubt. Or was it that twinkle in his blue eyes? That glitter suggested he was no older than Charles and much naughtier.

"My lord," she began, "you sound very familiar with—"

"Lord Dartmouth!" Marshall surged into the foyer. The short, round butler wore a cheek-splitting grin atop his simple livery. "How wonderful to see you again!"

"And to see you. Will you vouch for me to yon suspicious lady?" He clapped Marshall on the shoulder. "She seems concerned that I am a miscreant bent on mischief." He loosened the buttons on the front of his greatcoat. "Assure her that, with Oliver absent, there is no need for me to perpetrate any devilment."

Marshall nodded so vigorously that Joyce feared his head might pop right off. "Lord Blackburn would wish his friend to find welcome here, Miss Stuart. I am happy to reassure you that Lord Dartmouth is above reproach."

"No need to go that far," Lord Dartmouth said, his smile as wide as the butler's. "Miss Stuart has shown uncommonly good sense already, and she will question the validity of your words if you engage in such hyperbole."

Marshall chuckled warmly as he took her cloak and turned to Charles.

"Lord Dartmouth," the butler said, "your young friend is welcome as well."

Charles flinched, and a dozen emotions whirled through his eyes before anger flared in them. With taut, furious motions, he undid his coat.

"Marshall," Joyce said quietly, "Charles Everett is my guest. He will be our guest until his parents return to

Town. Charles, whatever you need, Marshall will be glad to help."

"I need to stop being passed about like a collection plate," he grumbled.

A surge of sympathy raced through her. She had been so intent on trying to figure out what she would do to keep a lad from being bored that she had not realized how distressed Charles must be. Mayhap he had wished to go with his parents to see France or to stay with friends of his own age. Instead, he had been handed off to a stranger who had not hidden the fact that she considered him a difficulty.

"You are welcome to stay here as long as you wish." She put her arm around his shoulders.

"Only because you have no one else to give me to!" he snapped, shrugging off her arm.

"She could have sent you to me." Lord Dartmouth smiled. "But then you would have ended up a refugee here once more."

Joyce glanced at him. What skimble-skamble was he talking about now? Before she could ask, Charles raced up the stairs.

"What did I say to cause him to do that?" Lord Dartmouth asked, astonished.

"Nothing, for he is hurt that his parents left him here in Town while they are traveling on the continent."

"Continent? Are they mad? The war is barely over!"

"Don't you know that half of the *ton* is en route to Paris or making plans to go?"

"Apparently not. And they call *me* want-witted!"

"If you will excuse me, my lord. I need to see that he is settled comfortably." Joyce put her hand on the railing, but drew back when a screech came from beneath the paisley shawl. She whirled at Lord Dartmouth's laugh. Her scowl had no more effect on him than Charles's had.

"Let the boy be," Lord Dartmouth urged. "No lad of that age wishes to be mollycoddled. He wants to sulk and enjoy his misery for a while. He will come about with time."

"You speak with a great deal of authority."

"Why not? *I* was a lad of that age and most exasperating temperament at one time." He handed his hat to Marshall.

The strange odor drifted from him once more. Her nose wrinkled before she could halt the involuntary motion.

Lord Dartmouth tapped her nose, shocking her. Again the tingle slipped through her, mysterious and maddening. She needed every bit of her wits about her to deal with this unpredictable man. To become enthralled by his bold touch would prove she wanted for sense.

"I see, Miss Stuart," he said, "you have taken note of my unique aroma. A bit of mishap at the place where I was staying gave it to me. The chimney seems to have been wanting for a cleaning."

"How horrible!"

"Not so horrible when it has sent me upon this adventure which led me to your door." He held his sleeve near his nose and took a deep breath. "I do smell like a member of the minor clergy, don't I?" He held out his arm under her nose. "What do you think, Miss Stuart?"

She stepped back. "I think even a chimneysweep would have the decency not to put his sleeve directly beneath my nose."

"And a charming nose it is." He arched a golden-brown brow at Marshall. "I think I owe this fine lady the duty of a few genuine compliments. We got off to an uneven start when I mistakenly called her 'Lady Blackburn.'" Unbuttoning his greatcoat, he said, "An honest error, you must understand. I had heard that Oliver had lost his heart to a lovely miss with curves that would hold any man's eyes. How was I to guess there would be two such paragons of perfection in one household, butler?"

"Lord Blackburn will be sorry he has missed your call, Lord Dartmouth." Marshall took the greatcoat and handed it to a maid.

"You do not expect him back soon?"

"He and Lady Blackburn are in Italy to enjoy their honeymoon."

Lord Dartmouth's brow furrowed in a baffled expression. "I had understood they were married months ago."

"Other matters demanded their attention until recently. They wished to be able to put all concerns behind them before they sailed," Joyce said in a tone she hoped would allow for no more questions. Just to be sure, she hurried on before Lord Dartmouth could reply. "My lord, your creatures need to get closer to a blazing hearth."

"A jolly notion." He lifted the cage and the carton. A yowl came from the cat, which clearly was tired of being imprisoned.

Joyce watched as a footman led Lord Dartmouth up the stairs to the sitting room above. In his wake, she hesitated. She should follow, for she owed him a duty as his hostess to be sure that he and his beasts were provided for.

She untied the pink striped ribbon beneath her chin and lifted her bonnet off her head. Her hair fell down her back, and she sighed. No doubt each of her hairpins was strewn across the walkway. What an ignoble end to a day!

"Well, well, this is, indeed, a pleasant surprise," said Marshall as he took her bonnet.

She wished she could agree. A surprise, yes, to have both young Charles and Lord Dartmouth propelled into her life. *Pleasant,* she feared, was not the adjective she would have chosen.

"Please have a second guest chamber made ready for Lord Dartmouth. One with lots of sun, for I know both cats and birds appreciate light."

"Of course, Miss Stuart." Marshall held out a folded slip of paper. "This was delivered for you."

She glanced at it, recognizing her friend Stella Richmond's effusive handwriting. Opening it, she read Stella's invitation to call as soon as she could. Odd, she thought. She was sure Stella had gone to the country several fortnights ago. "Thank you."

"Certainly." He started to turn away, then paused. "Miss Stuart?"

"Yes?"

"You seem unsettled by Lord Dartmouth's arrival."

"As you said, 'tis a surprise." She ran her fingers along the smooth bannister and looked up the stairs toward the railings edging each of the two balconies over the foyer. "So you know him well?"

"Lord Dartmouth's family and the Blackburn family have been allies and friends in war and in business since before anyone can remember. Lord Dartmouth and Lord Blackburn were like brothers when they were children. They attended school together and have worked together often in the past." His voice dropped to a conspiratorial whisper. "Even during the war."

"That ninny-hammer worked for the foreign ministry?" She bit her lip when Marshall frowned. Insulting

Lord Dartmouth before the butler who clearly welcomed him here would be opaque.

"Do not mistake a good sense of humor for all that is within the man, Miss Stuart."

Accepting the dressing-down because she knew it was deserved, Joyce winced when her toes slid about in her wet slippers as she climbed the stairs. Never had the idea of a cup of hot chocolate seemed as wondrous as it did just now. That and a chance to read while nestled under her blankets would have to wait until she was secure in the knowledge that both of her unanticipated guests were snug in their own chambers.

Three

As if she had guessed the course of Joyce's thoughts, Mrs. Englewood waited at the top of the stairs. The slender housekeeper's usual smile was strained, and strands of gray hair poked out of her bun—a most unusual sight, for Mrs. Englewood customarily was the pattern-card of serenity and propriety. The whole of the household had been thrown out of kilter by these two unforeseen guests.

"The lad requested that his evening meal be sent up to him, Miss Stuart." Disapproval warred with sympathy in Mrs. Englewood's voice.

"Tonight, do as he requests. He clearly wants some time to digest all that has transpired for him today." Joyce glanced toward the sitting room. "Is Lord Dartmouth in there?"

The housekeeper's reply vanished beneath a shrill meow. A flurry of gold, black, and white sped past them, vanishing up the stairs.

Joyce gasped, "What was that?"

"Josephine, I am afraid," Lord Dartmouth replied as he rested his elbow on the wide molding around the arched door to the sitting room. With his coat off and his cravat loosened above his green waistcoat, he appeared quite at home. "Like most cats, she resists any sort of change, and bringing her across Kensington and Mayfair has disturbed her greatly."

"Mayhap you should have let her remain behind."

"She would have been even more distressed by the workmen wandering in and out to tend to that blasted chimney." He tugged at his wrinkled shirt sleeve. "I trust you will forgive me for my casual appearance, Miss Stuart. That coat was so saturated with smoke, it was making me sneeze."

"Of course," she replied, glad he could not be privy to her thoughts. "Mrs. Englewood will have it cleaned for you."

"I thank you." He bowed his head toward both of them. "My wardrobe, at this moment, is understandably limited, so I appreciate your attention."

As Mrs. Englewood gathered up the coat and hurried away, Joyce walked into the sitting room. It was her favorite. Here she could sit and, on pleasant days, enjoy the sun shining through the tall window that swept nearly from floor to ceiling. The view of Berkeley Square was never the same, for every day brought different visitors and merchants.

The sea-blue carpet matched the striped wallcovering and the flowers of the settee's upholstery. Framed paintings of the current ships of the Blackburn Line flanked the chimneypiece, and log books of ships that had previously sailed for the Line were set on two wide shelves that ran the length of the room. She had found them interesting reading on a rainy day.

When Lord Dartmouth brushed brusquely past her, Joyce bit back her annoyance. He squatted next to the paisley-covered cage and slowly drew back the shawl.

"Do not worry about Josephine, Miss Stuart," he said

without giving her the courtesy of looking at her. "She will quickly accustom herself to this house, especially once she finds a mouse or two to feast on."

"What gives you reason to believe any rodents reside within these walls?"

"You have no cat here." He lifted the cage and set it on a table near the hearth. "I do not mean to disparage either your supervising of this household or the keen eye of your housekeeper. You need only ask butler—"

"Butler? You called Marshall that before. Don't you think that is rather rude?"

He laughed softly. Napoleon let out a raucous squawk, nearly drowning out his answer. "My dear Miss Stuart, I am often irreverent, occasionally witty, but never rude. I call him 'Butler' because that is the man's name."

"His name is Marshall."

"Who told you that?"

"Oliver—"

"Belongs to the only family I know which has a butler named 'Butler.' " He chuckled. "The Blackburn family and their butler Butler, in an effort not to disturb the gentlefolk of the Polite World, long ago agreed to use Butler's given name."

"I had no idea." She frowned. "Or are you hoaxing me?"

Geoffrey Wilcox laughed again. He was not teasing Miss Stuart, but doing so might not be a bad idea. Turning to face her, he enjoyed the most pleasurable sight of her in her pink gown with her black hair cascading over her shoulders. He guessed she usually wore it in prim curls swept up around her nape, but the damp ends warned it had come loose when they stumbled on the stairs. It would be a shame to restrain all that spun ebony.

The whole of this was an astonishment. Driven from his quarters by that dashed smoke, he had looked forward to sharing a few laughs and a bottle of blackstrap with his good tie-mate Oliver. Instead, his friend was enjoying a belated honeymoon, and this pretty brunette was here to entertain him. If only she were not wearing such a dour frown . . .

"Forgive me for distressing the lad and you, Miss Stuart." Mayhap an apology would be the route to bringing a smile, which he suspected would be utterly charming, to her face. "I make it a practice to give someone a look-in only when they are at home, but the events of this afternoon conspired to alter my customary ways."

"You would not have asked for such troubles to come your way." A hint of a smile stole the edge from her taut lips. "I was looking forward to enjoying a cup of chocolate on my return here, my lord. I would be glad to ring for a cup for you."

"Some port or, better yet, brandy would be more to my taste."

"I thought you might have been chilled."

"Obviously, Miss Stuart, you are not an aficionado of the fine ball of fire Oliver always manages to have waiting." He rubbed his chin and frowned at his rough whiskers. No wonder Miss Stuart regarded him with less than admiration. He was cutting a poor figure upon their first meeting.

"I prefer chocolate on an evening such as this." She reached for the bell-pull. "However, Marshall is sure to know where Oliver keeps his best brandy."

The butler arrived so quickly Geoffrey suspected he had not given up his habit of listening near the door. A good and faithful trait for any butler, but damn annoying if a chap wished to do more than share a cup with a lovely lady. He walked over to Napoleon's cage while Miss Stuart passed her request on to the butler. If she glanced in his direction just now, she might read the thoughts behind his smile. That would only exacerbate what was clearly a discomfiting predicament to her.

Napoleon glared as Geoffrey pulled the shawl from his cage and tossed it on the back of a nearby chair. With a move that needed no translation, he turned his back on Geoffrey and began to clean his feathers.

Geoffrey smiled at the silly bird which he had inherited along with his uncle's house. His smile broadened when he heard Miss Stuart whisper a question to the butler.

"Do tell her the truth of your names or she may begin to believe it is, in truth, Rumpelstiltskin," Geoffrey said, leaning his hands on the back of the settee.

Marshall's round face creased as he laughed. "Yes, Miss Stuart, Lord Dartmouth was being honest. My full name is Marshall Butler, as my father's was before me and his father before him. The Butlers have long served as butlers in this household."

"See?" Geoffrey asked. "I was not jesting."

"About that," she returned.

"About that." This was going to be most amusing. Behind that serene façade, Miss Stuart was struggling to conceal a honed mind and a sense of humor that might rival his own. "You must learn to be more trusting."

"I suspect I am as trusting as I ever shall be."

"A pity."

"Have you eaten?" she asked as she sat on a chair facing him.

"I assume a cake or two will come on the tray. That

will suffice for this evening. I ate my fill of smoke before I came here."

"And your creatures?"

"Napoleon is grateful for the seed he gets and an occasional treat." He smiled as he patted the cage. "And, as I told you, Josephine is quite capable of ferreting out her own repast." Coming around the settee, he sat. "How does young Charlie do?"

"*Charles* requested a tray in his room. I guess he plans to make an early evening of it."

"Or sneak out."

She came to her feet. "Do you think—I mean—" She grasped the bell-pull and tugged it wildly.

The butler popped back into the room as if he had been fired out of a pistol. "Yes, miss?"

"Marsh—But— . . ."

"Marshall will do, miss."

Geoffrey did not bother to hide his grin as the butler shot him a reproving glance. Marshall Butler should have learned long ago that such an expression was wasted on Geoffrey Wilcox.

"Marshall," Miss Stuart said, anxiety filling her voice, "Lord Dartmouth has acquainted me with the folly of not suspecting that our young guest might not be willing to stay here."

"I arranged for Toby to stay in Mr. Charles's dressing room, Miss Stuart, on the pretext that Toby would assist in any manner needed."

"Thank you!"

"Of course, miss." Marshall stepped aside as a six-pounder came into the room, carrying a tray with a steaming pot and a bottle of brandy.

The saucy maid eyed Geoffrey brazenly, and he returned the compliment. The newest Lady Blackburn must be very assured of her place in her husband's heart to have such a lovely, cheeky wench in her house, he mused. His attention refocused on Miss Stuart when she returned to her chair. He fought another smile as the maid flounced out of the room, making no effort to hide her disappointment at his lack of interest.

"Brandy, my lord?"

He accepted the cut crystal glass. When she took great pains to keep her fingers from touching his, he had the answer to the question that had taunted him from the first words they exchanged. Miss Stuart—cool, composed Miss Stuart—was not indifferent to him! These were the best tidings he had had all day, even though he had to own that he had suffered only bad news up until now.

Taking a sip of the flavorful brandy, Geoffrey asked, "Why have you remained behind?"

"I doubt if the newlyweds wished me to join them."

He laughed. "On that, we agree. However, that was not what I meant. You are here in Town when the rest of the *ton* is enjoying the winter in their country seats. The household here could manage well without supervision. They have proven that on numerous occasions in the past few years when Oliver was out on his ships."

"I was looking forward to the quiet of Town now that the Polite World has taken its leave."

"But you will miss the round of parties and balls and card games in grassville." He relaxed in his chair and propped one leg on the other knee.

"I realize that. I have heard much of the gatherings that are being held. The Season does not come to an end. It simply moves out of London to a wider setting."

"Yet you are still here."

"Yes."

Geoffrey waited for a pair of heartbeats for her to continue. As she stared down into her cup of chocolate, he took a deep breath and released it slowly. The silence weighed heavily on his ears. Her reticence told him more than words could have.

Miss Joyce Stuart was avoiding the *ton,* although she should be in the midst of the whirl of winter parties. He could easily imagine her riding by some handsome swain's side in a horse-drawn sleigh or twirling in a confection of white silk to a country dance in a ballroom brightened with candles as shimmering as the snow. With her cheeks rosered, her lyrical laugh would be as crystalline as the ice veneer on branches.

Yet here she was. A puzzle, and he adored puzzles, for it was always an adventure to decipher the truth.

When Lord Dartmouth's grin widened, Joyce wished she were not so aware of his gaze. In spite of his funning ways, he possessed an insight that unsettled her.

"You are welcome to stay with us for as long as you need," she said, taking another sip of the hot chocolate.

"I shall not be a burden for too long if all goes well." He broke off a piece of one of the cakes and held it out to Napoleon. Although Joyce half-expected the bird to snatch it with its beak, Napoleon very delicately plucked the crumbs from Lord Dartmouth's hand with one foot. Her surprise must have been bare on her face, for Lord Dartmouth added, "In spite of your first impression of us, Miss Stuart, I can assure you that both Napoleon and I have manners fit for the presence of a lady."

"And Josephine?" she asked, smiling at his feigned tone of having taken insult.

"A cat has rules unto itself. I assume she will act according to those."

"I trust you will feel free to run tame through the house, my lord."

"You may as well call me Geoffrey. It appears we shall be sharing this house long enough to make 'Miss Stuart' and 'Lord Dartmouth' absurd. Why not make this uncomfortable situation as comfortable as possible?"

Four

"I am sorry if you find this uncomfortable," Joyce said, unsettled by Lord Dartmouth's odd answer.

Lord Dartmouth leaned toward her and chuckled when she drew back. *"I* do not find it so, but you do. You are as jumpy as Napoleon when Josephine starts cleaning her whiskers. Are you always unable to say shoo to a goose, or do I merit special consideration?"

"You are certainly not shy, my—"

"Geoffrey, if you would please, Joyce."

Dear God, but the man was insufferable . . . and had the most bewitching eyes. Green-gray sparkles hinted at depths of emotion concealed behind his bonhomie. Mayhap he had not been jesting when he said, on the steps, that he was a dangerous man. She shook the unwanted thought from her head. He was simply a vexing man.

"No," he continued with a grin, "I was dipped in the Shannon at an early age, and I have long been accused of enjoying the sound of my own voice."

Joyce laughed. She could not help herself.

"Now that is a sound I enjoy even more," he said. "I trust you laugh more often than you have on this eventful day."

"I try to find joy in each day." Rising, she went to the

window. "The snow is not easing. We may be snowbound tomorrow."

"It is pretty, isn't it?"

She looked from the swirl of flakes to discover Geoffrey—it was not difficult to think of him that way—standing right behind her. The golden fire glowing off his hair matched the warmth in his eyes. Suddenly she was aware of how deserted the house seemed. Even though they stood in front of the window overlooking the Square, no one was without to take note of them.

When he settled the paisley shawl that had covered the bird's cage over her shoulders, he said softly, "You are shivering. It would be wise to rush to your bedchamber and a few thick coverlets."

"You give orders very easily."

"Which I suspect you will heed no more readily than Napoleon and Josephine do." His smile faded. "I appreciate that you have opened your door—however reluctantly—to me and my creatures when you did not know me from Adam."

"Marshall knew you."

"I am trying to compliment you."

She pulled the shawl up under her chin. "I do not need you to lather me with *bon mots*. You are wasting your breath."

"Why not? 'Tis my breath to waste, and I only wished to laud your kindness."

"Please do not."

As she started to edge past him, he put his hand on her arm. She pulled her gaze from his fingers that curved over her wrist. Looking up at him, she could not halt a gasp from slipping past her parted lips as his finger tipped her chin toward him.

His words were as low as the wind skulking past the windowpanes. "Being a gentleman, I would gladly traverse the Thames to rescue you from drowning. I would not hesitate to jump in front of a runaway carriage to keep you from being trampled. Nor would I pause if you needed help to clamber down from a mountaintop. However, I refuse to vow not to ply you with Spanish coin, for each bit of flattery is true."

"But I do not ask that of you." She turned her chin away from his finger. "Nor of any man. I know you think to captivate me with your words, but I find them a bag of moonshine." Bowing her head to him, she said, "I bid you good night. If you need anything, be certain to ask."

Again he put out his hand to block her path. "Do you mean that? Anything?"

She bit back the retort she should not speak. Egad, but this man made her think of uttering cant she had never even imagined before. Bidding him another quick good evening, she rushed up the stairs to her bedchamber.

She threw open the door, hurrying into the light green room which was nearly lost to the shadows. A single candle fought back the darkness. She closed her eyes and leaned back against the door. Her breath came as swiftly as if she had waded through waist-deep snow.

"Miss Stuart?"

She sighed as she forced a smile for her abigail. Hélène regarded her with dismay.

"Do not look so," she said, reaching for her nightgown as her abigail undid the back of her gown. "I had no idea the day would take this turn."

"You could not turn Lord Dartmouth from the door."

"Nor Charles."

"Poor *petit*." She sighed. "He is so furious with the

fates that have brought him here. Toby told me the lad has been nabbing his bib since he shut himself within his rooms."

Joyce blinked back the abrupt rush of tears that filled her eyes. "I guessed Charles had fled from the foyer so he would not weep in front of us."

Hélène picked up Joyce's slippers. "No child should have to be so brave."

"On the morrow, I shall devise some ways to make him forget his grief."

"How?"

"I had hoped you would have some ideas."

The abigail smiled ruefully. "None, for I was an only child."

"And I have only an older sister. I have no idea how to entertain a young boy, but mayhap Lord Dartmouth does." With a groan, Joyce dropped onto the stool beside her dressing table. "I suspect he already has many ideas, but, if all goes well, mayhap I can come up with a plan to amuse the lad before he does."

"I hope you are right, my lady."

Joyce silently agreed, but doubted if she would savor even a moment of the tranquillity she had been looking forward to just this morning.

The sitting room was quiet when Joyce passed it on her way to the breakfast-parlor. She paused in the doorway as she saw something move on the gold brocade cushions of the window seat.

Smiling, she entered slowly. "Josephine?"

The calico cat regarded her with a cool, yellow stare.

"May I?" she asked, pointing to the cushion.

The cat blinked.

"I shall take that as permission." Joyce sat by the cat. It stared at her, but a condescending nod graciously allowed her to continue petting its variegated fur.

This was the quiet moment she needed. A night with little sleep had left her exhausted and completely without inspiration as to lightening Charles's spirits. More than once during the night, she had heard his footsteps in the room across the hallway. Her one attempt to soothe him had been rebuffed as coldly as she had disdained Geoffrey's endeavor to tease her out of her dismal spirits last evening.

Looking out the window at the snow that was a bed of jewels in the sunlight, she saw the fall had been light. Just enough had accumulated to conceal the icy puddles that had been dirtied with soot and cinders. How simple it would be if it were possible to cover over harsh words so readily.

"What a lovely scene of household tranquillity!"

Her head jerked up as she stared at Geoffrey. In spite of herself, she could not keep from admiring how his shoulders strained the seams of his black coat. Oliver's coat, she suspected, for the sleeves were too long. A cool sheen across his cheeks revealed his recent shave, but nothing could detract from the stern lines of his face.

When he stepped into the room, his arm draped companionably over Charles's shoulder, she knew her face had revealed her shock. Both smiled as if they shared a joke she would never understand. Mayhap they were correct, for Charles had vented his frustration on Geoffrey even more last night than on her.

"Josephine has deigned to let me pet her," Joyce said, although she wanted to ask how this change had come about. She had to avoid embarrassing the lad.

THE WINTER HEART

Geoffrey crossed the room and scratched the cat under its chin. Josephine began to purr deeply and rose to stretch farther than Joyce would have guessed possible.

"She has me well trained," he said quietly, "to do exactly as *she* pleases." He raised his gaze to meet Joyce's. A smile twitched on his lips. "The goal of every female with her male."

"How cynical!"

"And how true." He sat beside her on the window seat. "I find it saves so much time just to speak the truth, even though it has not endeared me to some of the old toughs and the young misses. They prefer nothing-sayings and court promises. I hope you are different, Joyce."

"My dear late father was a pastor. Truth was considered essential in my household."

"So you speak nothing but the truth?"

She smiled. "I try, which often requires me to say nothing at all. What I have learned in the past year is not to believe everything I am told. Some people lie for their own benefit or simply for the enjoyment of it."

"Now that is being cynical."

"Honest."

Before Geoffrey could answer, Charles asked, "Why are you two so interested in that cat?" He rubbed his hand indelicately across his nose. "We have plenty of cats at Everett Park."

"But do you have something like Napoleon?" Geoffrey took the lad by the arm and steered him toward the covered cage. With a flourish, he pulled the shawl off and said, "Napoleon, you cantankerous old cuff, give our new friends a greeting."

The bird tilted its head and chirped, "Good morning."

"Rip me!" Charles cried. "The bird talks!"

"Amazing," Joyce said as she came to stand beside them. "Or is this a hoax, Geoffrey?"

"You wound me, milady faire." He put his hand to his chest and reeled backward.

"Bamboozled addle coves!" chirped the bird.

Joyce smiled. "He seems to know you well."

Straightening, Geoffrey laughed. "I do not put words in Napoleon's mouth. My late uncle worked long with the bird to give it a vocabulary that would put you to the blush. 'Good morning' is one of the few things I would beseech him to speak within earshot of a lady."

"A bird that speaks?" Charles asked. He squatted and put his finger out to the cage.

All amusement left Geoffrey's voice. "Be careful. He likes to bite."

Charles frowned. "He has no teeth, just a beak."

"Yes, but that can be as—"

The boy yelped and pulled back his finger. A streak of scarlet ran along it.

"It bit me!" Charles cried.

"I warned you."

"Stupid bird!" He jumped to his feet and raced out of the room.

Geoffrey set himself on his feet to follow, but Joyce stepped in front of him and said, "You were the one to tell me to let him be alone before."

"No lad should be left alone to lament his fortune endlessly."

"Endlessly? It has only been a day."

He took her hands and drew her closer. "Childhood is too short to waste it on boredom and disappointment. That is why I tried to lighten his spirits last night."

"He was smiling when you came in. That surprised me."

"I am glad."

"I am glad he was smiling, too. It—"

"No." He traced an ambling pattern across the back of her hand. "I am glad you were surprised. I think, Joyce, you could use more surprises. You seem too content with your life."

"Is that so horrid?"

"It can be." He took a step back into the middle of the room, pulling her with him. "One should always be on the lookout for possible adventures. You can never guess where they might appear. After all, would you have suspected yesterday at this hour that you would now be hostessing two strangers?"

"How could I?"

"Of course. How could you?" Drawing her even closer, he said, "That is the joy of pending adventure. You never know where or when one might come." He lifted her hand to his lips.

The tingle left by his touch became, beneath the teasing warmth of his mouth, a raging torrent that surged through her, threatening to weaken her knees and sweep her from her feet. It could not dampen the pulse which burned like the fire in his sultry, sapphire eyes. He certainly was not the most handsome man she had ever met, but he was the most compelling . . . and most outrageous. She pulled her hand out of his.

"See?" he asked, clearly not insulted by her coolness. "You could not have guessed I would take this opportunity to greet you as politely as I should have last evening. Adventures, grand and glorious as well as small and barely significant, await us everywhere."

"That is a most peculiar way of looking at things."

"I think it is most enlightened." He smiled and bowed. "Pardon me, Joyce, while I go upon the quest for something to break my fast. I find that, even though smoke is filling, it leaves one wishing for a more hearty meal."

"I was just on my way to the breakfast-parlor."

He offered his arm. "Then lead on, my dear Miss Stuart, and let us see what escapades await us over biscuits and eggs."

Five

Joyce doubted if anyone who might call would know which one of them was the host as Geoffrey led her into the white breakfast-parlor. He graciously sat her at the oak table and collected a plateful of food from the sideboard for her before selecting some for himself. His greeting to Mrs. Englewood suggested he had been served by the housekeeper and her staff many times in the past.

Watching in amazement, Joyce wondered how he managed to put everyone around him—save her—at ease with a few words. His compliments were not effusive and seemed unquestionably genuine. The kitchen maid was unable to restrain her giggles, but Joyce could not accuse Geoffrey of flirting. As lief, he simply treated everyone with that contagious warmth that made one feel so special.

That, she warned herself, was the very reason why she must ignore the delight quivering through her each time he touched her. With his easy charm, he could convince a woman she was the exclusive recipient of his attention when he meant nothing but to be pleasant.

She was no less baffled when she returned to her room after breakfast to collect the letters she needed to answer. With *Le Beau Monde* dispersed from London, many wrote to her, eager to hear of any tidings of events that might have transpired in their absence. For the first time during this winter, she had news to share. She wondered what her friends among the *ton* might know of Geoffrey Wilcox.

Stella! She must give Stella a look-in. Her bosom-bow had so many acquaintances among the Polite World. Surely, over a bit of scan-mag, Stella would be able to ease Joyce's curiosity. And, in addition, Stella had several younger brothers. Mayhap she could advise Joyce on how to keep Charles's smile from vanishing so swiftly.

Putting all thoughts of writing letters out of her head, Joyce went up the stairs with lighter steps. She hummed a tune under her breath. This was the best idea she had had since she went to call on her great-aunt. Not only would she be able to enjoy Stella's company and possibly learn more about Geoffrey, but she could have an hour or two away to sort out her thoughts.

She checked her appearance in the glass in her bedchamber. Wisps of black hair curled around her cheeks, and she pushed them away. Whirling around, she collected her favorite bonnet. It was lined with fur and warm about her ears when the weather turned chill.

Her abigail came in, smiling. "You have selected a lovely day for a walk. This frosting of snow is just what we needed after all the cold rain."

"Miss Richmond asked me to give her a call. You know she likes her callers to arrive before noon."

"Unfashionably early."

Joyce sat and took the high-lows her abigail brought to her. Slipping the ankle-high boots onto her feet, she said, " 'Tis a good thing I have never thrown off my country-put ways."

"You are no bumpkin," Hélène asserted faithfully.

"Mayhap not, but I am going to take advantage of this invitation to visit Stella." Heat burned on her cheeks. "Oh, dear. I should not have said that, but I do hope Stella can give me some guidance on how to be a good hostess to both of my guests."

Her abigail laughed. "It would appear, Mademoiselle Joyce, that you have been given the care of not merely one boy, but two."

"I am afraid you are right." She leaned her chin on her palm and looked out the window. The center of the Square was still pristine. Not a single footprint marred the fresh snow around the statue of King George III dressed in classical Roman garb. "I know nothing about boys. How can I hope to keep Charles from suffering from ennui?"

"As you said yourself last night, Lord Dartmouth should be able to help you find ways to amuse Mr. Charles."

"Or get him in trouble. Geoffrey has a maddening way about him."

The abigail laughed again. "My *maman* warned me when I was no older than Mr. Charles not to trust a man whose eyes twinkled like the sun on the sea. Such a man would be as fleeting and unobtainable as a sunbeam."

"Wise advice. I . . ." Her eyes were caught by a motion beneath the trees in the middle of the Square.

She came to her feet as a silhouette which was undoubtedly Charles Everett rushed out through the snow. He paused, scooped up some snow, and turned to throw it.

"Fiddle!" If the lad were aiming at Lady Brookston's carriage, which often left the Square at this hour, there would be the devil to pay and no pitch hot.

Leaving her abigail calling a question to her back, Joyce rushed down the stairs and out the door. She gasped as the cold struck her like a fist, knocking the breath right out of her. Pushing aside the thought that she should return inside for her spencer, she hurried to the walkway and crossed the street to the heart of the Square.

Her arm was seized. She shrieked as she was tugged to her left. A muscular arm swept around her waist and kept her from falling into the snow. She opened her mouth to scream again, but halted when a snowball struck the tree in front of her.

"That was close." Geoffrey laughed.

She stared at him in disbelief. "What is going on here?"

He gestured past her as Charles ran up to them.

Geoffrey laughed again and ruffled the boy's snow-flecked hair. "Why don't you gather some snow, Joyce? I could use some help. Charlie is quite a marksman." Brushing snow off his greatcoat, he added, "You can see he has proven that more than once."

"Charlie hit you with all that snow?" she asked, looking from one to the other.

Instead of answering, the lad crowed, "You are too slow!"

"When you are as *old* as I, you will be slower." Geoffrey stooped over like an old man. With a laugh, he straightened. "But let us see which of us truly has the better eye."

"A contest?" Charles asked.

"Why not?" He bowed toward Joyce. "In this fair lady's honor."

Charlie wrinkled his nose. "That is silly."

"Spoken," Joyce said, "like a boy who is much more mature at twelve than you are at your years."

"Ouch!" Geoffrey tapped his chest. "I can see you waste no time getting right to the heart of the matter." Bending, he collected a handful of snow. "Are you ready, Master Charles, for some competition?"

Charles looked from him to Joyce and shook his head. "No, thank you." He wiped his gloved hands together and started back toward the house.

"What did I say this time?" Geoffrey asked.

Joyce sighed. "You said nothing wrong. It appears that, although he has forgiven you for startling him upon your arrival, he is still very angry at me."

"Why? If it hadn't been for you, he might have no place to go."

"Exactly. Don't you understand? That is why he tried to come to my rescue on the steps. He feared, if I were hurt, he would have no one. Even an unwanted hostess is better than no hostess at all." She slipped her hands under her folded arms to keep them warm. "I wish my great-aunt had taken him with her to the country. Surely there must be more there for a boy to do than in London at this time of year."

"We can arrange for things to keep him entertained."

"No!"

"Joyce, no need to dismiss the idea out of hand," he replied, abruptly somber. "The boy wants to feel important to someone, for he clearly thinks his parents and all his connections consider him to have as much purpose as feeding a goose hay." Taking her hand, he drew her back toward her side of the Square. "Trust me. Everything will work out as it should."

"I am not certain that is a good idea."

"Do you have a better one? Get your coat and bonnet, Joyce. You could use some more fresh air."

"Really?"

"Really!" He opened the door and knocked mud and snow from his boots. "I must go to speak with the head of the workmen who should even now be at my house. When I hired them yesterday, he asked that I should prioritize the work that needs to be done."

"How much is there to do? I thought 'twas no more than a stuffed chimney."

"Why not come with me and see for yourself? I would not mind a feminine opinion on this."

"I think—"

"If you fear for your reputation, bring Charlie along as your *duenna*."

"The lad's name is Charles."

"His father's name is Charles, so he prefers 'Charlie.' "

She glanced up the stairs. "I do not know if he would wish to go with us."

"With you."

"You do not mince words, do you?"

"A waste of time when we can be riding across Mayfair." He tipped her face toward his as his voice dropped to a whisper. "I promise you excitement unlike any you have ever known."

She should have told him she had other matters that required her attention. The household accounts which Mrs. Englewood brought for her review once a week, a look-in on Stella Richmond, those letters which still waited to be answered . . . Each task was forgotten as she stared up into his smiling eyes. She could imagine excitement with him so easily if the passion in his eyes swept over her, bewitching her with thoughts she should not be having.

"Will you come with me on this adventure?" he whispered, holding up his hand.

She placed hers on it and watched his smile broaden. A shiver slid down her back. A shiver of dismay . . . and anticipation.

"London has a different air during the winter," Geoffrey said as the carriage bounced in a chuck-hole. He put up his hand to keep the top of his hat from hitting the roof and steadied Napoleon's cage on the seat next to him. The bird squawked its outrage from beneath the paisley shawl, then subsided with a mutter of something Joyce decided was better left unintelligible.

Joyce grasped the door as she heard Charles chuckle from up on the box where he was riding with the coachee. She hoped the lad was not driving, for she guessed this would be only the first hole the carriage struck. No, Oliver's coachee would know better than to let a sprig handle the reins.

"I'm learning about the differences," she replied, settling back on the leather seat and sticking her fingers into her muff. Despite her fur-lined bonnet and heaviest wool spencer, the day was damp and chill.

"Is this your first winter in Town?"

"Yes."

"Have you come often for the Season?"

"No." Her hope that he would take the hint from her brusque answers and change the subject was futile.

"Did I venture too close to that forbidden territory again?"

"Simply because I do not wish to lay bare my past is no reason to continue to probe it." She looked out the window at the street. It was nearly deserted beneath the sky that threatened more snow.

"I possess a curious nature."

"Your bad luck, my lord."

"Egad, I must have overstepped myself." His finger under her chin turned her face to him. "Not only are you giving me monosyllabic answers, but I am once more 'my lord' to you."

She dug her fingers more deeply into her muff and lifted her chin away from his beguiling touch. How was it that a man who was so dashedly irritating could make her heart beat more swiftly with such a simple touch? Fiddle! She should have insisted that Charles ride with them in the carriage.

"You are speaking nonsense," she said in the stern tone she copied from her great-aunt.

"Probably."

She stared at him.

"I do not wish to have a brangle with you *again*. Is it possible we might be able to enjoy some conversation?" His eyes began to twinkle anew. "Conversation, not brown talk. I have no wish to return to the artificial proprieties of 'my lord' and 'Miss Stuart.'"

"I suppose we can."

"Ah, a good hostess to the very end."

"End?" she asked, startled.

"Of our journey." He pointed out the window as the carriage slowed. "Here we are at the very spot where disaster propelled me upon your benevolence."

Joyce decided she would hold onto what small bit of dignity she still possessed by not replying to his hanking.

As he handed her out, he held her fingers no longer than propriety allowed. She was shocked by the abrupt melancholy swirling within her when he turned to lift the birdcage out of the carriage as he spoke with Charles.

This was beyond absurd! One moment, she wished he had never been catapulted into her life along with his menagerie and that he would stop intruding into her every thought. The next, she suffered this sense of loneliness that he was paying her no mind. She had no more sense than Napoleon.

Hoping she could leave her bafflement on the walkway, Joyce walked with Geoffrey and the lad to the front door, which was ajar. The house, set alone at the end of a narrow street, had the air of having been built years before and was waiting for the city to grow out to it. Two wide chimneys claimed either end of the house. Between them, simple windows were set in neat precision. The door with its Corinthian columns was set in the brick façade four steps up from the walkway.

As they entered the octagonal foyer, a longcase clock by the curve of the stairs leading to the first floor gonged a mournful dirge. Joyce stared about in dismay as Charles whistled under his breath.

Soot outlined spider webs on the ceiling and added ebony fringe to each of the drapes in the sitting room to the left. The once white upholstery had become a dreary gray. Black footprints crisscrossed the carpet from the hearth to the double French doors at the back of the room.

"I had not guessed it would be this appalling," Joyce said as she inched around the ruined settee. Something crunched under her feet. She looked back at Geoffrey who was setting Napoleon's cage on the foyer floor and drawing off its covering. "All these cinders? You mentioned nothing of a fire."

"It was not a large one."

"Hardly worth mentioning?"

"Exactly." He crossed the sitting room and ran his finger along the charred mantel. "I did like this, though. Mahogany and marble. I wonder if it can be reconstructed."

"Have you lived here long?"

"I was here often since I was in short coats." Folding his arms in front of him, he glanced around the room. "The house has been empty for many years, so I should have guessed the chimneys were in dire need of attention."

From the foyer, she heard Charles shout.

"What is it, Charlie?" Geoffrey called back. He flashed her a grin when he used the nickname, but even that could not disguise the sorrow in his eyes. Striding toward the foyer before she could speak, he kept her from offering him any sympathy.

Joyce glanced around the room again. Most of the damage, she noted on closer scrutiny, was from smoke and the water used to put out the blaze, which must have exploded right out of the hearth. Although the furniture closest to the fireplace was charred beyond repair, the rest of the pieces could be salvaged if Geoffrey wished. She had no idea if he possessed plump enough pockets to buy all new furnishings or if he would choose to have these restored. Mayhap these things had a sentimental meaning which no amount of money might replace.

She knew so little about him. His sense of humor and delight in the bizarre raised an effective barrier which she had not realized existed until now. When he preferred to speak of Napoleon and Josephine as lief his own despair in the wake of the fire here, he had prevented her from asking any questions he did not want to answer.

Until now. The flash of grief in his eyes had revealed more than he might have suspected. She would not be bamblusterated by his jobbernowl ways again.

Six

Wandering out into the foyer, Joyce paused to check Napoleon. The bird glowered at her and spat an obscenity.

She laughed as the bird continued to air its vocabulary. Geoffrey had not been exaggerating. Napoleon had a gift for curses that would make a conveyancer flush, although, even though she was the daughter of a minister, she heard nothing she had not before.

"You will have to do better than that," she said, bending to meet the bird eye-to-eye.

"Bamboozled addle cove!"

Laughing again at what the bird must think was its worst insult, she followed the sound of Charles's eager questions toward the back of the house. She could not silence her gasp of astonishment when she entered a room that was a twin in shape to the foyer, save that no staircase edged its left side. A hearth stood, cold and lifeless, opposite her, but she gave it barely a glance as she stared at the collection of animal heads ringing the room. She could not name more than half of the animals, for she had never seen their like.

Geoffrey turned and grinned. "Come in, Joyce, and see what may be unique in Town."

"Where did all these beasts come from?"

"My uncle enjoyed the hunt whether in England or

abroad." He stretched up to pat a stuffed zebra on the snout. "This was a favorite of his, for it was the first beast he shot in Africa. The rooms above are filled with more of his trophies."

Joyce wrinkled her nose. "I do not like the idea of living with stuffed beasts about."

"At least, these are only stuffed," Charles said in a gloomy tone. "That is, more bearable than some stuffy folks in London."

Geoffrey laughed and slapped Charles lightly on the shoulder. "A fine turn of the phrase, my boy, but no way to speak of the *ton*."

"Not all the *ton* is stuffy. Just some of them." He looked at Joyce.

She forced a smile. The lad had tried to infuriate her at every turn and had succeeded admirably. No more. If she hoped for any sense of peace in her household until his parents returned, she must not react to his inflammatory retorts.

"I agree," she said quietly. Walking to the other side of the room, she added, "This lion reminds me of a fisherman who lived near where I spent my childhood. He had hair as wild and an expression as dour. Like a lion, he would roar at anyone who came too near his cottage when he did not wish to be disturbed."

"Were you scared of him?" Geoffrey asked.

"No, for he also spun the most wonderful tales of things and creatures upon and beneath the sea. I daresay he believed in many of them, although, even then, I knew the tales could not all be true."

Charles surprised her by asking, "What kind of creatures?"

She looked at Geoffrey, and he gave her an encouraging smile. Was it possible the three of them could achieve some sort of compromise and live serenely together?

Turning to Charles, she said, "Creatures that are half human and half fish. Creatures as big as a brigantine. Creatures that glow in the dark like stars caught beneath the waves."

"Imaginary creatures."

"Not to Salt Jack." She went to the doors leading out into the garden, which was sculptured into frozen shapes beneath the thin layer of snow. "I believe he came to accept his stories as gospel." Facing them, she smiled. "When he told his tales it was difficult not to believe, too."

"Some of our grandest adventures take place within the confines of our imaginations," Geoffrey said as he patted the horn on the front of some beast Joyce could not name. "That is all to the best, because then there are no limits on what we might do."

When the lad asked a question about one of the other animals, Joyce went back out into the corridor. She peeked down the stairs into the kitchens. They were blackened with the same smoke that had redecorated the sitting room. A door was open, and snow had drifted across the stone floor.

Geoffrey was going to need a place to stay for at least a pair of fortnights. Even as her heart throbbed with pleasure at the thought, she groaned. Her quiet time before the Season resumed was doomed.

Going back into the sitting room, she smiled. This room was not so bad on second appraisal. Paint and some wallcovering would conceal the scorched marks on the wall. The rug was burned in only one spot. If turned, the ruined part could be hidden beneath a draped table. Only the mantel and the few pieces of furniture nearest to the hearth were destroyed beyond a quick repair.

Joyce tried to disregard the crunching beneath her shoes as she went to the hearth. Her toe hit something that bounced across the cinder-covered rug and onto the marble floor beside the hearth. Bending, she picked up what she realized was a double gilded frame. She turned it to see broken glass covering a set of miniatures. Two unsmiling faces peered back at her. Geoffrey's parents? She saw some resemblance in each face, for they looked not much older than he must be now.

"Joyce?"

At Geoffrey's call from the doorway, she spun, hiding the frame behind her back like a naughty child who had pried where she should not. She frowned as shards of glass fell from the frames to shatter on the marble.

He said nothing as he crossed the room. He simply held out his hand. When she gave him the broken miniatures, he glanced at them and then folded the frame shut. He set it on the table.

"We can take it with us," she said. "I am certain someone at Oliver's house knows how to cut and fit glass back into the frames."

"I will have everything repaired in time." Again he kept her from voicing her questions by adding, "Come along. We must not linger here any longer. Napoleon will take a chill, and I have seen all I need to so I may give instructions to the workmen."

"Geoffrey?" She did not move as he walked to the door.

His back was to her as he asked, "Yes?"

"I am so very sorry."

He put his hand on the molding, but did not turn. "About what?"

"About all this."

"You need not waste your pity on me, Joyce." Slowly he faced her. "The house can be repaired to the way it was, for my memories of it are intact." He ran his hand along the door frame. "And the parts I never liked, like this molding, can be replaced. It is just a house. It does not matter as much as you seem to think."

A shout from Charles, who clearly had continued his exploration upstairs, echoed down the stairs. Geoffrey strode away to answer him.

Joyce stared after him. For the first time, Geoffrey was plying her with balms. She suspected he was hiding the truth from her . . . and from himself.

The small parlor was aglow with dozens of candles. Joyce wondered how many servants were required to keep the wicks trimmed and the candles replaced and when they managed such a task. On the many calls she had made to Stella Richmond's home on Hanover Square, she had never seen the room lit with less than a score of candles. Even in the middle of the day, when the sunshine slithered across the Persian rug, each of the cherry and marble tables was topped with a flickering candle.

Surrounded by all the light, Stella greeted her guests. Stella was older than Joyce by a decade, but the efforts of her abigail and dresser hid that fact. With her lush blond hair and elegant figure, she was the center of attention wherever she went. She had buried one husband more than a year ago, and now she had set her eye on obtaining a new one. And not just any husband, but Lord

Markham, a plummy marquess with a splendid country seat not far from her parents' home and an even grander home here in London. It was for that reason, more than any other, that Joyce was astonished her friend had returned to Town.

"You took your merry time coming to pay me a call." Stella's smile softened her scold as she motioned for Joyce to come in and sit on the silvery settee across from where she lounged on its twin. Sitting straighter, she smoothed her ivory teagown around her. "I sent you that invitation to call almost a week ago. I do believe I said I hoped you would visit with all due speed."

"Playing the hostess gives me little time for myself." She clamped her lips closed. No need to down-pin Stella with the tale of what had been taking place on Berkeley Square for the past seven days. She doubted if she could choose who had been more exasperating, Geoffrey or the boy. They had become partners in an effort to keep the household atwitter with laughter and vexation.

"Hostess?" Stella offered Joyce a cup of tea and smiled. "Ah, yes, I do recall hearing that Lady Eloise asked you to look after the Everetts' boy. A burden, I know, and one which will keep you from joining the rest of us in grassville."

"But you are not there. What brings you back to Town?"

Stella poured more tea into her cup and selected a cake from the plate. "My sister's baby kept everyone awake for a week. I decided the only way I would be able to get enough sleep so I would not go to Lord Markham's *soirée* with gray circles under my eyes was to come here and enjoy the silence."

Joyce could easily commiserate, and she wished Stella

better fortune than she had had. The only quiet times she could steal now were when everyone had sought his or her bed. Even then, she had been wakened just last night when Geoffrey was pointing out the constellations in the winter sky. She had tiptoed out onto the back balcony and watched how he traced their paths through the sky. She had been as mesmerized as the boy. Something about Geoffrey was undeniably beguiling . . . when he was not being irritating with his determination to turn every event into a grand escapade.

"If Lord Markham saw you with circles beneath your eyes," she said when she realized Stella was waiting for an answer, "he might not think you had been dreaming of him."

"As you have been dreaming of Geoffrey Wilcox?"

"Geoffrey?" She laughed, glad it sounded sincere. "Who has been filling your head with such pap? If he intruded on my sleep, it would be more as a nightmare than as a dream."

"I have heard—"

"Heard? Where? So few of the Polite World remain in London."

"At my sister's house—"

"Your sister's house?" Standing, she set her cup on the table. "How is it that a simple show of benevolence is of such interest to the *élite?*"

Stella came to her feet. "Dear Joyce, you know that anything you do intrigues those who have nothing in their lives but the enjoyment of poker-talk. There is still talk about how you saved your sister's reputation in that accommodation house."

"Stella!"

"You need not be ashamed of your courage and foresight."

She tapped her foot on the floor as she frowned. "I just have no wish to have every move I make displayed in the air by witless blocks."

"Do not take the owl. Anger will gain you nothing." Stella's lips tilted in a smile. "Besides, it is a waste of time to be in a pelter when people simply wish to admire what you have done. On my say-so, Joyce, I have heard only amazement that you have taken in both young Charles Everett and Lord Dartmouth, who is well known to be queer in his attic."

"He is not insane." She relented from her scowl enough to smile. "A bit eccentric mayhap, but he is not mad. If not for Geoffrey, I fear the situation with Charlie—" She guessed her cheeks were a ruddy shade, for warmth burned on them. Dash it! How ironic she should take on Geoffrey's bad habits when none of her *good* ones seemed to be making any inroads on his behavior. "I mean, the situation with Charles would have been intolerable if Geoffrey had not been there to help." Sitting again, she picked up her cup. "I own that Geoffrey has some odd ideas, but he makes the lad forget his parents are far away."

"You defend him with such fervor."

"I am simply thankful to him."

"Are you certain?"

"Stella, do not look for something to put upon the *on dits*. I thought you were my bosom-bow."

Stella sat facing her once more. "I am your dear friend. That is why I am trying to help you see what you clearly wish to ignore. You are intrigued by Lord Dartmouth."

"He is a bothersome, stubborn man."

"Making him the perfect match for you."

"Now you sound like Lady Eloise. Since I have known her, she has been after me to find a man to buckle myself to with all alacrity."

Stella rolled her eyes. "I see I have touched upon a sensitive spot." Clasping her hands in her lap, she said, "Joyce, I do not want you betrothed and married to such a quiz. I simply wish to warn you that he has not been quite the same as anyone else since he was a young child."

"What do you mean?" She stared at her friend in consternation. "I own that he has a unique way of looking at the world, but he has been the epitome of kindness to Charles."

"And well he should. He knows well what the boy is feeling with his parents gone."

"Geoffrey's parents were gone often?"

Her voice softened into sorrow. "I thought you would know, Joyce. Lord Dartmouth's parents died in a horrible carriage accident when he was not much more than a babe. He had only an unmarried uncle left. The man traveled often and had little time for such a small child." She picked up her teacup and ran her finger around the top as she stared into it. "Lord Dartmouth was much alone until the Blackburns made him a part of their family after he and Oliver Blackburn met at school. He spent all his holidays with the Blackburns. When he finished with school, Lord Dartmouth seems to have assumed a life much like his uncle, for he traveled often. He came back to London only a few months ago when he inherited that bizarre house that belonged to his uncle."

"Oh." She was not sure what else she could say. So much came clear with this vital bit of information: the obvious, long-standing friendship between Geoffrey and

Marshall, Geoffrey's patience with Charlie's tempers, the sorrow that had stolen the smile from him when they went to the fire-damaged house in Kensington. Tears rolled heavily into her eyes, but she blinked them away. Geoffrey did not want her sympathy.

"Just be grateful the boy is there. To have you and Lord Dartmouth sharing a house would cause such a to-do it would reach every ear, even with the *élite* scattered throughout England." Stella took a sip and smiled. "We must think of some way to handle this dilemma, Joyce."

"I am sure something can be arranged. Geoffrey must have other friends in London, but, of course, as Oliver's tie-mate, he must be made to feel welcome for as long as he wishes." She clenched her hands as she fought back the delight that pulsed through her when she thought of Geoffrey staying longer at the house. Was insanity catching? She feared she had been infected.

"Leave it to me. I know every member of the *ton*. I am certain I can work something out to your satisfaction."

"I hope so."

"Trust me, Joyce. Everything will work out as it should."

She heard the echo of Geoffrey's voice telling her the same thing. She wished she could believe it.

Seven

"She is angry that I am here." Charlie slumped in his chair.

Geoffrey reached for one of the pairs of dry socks that had been brought for them after their walk in Hyde Park. "No, Miss Stuart is not angry you are here."

"You are wrong!" He propped his chin on his fists and glared out the window. "She is just too polite to say anything. If she could pass me off on someone else, she would do so."

"I own she can have an adder's tongue, but if she has taken a snuff at anyone, it is not you."

"Oh, she does not like you being here either." The boy spoke without rancor.

"Now, on that, I will agree with you wholeheartedly." Chuckling, Geoffrey stood and wiggled his toes. Warm, dry socks were the grandest thing he could imagine just now. *The next to grandest thing,* he corrected himself. Joyce's fingers against him, chaste though the caress had been, had been an even sweeter sensation.

"Mayhap we should just leave."

"Leave?" He looked at the boy, who was still staring out the window. "Exactly where do you intend to go?"

"Somewhere. Scotland or mayhap Africa or someplace exciting."

"Africa is, indeed, exciting."

Charlie spun, his face alight with eagerness. "You have been there?"

"A few times." He bent to watch Napoleon clean his feathers. "As you saw in Kensington, my uncle enjoyed that unknown land. He had holdings there, and I traveled to visit him on the occasional holiday."

"Did you like going there?"

"Each trip was different from any others. I always enjoyed the opportunity to see the people and animals who live there. They are nothing like those on our staid island."

"So let's go."

"Now?"

"Why not? Miss Stuart does not want us here, and we don't want to be here. What can you imagine that would be more perfect?"

Geoffrey was tempted to reply with the truth. The most perfect thing he could envision was enfolding Joyce Stuart to him. Blood and 'ouns! He had to be grateful that Oliver was not here to see him acting as moony as a young sprig dallying after her. Mayhap he should take the boy's suggestion. If he were this sweet on her when he had done no more than touch her hand and look into her eyes, he did need a bit of fresh air to clear his head. A change of scenery was what he needed, but not, he had to own, what he wanted, for he relished every moment when his gaze could settle on Joyce.

"An ocean voyage this time of year is horrendous," he said in lieu of his true thoughts.

"We could weather it." Charlie's thin chest puffed out with mock pride. "I am not afraid of waves and wind."

"Have you ever suffered from carriage-sickness?"

When the boy nodded, Geoffrey arched a brow. "Seasickness is even worse, because, unlike a carriage, you cannot stop the ship and walk about to ease the nausea. This time of year, the sea is as savage as Josephine's wild cousins in Africa."

Charlie's smile faded as he nodded. "It would have been fun."

"Great fun."

"What would have been fun?" asked a lighter voice, the same one that had lilted so pleasantly through Geoffrey's dreams last night.

Joyce held out a plate of iced cakes as she came into the sitting room. She looked as luscious as any of the sweets, and he would as lief taste her lips than sample one of the cakes.

An air-dreamer! That defined what he was. Miss Joyce Stuart had very graciously let him know that he was an inconvenience she hoped would soon be gone from her life. She wanted peace and quiet. He detested the same. They had nothing in common, save, he hoped, the pleasure even a vagrant touch sent leaping through him.

"Charlie and I were talking about taking a sojourn," he replied quietly.

Her smile vanished even more swiftly than Charlie's had. "You should not plant impossible hopes in his head. You know, we must wait here for his parents to return."

"Why?" demanded Charlie.

Geoffrey put his hand on the boy's arm and was not surprised that it quivered with barely suppressed emotion. "Do not give Joyce a wigging when you know she is being honest."

"I do not want to stay here in Town. It is beneath boredom."

"Only if you make it so," Joyce said. "If—"

Napoleon piped up, "You go before your mare to market."

"See?" Geoffrey gestured toward the bird. "Even the bird knows you are being ridiculous."

"Bamboozled addle coves," Napoleon retorted.

He laughed again. "So we are, and we must do something to alleviate that ennui." He took the tray and set it on the table. As he watched both of them sit an arm's distance away from each other on the settee, he smiled. "There is but one thing to do, and I hope our hostess will agree. We must hold a gathering."

"A gathering?" Joyce asked in astonishment. She had not expected such a mundane suggestion when his eyes were shimmering like heat rising from a lush field on a summer afternoon.

"Why not?" He drew up a chair and sat facing her. "Is that not how the *ton* entertains itself throughout the Season? As I missed the last one—and the one before that, I must own—it would be intriguing to create our own small version right here."

She shook her head. "I do not think that is an inspired idea."

"But it is, Joyce." He grasped her hands and folded them between his wider ones. "Imagine the fun we could have if we hosted such a gathering."

"We?"

"I would be delighted to assist you in the necessary tasks." He leaned back in his chair, drawing her toward him. "And it will give Charlie something to do." He winked at the boy, whose face was decorated with the green icing from the half-eaten cake in his hand. "We do not want the poor lad to suffer from ennui. That is a sorry state for any kiddy of his age."

"He has not—thanks to you—been bored."

"But I shall not be here much longer. I cannot infringe on Oliver's hospitality along with yours when my chimneys should now be clean. It will not take long for the house to be repaired to a point that I may resume residence there."

Joyce bit her lip to silence the words she must not speak. How was it that, in just this short time, Geoffrey had become such a part of her days—a most exasperating part, to be sure—that she could not imagine him leaving? He had altered all her plans for a quiet retreat from the hubbub of the *ton,* when he burst into her life with his bird and his cat and his peculiar outlook.

"Oh, do let us have a gathering," Charlie implored, grinning at her through the frosting.

"But what shall we do at this gathering?" A sense of being out-flanked filled her. She knew there was a good reason not to have a gathering, but it had disappeared from her head at the moment Geoffrey said he would be leaving soon. She should be thrilled. She was miserable.

"Leave that to Charlie and me," Geoffrey said. "Meet us in the breakfast-parlor in an hour." He stood and gestured toward the door. "Let's go, my boy."

With an excited whoop, Charlie rushed out the door.

Her breath caught as Geoffrey put his hand on the arm of the settee and leaned toward her until his breath warmed her face that was both too hot and too cold. When his fingers lightly brushed her cheek, she put her hand on his arm. She could not halt herself. She wanted this indescribable sweetness of touching and being touched. His lips grazed her cheek, a chaste salute that was gone in a heartbeat, but the heat seared to the very tips of her toes.

"Thank you," he whispered.

"Thank you?" She should be the one thanking him for this delight.

"You will be glad you agreed to this *soirée.*"

"I hope so." She wished he would stop prattling and kiss her again, and not just on her cheek this time.

"Trust me." He squeezed her hand, then turned to hurry out of the room with a youthful anticipation that rivaled Charlie's.

"I wish I could," she murmured in his wake.

Eight

Joyce heard excited voices before she reached the breakfast-parlor door. Pausing in the doorway, she stared about the room. Most of the household must be gathered within. Not just the young maids and the cook's assistants who giggled and batted their eyelashes each time Geoffrey walked past them, but Cook and Marshall and Hélène as well. She wondered what Geoffrey had told them about his plans.

"And here is Miss Stuart now." Geoffrey held out his hand to her. "Do come and join us, Snow White."

"Snow White?"

He grasped her hand and drew her to the table where Charlie sat scribbling with the intensity of a scholar about to make a great discovery.

Geoffrey said, "Show Miss Stuart what you have completed so far, Charlie."

The boy held up a page. At the top was written *The Story of Snow White—A Play by Charles Everett of London*. "I have only the first scene written, but the rest will be done in a streak."

"See?" Geoffrey tapped the page. "Here are your opening lines, Joyce."

Handing him the page, she sat on the chair closest to the door, saying, "You are mistaken. I shall be the hostess

THE WINTER HEART

of this gathering. I cannot take time from my guests to take a part in this play. I shall simply be an interested observer."

"Observer?" Charlie jumped to his feet. "Miss Stuart, you must be part of our play."

"Why not ask Gwen?" She motioned for the plump serving lass to step forward. "She has the coloring and is of an age to be your Snow White."

Charlie's smile became the scowl she had become all too familiar with.

"Joyce," Geoffrey said quietly, "let us talk of this out in the corridor." He raised his voice. "Butler, I leave to you the choice of which of the lads would be best suited to play our septet of dwarves."

Joyce thought of a dozen things to say as she went with Geoffrey to the sitting room. When he closed the double doors, cutting off the rumble of conversation that had followed them from the breakfast-parlor, she said none of them. She was caught by his gaze as he walked toward her. She clasped her hands behind her, so he might not see how they trembled when she realized how alone they were. No one in the household would intrude without knocking first.

When he walked past her, she whirled, shocked at his cool action and her despair that he seemed to have forgotten the kiss—albeit on the cheek—that he had given her here such a short time ago.

"Please sit, Joyce," he said in an unemotional tone that unsettled her even more.

Carefully she lowered herself onto the nearest chair. She dampened her lips as she stared at him.

He gave her a cold smile. "Why are you frightened to be in our play?"

"I don't understand you."

"I suspect you do."

"I do not have stage-fright. As I told you, I shall be so busy with our guests that—"

"You know that is not what frightens you." He walked around her chair. When she would have turned, he put his hand on her shoulder. He bent forward, so his mouth was against the curls just above her ear. They fluttered, tickling her, as he murmured, "You are frightened to feel anything, even in the framework of a play written by a twelve-year-old boy. For some reason, which you have been most punctilious to conceal, you have made your heart as cold as the winter wind battering at the eaves. It is compounded by the fact you are as stubborn as a toothache."

"You are another!"

"I readily own to that." His finger followed the curve of her jaw in a feathery caress.

She wanted to give him a back-answer, but every word was lost in the pleasure swelling outward from his touch. As his fingertip trailed along her cheek, brushing the corner of her mouth lightly, she closed her eyes to savor the sensations that she should not be feeling. She had vowed not to enjoy a man's touch like this again, for she knew how easily this longing had betrayed her before.

"You need not be so stubborn, Joyce. I know you think I am a quarter flash and three-parts foolish, but you can trust me." He came around the chair and knelt beside it. Putting his hand on its arm, he did not touch her. "I am not him."

"Him? You know—"

"Nothing, as you have wanted to tell me on more than one occasion." His crooked smile was as endearing as a child's, but there was nothing childish about the sweet fire pumping through her veins. " 'Tis nothing more than what I have learned by being an interested observer."

"Two muffs!" squawked Napoleon before grumbling to himself.

At the bird's insight into their silliness, Geoffrey kept his laugh from bursting forth only because he knew it would add to the pain dimming Joyce's eyes. He should have considered this when he had agreed to Charlie's suggestion that they perform a play to bring a bit of lightness and laughter to this household. In the days since he had come to this house, he had been careful not to probe too deeply into whatever stole the scintillating glow from Joyce's smile. He had considered, more than once, riding out into grassville and calling on one of his friends to discover what might be known of Miss Joyce Stuart.

Now he did not need to, for a single guess had exposed the truth. She could not trust him—or any man, he reminded himself, not wanting to believe her distrust was aimed solely at him—because some other man had betrayed that trust. She yearned for a quiet life where she could molder away along with the furniture, because, he was beginning to believe, she had suffered from some adventure that had gone awry.

It mattered nothing to him who the blackguard might be or what enterprise she had been upon when she was confronted with disaster. He wanted only to persuade her to give this adventure, when they had been thrown together by the whims of fate and a clogged chimney, a try.

Sitting beside her, he folded her hands between his. How delicate they seemed. Not like a caged bird's, for he would not make the mistake twice of believing Napoleon was a fragile creature. He had the scars on his arm to prove the price of his misconception. Her hands reminded him of the caress of a sunbeam, sweeping into a room, touching everything with its brightness, but never lingering.

"Joyce, Charlie is anxious to do this play."

"And I am anxious for him to do it. You are asking too much for me to play both the hostess and Snow White."

"You know that is not true. If we have as many guests as we can count on one hand, it will be a smashing success." He could not resist putting his finger beneath her stubborn chin and tilting her face toward him. His breath cramped in his chest as he was confronted by the sorrow in her eyes. Smoothing the lines from her brow, he said, "Do this, or you may regret it always."

"Regret making a blind buzzard of myself?"

"Regret that you let go of your last hold on life. Do not find yourself, years from now, realizing you have spent those years existing, not living."

"You make it sound so simple."

"It is." His fingers slid down her cheek as he guided her mouth toward his. "As simple as this." When her eyes closed to let her dark lashes brush her cheeks, he knew he had wanted nothing as much as he wanted to taste her warm lips.

The door crashed against the wall. Joyce bounced away from him so sharply her nose struck his. He yelped, then turned to find out who had been so thoughtless as to interrupt them without the courtesy of a knock.

Charlie grinned as he rushed to them. "Is it all set?"

"Is it?" Geoffrey asked, catching her eyes again. They were bemused with a softness he had never seen in them before. He wanted to see it again as they closed in an invitation to kiss her.

"It?" Her voice quivered on the single word.

"The play!" Charlie could not hide his impatience. "Will you be in the play, Miss Stuart?"

She glanced at Geoffrey and nodded. "It appears so."

"Allow me," Geoffrey said with a broad smile, "to introduce you, Snow White, to your Prince Charming." Standing, he drew her to her feet before he slipped his arm around the lad's shoulders. "Prince Charlie Charming, to be exact."

Joyce dipped into a deep curtsey. "Your highness, I am honored to be in your presence."

Charlie blushed so brightly his tawny hair seemed to be growing out of a ripe apple. Then he grinned. "This could be fun."

"Exactly." Geoffrey draped his arm over Joyce's shoulder as well. "It shall be extraordinary fun."

Nine

The snow continued to drift down in slow circles as Joyce stepped out onto the church's porch. Few vehicles stood in front of the church, but that was to be expected when most of the pews had been empty. Last night, the storm had begun. Enough snow had piled up around Mayfair for Charlie to convince her to use the sleigh as lief the carriage. She had to own she had not needed much persuading, for she loved the sound of the bells the coachee added to the reins.

"Good!" cried Charlie as he jumped down from the steps. "It is still snowing!"

She smiled as Geoffrey offered his arm. The risers glittered prettily, but she knew a single misstep could send her flying into an ignoble mound on the walkway.

"He is much happier," she said, bowing her head so the snow did not strike her face. "That is your doing, Geoffrey."

"A child simply needs something to laugh about. Laughter drives away all fretting. It is not easy to be abandoned by those you have trusted to be there forever."

She glanced up at him, startled, for she had never heard him use such a dolorous tone. Recalling what Stella had revealed, she gently squeezed his arm. She must respect his need not to talk about his past, even though he was blastedly intrigued with hers.

His light tone returned as he continued, "There is no need to go directly back to Berkeley Square."

"Where would we go? No shops are open. I know of no at-homes today."

"That is all for the good." He included the lad in the conversation as they paused by the bright red sleigh. "We do not want to be bored by shopping or making calls, do we, Charlie?"

"No." He sounded dubious, like Joyce uncertain what Geoffrey intended.

"Let me take all of us for an adventure."

"Adventure?" She wiped away a flake of snow that landed on her nose. "Isn't the weather a bit inclement for adventures?"

"Of course not!" He glanced at Charlie. "An adventure is much more interesting if a challenge is included. Am I not correct?"

"A challenge?" the boy asked, his eyes widening.

"Certainly it would be more fun to cut through the jungle if snakes lurk in the undergrowth or a tiger or a maddened elephant."

"None of which we shall encounter today, thank goodness," Joyce said.

"Not tigers or an elephant."

"Or snakes!" she cried.

"That," Geoffrey said, his eyes sparkling as brightly as the fresh snow, "is something I cannot guarantee, although I doubt if any are out sunning themselves on such a cold, dreary day."

"Mayhap we still can find one." Charlie laughed as he

clambered into the back seat of the sleigh. "Napoleon would like a snake or two for his next meal."

Geoffrey shook his head, sending the flakes clinging to his lashes onto his cheeks. He did not brush them away as he handed Joyce into the sleigh's front seat. "Better to feed them to Josephine. Snakes enjoy eating birds like Napoleon, so the sight of one, even dead, in his cage is sure to bring on apoplexy."

Joyce listened to the two tease each other as Geoffrey drove the sleigh away from the river. Her first thought that he might be taking them to Kensington vanished. They were bound along Oxford Street toward the unbuilt land beyond Mayfair.

Snow was whipped up by the horse's hoofs, and the wind tugged at her bonnet. Drawing closed the collar of her spencer, she pulled her scarf up to protect her face.

The buildings thinned. Suddenly they were traveling between fields that slumbered beneath their wintry blanket. She glanced back, but the city was nearly lost in the gray of fog and snow.

When Geoffrey slowed the sleigh in front of an elegant house that was under construction, he rested his elbows on his knees and said, "I suspect someday this land in Marylebone Park will be as grand as Berkeley Square. Mayhap I should simply sell my uncle's house and commission a magnificent terrace house here."

"You certainly would have privacy," Joyce replied. "So much of the construction here has come to a halt."

Charlie leaned over the back of the seat. "Can we look about?"

"The owners may not like that," she said.

"The owners are not here."

Geoffrey chuckled. "You cannot argue with that fact."

Stepping out of the sleigh, he asked, "Shall we have an exploration?"

She looked at the house. The outer walls seemed to be standing upright only through the grace of God. She guessed the interior had had little done to it. The empty eyes of the glassless windows gave no hint as to what might be within. "Not inside," she said. "It may be too dangerous."

"You heard Snow White," Geoffrey said, surprising her at his acceptance of her limitations on his adventure. "Let us look about the exterior and see what we may find to amuse us. Coming, Joyce?"

She looked at how deeply his feet had vanished into the snow and shook her head. "I will stay here in case one of you brave explorers suddenly finds yourself in need of the services of a doctor."

"Let me show you how careful we shall be." He laughed and walked around a stack of something that was masked by the snow. Pulling out two thin boards, he handed one to Charlie. The boy regarded it with confusion until Geoffrey held his up like a rapier.

"En garde!" shouted Geoffrey.

With a laugh, Charlie swung his strip of wood.

The two swords met with a resounding crash. They parried and circled, testing each other for weaknesses.

Joyce leaned forward in the sleigh, wanting to warn Geoffrey to take care not to injure the boy. She relaxed when she saw Charlie slash at his opponent with obvious skill. Charlie bit his lip in concentration, but his eyes glittered with a delight she had not seen on his face before.

Thank goodness for Geoffrey! She almost laughed at the thought, for she had wondered so many times in the past days what curse had been inflicted upon her along with him. But she would not have known how to amuse Charlie like this. Something about Geoffrey remained delightfully child-like, so he could guess what Charlie would like to do and found ways to make the sullen child smile.

She flinched as Charlie shouted.

"Be careful of him, Geoffrey!" she called.

"Careful of *him?*" Geoffrey jumped back as Charlie swung his make-believe sword wildly. "He is going to disarm me before—"

Charlie swept the lath toward Geoffrey again. Geoffrey's piece of wood sailed up into the sky and landed with a crash on the steps of the house.

Geoffrey held up his hands. "Dear Prince Charming, do not slay me."

Holding the sword to Geoffrey's chest, Charlie shouted, "I win!"

"So you do." Geoffrey steered the board away from the front of his snow-dusted coat. "And your reward is to have any wish you want granted by yon princess." He bowed with a flourish toward Joyce.

"Any wish?"

"Any wish a princess could make come true," Joyce said with a smile. Charlie's grin was as infectious as his excitement.

Shock stole the smile from Geoffrey's face as the boy threw his arms around him and said, "I want to stay with you and have adventures. I wish my folks would never come back."

When Geoffrey said nothing and his face became as gray as the sky, Joyce jumped down from the sleigh. She took Charlie's arm and drew him back from Geoffrey.

Keeping the boy's back to Geoffrey, she forced her smile to stay in place.

"I can grant you part of that," she said, trying to keep her voice light as she watched Geoffrey turn away. She feared her heart would break when he picked up the two pieces of wood and threw them with all his might toward the back of the house.

"Which part?"

She looked again at Charlie. He had not meant to wound Geoffrey with his wish, and she would not ruin the lad's day by warning him to choose his words with more care. Ruffling his damp hair, she said, "You shall stay with us and have adventures . . . for a while. That should give you time to learn to have adventures on your own."

"I want to stay with you and Geoffrey."

Again she was amazed, but this time at Charlie's acceptance of her. All anger had left him.

"And you shall . . . for a while." She patted his arm. "Back in the sleigh. Cook is going to be distressed if we are much later for our meal."

As the boy scrambled into the sleigh, Joyce turned to discover Geoffrey walking toward them. He said nothing as he handed her in and picked up the reins. For once, he remained silent all the way back to Berkeley Square. Only Charlie seemed oblivious to the tension. He prattled like Napoleon until, upon their arrival, Joyce sent him upstairs to change into dry clothes.

Taking off her bonnet, Joyce handed it and her coat to the serving lass. She waited until Geoffrey had divested himself of his greatcoat, then she said, "Please join me in the sitting room."

Again he said nothing, but he went with her. This time,

she was the one who closed the doors behind them. Geoffrey went to pour himself a glass of brandy as she sat on the settee and drew off her damp slippers.

Looking up, she said, "I know about your parents' deaths, Geoffrey. I am sorry you were so distressed when Charlie said he wished his were never coming back."

"You call him Charlie now, too, I see."

"You are changing the subject, *I* see."

Taking a slow drink of the brandy, he said, "That sounds like an accusation."

"Don't confuse accusations with the truth. I am simply trying to be compassionate."

"Pity is something I never have found palatable."

She gripped the arms of her chair and pressed her feet to the floor, fighting the urge to throw her arms around him and tell him how sorry she was for the grief he had suffered at such a very young age. Her voice sounded strained and brittle in her ears as she said, "Yet you pity Charlie." She swallowed around the frustration filling her throat. "And you pity me."

"True."

"So the compassion may go only in one direction?"

"I am afraid so."

She resisted the urge to argue. It would gain her nothing now. "Very well, Geoffrey. I shall set my compassion aside if you will return the favor and not keep trying to discuss parts of my life that are past."

"You demand a hard bargain."

"The choice is yours."

"Then I must agree."

"As you wish." She rose and walked toward the door.

Joyce sighed silently. She had to respect the bargain she had just made with Geoffrey, even though the thought of merely being acquaintances who never delved past bibble-babble sent renewed pain through her. It was as if a door that she had dared to open even a trace had been slammed in her face. That loss hurt with every breath.

She flinched when Napoleon called, "Bamboozled addle coves!"

When she glanced back, she saw Geoffrey drain the glass and reach again for the bottle. She swallowed her sob of despair as she rushed up the stairs, trying to persuade herself it was better this way. He soon would be gone in search of a new adventure. It was better to be no more than friends.

Yet, if that were so, why did her heart ache with every beat as if it might break?

Geoffrey was an exacting director, shouting orders and correcting his actors as if they were about to take the stage in Drury Lane. With Napoleon sitting on his shoulder, he looked like a cross between a maddened pirate and a resident of Bedlam.

"More emotion, Hélène! You are Snow White's wicked queen. Wicked, wicked, wicked!" He screwed up his face and leapt about the room.

"You look like a monkey," Joyce said as he rushed past her. "Not a wicked woman."

He whirled and pointed at her. "Could you do better?"

Slowly she came to her feet. Smiling, she said, "Of course."

"Then by all means, emote." Stepping back, he gave her a sardonic bow.

She did not hesitate, as she wondered if anyone guessed that she was putting on a performance even now. Since the discussion in the sitting room in the wake of the sleigh ride, she had pretended, as Geoffrey had, that nothing was amiss between them. Mayhap if they pretended hard enough, the lie would become the truth.

Joyce took the queen's cloak from her abigail. "Hélène, you be Snow White."

"As you wish, *Mademoiselle* Joyce."

Instead of hunching beneath the cloak as Geoffrey had, Joyce straightened her shoulders. She kept her steps slow as she imagined a regal, proud queen would. With a graceful gesture, she motioned for all those around her to genuflect. She did not pause to see if the others had obeyed, for she wanted nothing to ruin the image of her assumed majesty.

She cupped Hélène's chin in her hand and looked down her nose at her abigail, who was struggling not to smile. "My dear, dear, dear Snow White, what a charming child you are! I swear the day will come soon when we shall be mistaken for sisters."

"Your highness—"

"Do not interrupt your queen, my dear child." Turning, she tapped her own chin as if in deep thought. Looking back at Hélène, she let a cold smile inch across her lips as she added, "I believe you have been spending too much time at your chores in the castle. Why not go out into the forest to enjoy the fresh air? I shall have my most courageous huntsman go with you." She gave her abigail a more beneficent smile. "Doesn't that sound like a wonderful idea?"

"If you wish, your highness."

Joyce swung the cloak off and dropped it in her abigail's lap. *"That,* Geoffrey, is how one should play a deliciously wicked queen."

Applause filled the room.

Hélène said, "My lord, mayhap *Mademoiselle* Joyce should be our wicked queen. She is so good at it."

"She is, isn't she?" Geoffrey clasped his hands behind his back. "Who would have guessed Joyce Stuart would have such a streak of wickedness?"

Charlie jumped to his feet. "No, she must be Snow White. Do not make her the wicked queen, Geoffrey! You said she would be Snow White!"

Geoffrey patted his shoulder. "Do not worry, lad." Without a pause, he added, "Joyce, may I speak with you a moment . . . alone?"

Not able to guess what he intended to say, she nodded and walked with him out into the hallway.

As soon as they reached the stairs and were out of earshot of the others, he smiled and said, "Although even a day or two ago I would have deemed it impossible, I believe Charlie has developed quite a *tendre* for you. He is eager that you will be the princess and he the prince. You must be careful. The only cure for calf love is time."

"Charlie is but a boy."

"But even a boy is rolling enough to admire a woman for her gentle loveliness. Charlie has more wit than many a man twice his age."

"Like you?"

"*Touché*. Or should I say *'en garde'*, for it is clear that you are ready to spear me with cold epithets to outline every shortcoming I possess?"

She ran her fingers along the bannister. "I do not wish to send you up to the boughs, Geoffrey."

"Nor do I wish to go there." He rested one knee on the stair and folded his arms on the bannister, pinning her hands beneath his. "I want to stay right here with you and see you smile. It is a rare treat."

"Please do not do this." She drew her hands out from beneath his.

"Do what?"

"Dally with me one moment and push me away the next. You warn me about hurting Charlie, but . . ."

"But what?"

She wanted to tell him. As she looked into his cobalt eyes and saw the swirl of emotions, she feared they were creating an eddy that would draw her more and more deeply within until she was brought to disaster. She must not speak the truth, for she was unsure of it herself. This man was unceasingly vexing. Even so, he had invaded her dreams and her thoughts with a desire to be in his arms, his mouth on hers.

Pushing herself away from the stairs, she threw over her shoulder, "The others are waiting. We must continue our practice."

She did not wait for his answer. She could only hope that, by losing herself in Snow White's problems, she could avoid confronting her own.

Ten

Joyce relaxed against Stella's settee. Coming here on this call today had been an inspired idea. Geoffrey had taken Charlie to Bond Street to pick up the items he had ordered for the costumes for their play, although Joyce had no idea where such things might be found. Sitting here, listening to her friend fill her head with the latest *on dits,* she could forget about the tug-of-war within her.

"I am so glad you could give me a look-in before I returned to grassville," Stella said.

"Lord Markham's assembly must be soon."

"At the end of the week. If all goes well, I shall be at my father's house with a day to spare." Dimples sank into her cheeks as she added, "And I shall sleep the sleep of a baby."

"If your sister's baby sleeps?"

"I hope that will be so. I wish you were going to be there for the gathering."

Joyce almost said she wished she could go, too, but that would bring a barrage of questions she was not sure she could answer. "I hope you will write and tell me every detail."

"I—" She looked toward the door. "Yes?"

Her butler entered, his livery of the same silvery cloth

as the settee where Joyce sat. "Another caller, Mrs. Richmond."

"Who is it?"

"Lord Dartmouth."

As Joyce groaned silently, Stella's eyes lit with delight. "Show him up with all speed." She captured Joyce's hands. "He must miss you with the deepest affection if he pines for your company so much that he has come seeking you after such a short call."

Trying to devise some out-and-outer that would allow her to excuse herself, Joyce failed utterly. She had no choice but to sit while Geoffrey entered with the graciousness he had shown her from the beginning. She listened to Stella twitter a greeting, but she was unable to pull her gaze from his face. His warm smile had not been aimed at her for nearly a week, and she had not discerned how much she missed it until now.

Geoffrey bowed over Mrs. Richmond's hand and stole a quick glance at Joyce. By the elevens, Joyce Stuart was beautiful, but he wished to see her face alight with a smile. This was his doing. He had vowed last night when he heard her pacing in her room while he was doing the same in his own chambers that something must be done to change these awkward circumstances. He was still waiting for inspiration and hoped this call on Mrs. Richmond might be the answer.

"Thank you," he said when Mrs. Richmond urged him to sit. He chose a chair across the low table from Joyce. That allowed him a pleasant view while he searched his brain for a solution. "I hope you can forgive this uninvited call, Mrs. Richmond."

She gave him a smile which he knew had been the downfall of several men before she accepted her late husband's proposal. Now she was ready to wed again, if the poker-talk were to be believed.

"I am delighted you have beat up my quarters, my lord, before I return to the country tomorrow."

"Tomorrow? You will miss our grand production of *Snow White*."

"Production?"

Geoffrey glanced at Joyce and grinned. "Can I believe Joyce has said nothing to you about her new avocation as an actress? She soon will be walking the boards here in London."

"An actress walking the boards?" Mrs. Richmond's eyes grew round. "Joyce, did you lose your good sense? Your reputation barely was redeemed when it was learned you were in that bordello—"

"You were in a school of Venus?" Geoffrey asked. "Miss Joyce Stuart, the pattern-card of propriety?"

"It was in extenuating circumstances, and my sister and Oliver were there as well." Joyce avoided looking at him. "Do not make something of nothing."

"But you as an actress?" gasped Mrs. Richmond. "You will be labeled a willow for having such a scabby reputation."

"Calm yourself, Stella." Setting herself on her feet, she said, "Geoffrey is jesting you, for he devised this play to amuse Charlie. It shall be seen by no one beyond our household and the few friends who will be about Town to attend."

Geoffrey closely watched Mrs. Richmond take a deep breath and release it. That way, he could resist staring at Joyce. A brothel? The very idea threatened to send him into whoops. Joyce Stuart was continually more interesting, not like the other women who had seemed fascinating but soon left him irritated, suffused with ennui. Blast their bargain not to ask about each other's pasts while they resided under the same roof.

"I have the answer," Mrs. Richmond said with a laugh. "It is so simple. You all must come to daisyville with me."

"Impossible!" Joyce exclaimed.

At the same time, Geoffrey replied, "Why not?"

Joyce fired a frown at him, but he refused to be scorched by its furious heat. "You know why not. We must be here when the Everetts return from France."

"They made their son wait for them. Why not let them wait for their son?" He smiled as he looked from Joyce's amazement to Mrs. Richmond's delighted grin.

"And you can do your little play to entertain us one evening," Mrs. Richmond said.

Joyce shook her head. "Do not be absurd! Moments ago, you were chiding me for being so bold as to act in a play. Now—"

"Now," Geoffrey interrupted smoothly, "Mrs. Richmond knows she will have the chance to see what our hours of practice have wrought."

Mrs. Richmond clapped her hands. "Do you suppose there is a small part for me?"

"You can play Snow White!" Joyce strode with unladylike speed to the door. "I shall not."

Her bosom-bow rushed to her side. "Oh, Joyce, I did not mean to distress you." Tears glistened in Stella's eyes. "My dear, dear Joyce, I asked you to join us only because I wished to have you by my side when . . ."

"Lord Markham speaks of his intentions to you?" she asked gently, vexed at herself for losing her temper.

"Is it so obvious how I feel?"

"I hope he shares your fervor."

"I believe he does." Charming color splashed on her cheeks. Stella grasped Joyce's hands. "Do say you will come to the country with me."

"If you wish, but about the play—"

Again, as he had too often in Joyce's estimation, Geoffrey intruded to say, "It will provide the perfect foil for the attention of Markham's guests, so he might pledge his troth to you, Stella."

"Exactly." Stella's smile became predatory. "As soon as you spoke of how you planned to perform it at an intimate gathering, I knew it might be just the dandy." Squeezing Joyce's hands, she asked, "Will you perform the play, Joyce?"

Geoffrey echoed, "Will you perform the play, Joyce?"

"Please do," urged Stella.

"Yes, please do," seconded Geoffrey. He drew Joyce's hands out of Stella's and folded them between his. "How can you disappoint such an eager public?"

She arched her brow in an imitation of his favorite perplexed expression. "It appears I have little choice."

He grinned. "None at all."

Eleven

"Joyce?"

She blinked open her eyes, but only a soft glow surrounded her. Moonlight, she guessed, filtered through clouds and mist. *The middle of the night.* That thought formed in her head even as her interrupted dream wrapped its enticing tendrils around her, urging her to slip back into sleep.

"Joyce?"

Geoffrey? Why was Geoffrey at her bedchamber door? Oh, dear God, could something be wrong with Charlie?

Pulling on her dressing gown, she jumped down from the bed. She sniffed as she rushed to the door. No, she could not smell any smoke other than the usual from the hearths, so the house was not afire. Then why was he at her bedchamber door in the middle of the night?

She threw open the door and stared. He wore his greatcoat and high boots. Holding his hat in one hand, he held out the other to her.

"What is it?" she asked.

"Josephine is not in the house."

"She is a cat. Cats wander about as they please."

"But it is snowing."

"What?" She swallowed a yawn. "Did you wake me

simply to tell me it is snowing and that the cat is out-of-doors? It has snowed nearly every day for the past week."

He grasped her hand and drew her out into the hall. "No, I woke you to ask you to join me for a visit to a magic place."

"Pardon me?"

"Get dressed in your warmest clothes. I will wait for you in the foyer."

"I am not going anywhere at this hour. It must be nearly midnight."

"To own the truth, it is more than an hour past midnight. Why don't you come with me and we will see what we can see while we trail Josephine?"

"You are dicked in the nob!"

"Mayhap, but do not tarry. The stars will not be as bright once the moon rises."

"Geoffrey, this is madness."

"Isn't it, though?" He whirled her about and shoved her gently toward her door. "Get dressed in your warmest clothes. You have five minutes. If you are not downstairs by then, I vow I shall come up and get you, dressed or not."

"You would not dare!"

"Wouldn't I?" He gave her a roguish grin. "In five minutes, Joyce, you are going on an adventure while we look for Josephine. 'Tis your choice what the adventure shall be."

Seeing the truth in his eyes as his gaze slid over her *déshabillé*, leaving sweet sensations in its wake, she nodded. She might be safer in going with him and Charlie on whatever jaunt they had planned than to tempt Geoffrey . . . and herself.

It actually took her less time than that to meet him in

the foyer. Giving her only enough time to button up her coat, Geoffrey swept her out into the night. The sleigh waited in front of the house. A disgruntled stableboy, who made no effort to hide his yawn, only grunted in reply to Geoffrey's thanks.

She shivered as she sat on the cool seat, but an even deeper chill cut through her when Geoffrey sat beside her and gave the order for the horse to go.

"Wait!" she cried. "What about Charlie?"

He grinned at her. "Are you advocating awakening a growing boy at this hour of the night? Just to find a cat? I would suggest, as well, Joyce, that you lower your voice. You do not want to wake everyone on the Square."

"Turn around!"

"Why?"

"Josephine would not have come this far."

"True."

"Then where are we going? I thought we were going to search for the cat."

"We may find her while I take you somewhere magical."

"Are you crazy?" she gasped. "If we were seen—"

"Who will see us? Everyone is asleep." His voice softened to the texture of the snow falling around them. "Trust me, Joyce. I have no interest in damaging your reputation. I only wish to share something special with you."

"That something special could be the devastation of my reputation."

He laughed without restraint and slipped his arm around her shoulders. Drawing her closer to him, he said, "Your own thoughts are more of a threat to you than I am. Relax, for you know I would not do anything to hurt you."

She did know that, but she did not want to own to that just now. Not that it mattered. The sleigh was gliding along at a speed that would have been impossible during the day when other traffic was about. She did not dare to relax, for then she would find it too easy to put her head against his strong shoulder and close her eyes as her dreams came to life.

No! She must not!

When he turned the sleigh into Hyde Park, she was not surprised to discover it was deserted. From between the clouds, starlight sparkled on the fresh snow, spiraling like an ever-changing tiara of gems draped from one bush to the next. Not a hint of breeze swept the smoke-filled fog into the park. Vagrant snowflakes drifted down along invisible paths through the sky as he drew in the sleigh beside an open stretch.

Geoffrey jumped off and helped her out. "Here we are. Isn't it perfect?"

"For what?"

"Snow angels."

"I don't understand. What is a snow angel?"

He said, "Just take a big step backward."

"And then?"

"Don't you trust me?"

She flinched, not wanting to answer that question which probed too closely to the truth. "I have no interest in playing the jack for you."

"Just the angel." With a laugh, he pushed against her shoulders.

She dropped back into the snow. Before she could remonstrate, he sat as well.

"Lie back," he ordered.

"Geoffrey, you said you would do nothing to—"

"Watch if you cannot trust me."

In amazement, she stared as he fell onto his back. He began to move his arms and legs through the snow as if he were having a fit.

"Try it!" he ordered without looking at her.

"I will get snow down my collar."

"Not if you keep your head still. Try it, Joyce! Are you so afraid of even this tiny adventure that you will just sit there and shiver?"

Telling herself she was half-frozen already and she had nothing to lose, she dropped back into the snow. It puffed into her face, and she sneezed. She heard Geoffrey's laugh, then his order to move her arms and legs as he had. The snow was harder to move than she had guessed.

"Do not stand," he cautioned. "I will help you." He drew her to her feet. "Look behind you."

She turned and smiled as she saw the silhouette indented into the snow. What she had considered the silly motions had created the image of an angel's wings and gown. "It *is* an angel. An angel that has come right down to earth."

"You didn't believe me, did you?"

"I am never quite sure what to believe about you."

"But you are that angel. See?" He leaned past her to point at the crushed snow. "Your hair there and here." He twisted a finger through her hair. "Of course, there are some parts of that angel I must only imagine here in the darkness. Such as your lustrous eyes."

Her breath caught as he turned her to face him.

"And I can only imagine an angel's mouth," he whispered as his finger brushed her lips. They parted as her heart drummed against her chest.

His voice deepened to a husky whisper. "I can see how that angel's hair brushes her shoulders just as yours does when it falls out of place. And how her gown matches yours." His finger glided along her shoulder in a slow stroke, then dipped lower along her spencer. "I imagine it clinging to her breasts there as—"

She pushed away from him. "You need not add more. I know exactly where my body parts are."

"As I do after intense study from a distance, but I wish to learn better from much closer investigation." He caught her arms and whirled her to face him. He captured her mouth before she could protest. His feverish kiss banished the chill of the night. Slowly her hands slipped up his arms. She wanted to touch him. It might be madness, but she wanted this madness.

She moaned as he drew away, but gasped when his breath burned along her face as he tasted every downy curve. She swept her fingers upward through his hair to let it flow in a satin shower between them.

Raising his head, he gazed down at her. His eyes were only a wish away. He groaned, and his hands tightened on her, crushing her to his hard body as his mouth claimed hers once more. His tongue teased the half shell of her ear, and she moaned with the pleasure that refused to be restrained. She yearned for him to delight every inch of her with the liquid ecstasy left by his lips.

Suddenly he released her with a curse that would have made even Napoleon stop prattling in admiration. Joyce grasped his sleeve to keep from rocking backward. She opened her mouth to ask what was wrong, then closed it as she stared at the pair of knights of the road.

Geoffrey snarled another oath as he drew her closer to him. The shabbily dressed men raised their glim, its dull light barely reflecting off the snow.

" 'Tain't no way t'bid a chap a g'd evenin'," said the taller of the two men.

Joyce shook her head. "If this is your idea of a jesting adventure—"

"This is no jest," Geoffrey said tautly. "The only adventure I planned for tonight was snow angels and a kiss or two."

Her eyes widened. "They are real?"

The taller man slapped his companion's arm and guffawed. "Real as rain, m'lady. 'Ow 'bout that g'd evenin'?"

"Good evening to you and be on your way," Geoffrey returned. His hand slipped toward the deep pocket of his greatcoat.

A knife appeared in the thief's hand and flashed in the dim light. "There, there, m'lord. No need fer ye t'be a 'ero."

"Be on your way," he repeated.

Joyce choked back a shriek when something cool touched her hand. The thief squinted at her.

"Fine lady-dove ye 'ave, m'lord."

"What do you want?" Geoffrey's voice was as frigid as the night.

Joyce's fingers were curled by his broader ones over what she realized was the haft of a knife. It weighed heavily in her hand. She glanced up at Geoffrey, but his gaze was focused squarely on the two Tryburn blossoms. He did not expect her to protect them from these beastly creatures, did he?

"Fine chap ye be, m'lord. Now 'and o'er what gold

ye've got." He gave them a ragged-tooth grin. "Wouldn't want yer lady love t'be mournin' ye."

Joyce drew in her breath at the threat. "Geoffrey, be careful."

"Aye, *Geoffrey,*" taunted the fleecer, "be careful, but give o'er yer gold."

Geoffrey whispered, "Run!"

"What?" she asked as softly.

"Run!" His shout resounded through her as he propelled her toward the sleigh.

She lurched several steps forward through the snow, then turned to see Geoffrey launch himself at the thieves. Was he crazy? If—

Her arm was grabbed. She swung the knife before she could think. A howl of pain erupted into the night. The knife jerked from her hand as the man disappeared into the darkness.

Arms enveloped her. She drew in breath to scream, then shuddered as the luscious warmth of Geoffrey's touch surrounded her. He took her by the elbow and steered her toward the sleigh.

He asked, "Are you all right?"

"I am fine!" Her voice clipped each word with fury.

"You do not sound fine."

"I said I was fine. I have not been speaking bangers to you, my lord."

"My lord?" Geoffrey stared at her in amazement. Would he ever understand this woman? He had just saved her virtue and mayhap even her life. Although he had not expected her to fall upon him weeping with gratitude, he had thought she would be more than barely civil. Handing her in, he did not release her hand. "Joyce, what have I

done to make you fly off the hooks? Would you have me leave you to suffer the demure hits of those beasts?"

"You should never have brought me here at this hour in the first place."

"I thought—"

"No," she said, and he could not doubt the sorrow in her voice, "you do not think, Geoffrey. You act no older than Charlie, seeking any adventure that will bring you a brief spurt of happiness."

"And what is wrong with that?"

"You are a man grown."

He smiled. "I thought you might have taken note of that when you were so soft in my arms."

"I shall not be part of your adventure here in Town."

"Why not?"

"I have had enough adventures to last me the rest of my days."

"Mrs. Richmond hinted at that." His finger slowly climbed her arm. "I must own I am intrigued at what the virtuous Joyce Stuart was doing in a brothel."

She said her prayers backward under her breath before snapping, "My sister had been tricked into going there by a man we both foolishly trusted. I owed her the duty of saving her. There is nothing more to the matter than that."

"But it was an adventure."

"My last one, I vowed!"

His hand curved along her nape as he leaned into the sleigh. With his lips so close to hers that a snowflake could not have drifted between them, he whispered, "Do not be a complete block. So many adventures await us. The one I wish to enjoy now is on your lips."

THE WINTER HEART

Joyce pulled away again. "You will share no more adventures with me." She slapped the reins on the horse.

Geoffrey jumped aside as she turned it toward Berkeley Square. She did not look back. She knew if his gaze caught hers, she would be drawn into his air-dreaming ways once more. She must not. No matter how much she longed to be in his arms, she must not.

She would not be want-witted for a man who promised her more than was humanly possible . . . again.

Twelve

Joyce should have been completely delighted from the moment she arrived at Stella's parents' house in the country. Lord Albanton and his wife welcomed Joyce with as much enthusiasm as if she had been a long-lost daughter. They had been gracious enough to extend that welcome to Geoffrey and Charlie and to Napoleon, who made no secret of his disgust at the snowy ride from town. The viscount and his wife were especially thrilled with the idea of a play being performed just for them.

This glorious room she had been given with its view of an evergreen maze and a frozen pond, where the guests were supposed to go skating on the morrow, should have filled her heart with joy. Yet, as she sat on a rattan chair in the window bay, she was fighting back tears. These were the same burning tears she had endured since the harsh words she had spoken to Geoffrey the previous night in the park. And the harsh words he had fired back at her.

Over and over, she had let the words echo through her head. Each time, she had sought an alternative that would not have ended with those cold words which left her frozen soul-deep. And, each time, she failed.

She had been honest. She wanted no adventures in her life. She had had enough to last her forever. She dreamed of a commonplace life with a commonplace family ... and, she had to own, an extraordinary love.

Rising, she paced from one side of the generously proportioned room to the other. Her footsteps were silenced by the thick carpet, but she knew she need not worry. On the floor below, many of the other guests had gathered. Their prattle would swallow any sounds she might make.

She paused when the door opened. Her eyes became as round as her mouth as she gaped at the red-haired woman entering the room. "Charity! What are you doing here?"

Her sister tossed her bonnet onto the bed and flung her arms around Joyce. "Do you think we would miss your début on the stage?"

"How did you hear of that?"

"When Oliver and I arrived home this morning, Marshall told us where you were and what you had planned. How could I resist coming to be a witness to this?" Stepping back, she wagged a finger at her sister. "Who would have guessed that Reverend Mr. Stuart's younger daughter would end up vowing to become a pit-raiser as she assumes the role of Snow White?"

"I would as lief not."

Charity's eyes became slits as she sat. "Joyce, what is amiss?"

"What else did Marshall tell you?"

"Nothing, save that you had come here with Geoffrey and Charles Everett. He need not have said more, for it is obvious from your curt answers you are distressed."

Joyce smiled wryly. "I never could hide anything from you, Charity. Sooner or later, you discovered how I felt."

"Why not save some time and tell me now?" The sunshine glowed off her auburn hair when she motioned for

Joyce to sit. "Are you still troubled by our great-aunt giving you the responsibility of caring for the Everett boy?"

"Charlie has been no problem."

"Charlie?"

Perching on the edge of a chaise longue, she said, "The boy prefers that name."

"Which Geoffrey gave him."

"How did you know?"

Charity laughed. "Oliver has told me many stories about Geoffrey."

"Then you should understand why I am distressed."

"Geoffrey is the cause of this sulk?"

Irritated at her sister's choice of words, Joyce said tautly, "You clearly do know him if you are able to surmise that so quickly."

"I have never met the man."

"Then how—?"

"Oliver speaks of him as often and with as much affection as I speak of you. When we heard from Geoffrey before we left for Italy, Oliver suggested Geoffrey call on you when we learned he was coming to Town to take possession of his uncle's house." Her lips tilted slightly. "Neither of us could have guessed a chimney fire would throw you two together so precipitously." Sorrow crept into her voice. "This is so dismaying. We had guessed you and Geoffrey would enjoy each other's company."

"Oh, no, Charity, do not become the matchmaker, too! I have endured Lady Eloise's hints of the men she intends to invite to call when the Season begins anew."

She smiled. "I will not take the blame for another's doing. Oliver suggested we introduce the two of you. He thought you would find Geoffrey amusing."

THE WINTER HEART

"He is impossible!" Heat slapped her cheeks. "Not Oliver. Geoffrey!"

"How?"

"In every way!"

Charity's smile vanished. "Joyce, you are talking to *me!* Do not think you can act as stubborn as Papa always did. Do you expect that I shall just tire of this conversation and leave you alone to sulk? Oliver thinks of Geoffrey as he would a brother. Everything he has said to me about Geoffrey has been complimentary."

"Even about his bizarre sense of humor?"

"One needs a sense of humor when their lives cross ours."

"Charity!"

"Joyce!" she returned in the same exasperated tone before adding, "Geoffrey Wilcox is a fine man who has overcome as much sorrow as we have. More, for he lost both his parents when he was as young as you were when Mama dropped hooks." She knelt beside Joyce. "Think of it. He has no one. We had each other."

"He had Oliver's family."

"That is most uncharitable of you to say that."

"As I have told you before, you were named for a virtue, not I. I need not be charitable."

Charity stood and sighed. "I see you will be as intractable about this as you always are when you do not want to heed good sense. Joyce, I ask you to rethink your vow to have nothing to do with Geoffrey. It is not as if I am asking you to buckle yourself to the man. He will be a frequent caller, so I simply want you to enjoy his company again."

"I am not sure I can."

"But—"

She wove her fingers tightly in front of her. "Charity, please listen to me. I have no idea what you have heard, but the truth is that he is, in many ways, no older than Charlie Everett. He thinks only of what great adventure he can enjoy next."

"You once thought the same way. When we lived with Papa, you often liked to explore along the strand. Then, when we came to London, you enjoyed many walks around Grosvenor Square."

"But I have matured. I know life is not an adventure."

Charity's eyes filled with tears. "Oh, my dear sister, you are so wrong. Life is a grand adventure. Who would have guessed a year ago that we would be part of a London Season and that I would be so happily married?"

"But adventures lead to ruin."

"Now *you* sound like our great-aunt." Charity shook her head. "Whatever made you change from the curious, courageous sister I once knew?"

"I saw how my search for adventure nearly cost you your life. If Oliver had not saved you from that horrible man—"

"With your help."

Joyce nodded. Of all that ignoble event, she was most grateful for the courage that had been hers when she rushed to her sister's assistance.

Charity put her hands on Joyce's arm and whispered, "Sister dear, if we had been fearful of adventure, we would be, even now, sitting in some humble cottage, unwilling to open our door and frightened of the wind rattling the windowpanes. Instead we dared to come to London and embark upon our first Season with Lady Eloise as our sponsor. I even came to believe in love again." Kneeling beside Joyce, she wiped a tear away.

"Everything we do, from the moment we take our first breath until our last shudders from us, is an adventure."

"Geoffrey spouts constantly about seeking adventure at every turn, for the opportunity is always there."

"Yes, for it is the truth." Setting herself on her feet, she smiled weakly. "I hope you remember that, Joyce, for once you held that truism in your heart. Do not close your heart in fear of it risking the danger of feeling something wondrous. That will close your heart to everything." She kissed Joyce's cheek. "Do think carefully on this. I do not want you to remain unhappy forever."

"I am not unhappy."

"Are you happy?"

Joyce hesitated.

Charity nodded. "I thought as much. Think on this deeply." Her smile returned. "I will leave you to prepare for your grand opening tonight. Oliver and I will be sitting right at the front to cheer you on."

"Thank you."

"I am your sister. I am here to help you, as you have helped me." Charity hugged her again before leaving.

Joyce had no time to think about her sister's advice. Hélène came into the room to help Joyce get dressed for the play. As Geoffrey had promised, each of them had costumes appropriate for their character. Her dark red gown, which reached an immodest height up her calves, was gathered at the waist. A forest green vest reached to the skirt's hem and matched her stockings. She wore her own slippers.

While her abigail plaited her hair into two braids, Hélène kept up a steady patter. Joyce guessed Hélène was suffering from stage nerves, so she did not halt the prattle. Her head throbbed with an ache that started right behind her eyes and reached deep into her skull. She could not wait for this evening to be over. At the same time, she wished the clock would slow its ticking. Once the play was performed, she doubted if she could avoid Geoffrey. Stella's parents planned a late supper for all the actors and the family's guests.

Her dread haunted her until she stepped onto the makeshift stage set up in the ballroom. Losing herself within the life of Snow White, she let her fear of what awaited her fuel her portrayal of the young princess's fright. The words, practiced so often on Berkeley Square, flowed from her lips as if they were her own. Even Charlie, who stumbled over both his feet and his lines, soon relaxed and began to sound comfortable.

Only when Joyce was lying on the bier in the wake of taking a bite of the poisoned apple did her thoughts return to plague her. She tried to concentrate on what the other actors were saying and doing as they mourned for their dead princess. Instead, across her closed lids splashed the memory of Geoffrey's face when she had driven away, leaving him at the park. He had said nothing of that when they left Berkeley Square this morning. He had said nothing *at all* to her.

She struggled not to smile when Charlie missed one of his lines and muttered a curse under his breath. She would have to chide him later for speaking thus in the presence of ladies. No doubt Geoffrey had granted him leave to use such cant.

Geoffrey! She did not want to think of him now. Why couldn't she clear her head of him? It was not as if she had fallen in love with him . . . or had she? He irritated her beyond reason, and still she could not keep from thinking of him and of his gentleness with Charlie and of how he had revived a part of her soul she thought was dead. And his kisses . . . No, she must not be seduced into madness by her own longings.

"She is so beautiful," Charlie said. "I must bring her to my castle, so that I might be with her always."

Strong hands settled on her arms. Shock pulsed through her, followed by a throb of sweet warmth. Charlie? No, it could not be Charlie. Only one person's touch elicited such pleasure from her. Only one person could make her heart shimmer with delight. Only one per— . . . Only one man had chipped through the ice around her heart to bring it back to life.

The strong hands curved along her face. She opened her eyes and stared up into the twinkle in Geoffrey's. From a distance, past the rapid cadence of her heartbeat, she heard Charlie speaking Prince Charming's lines. He was speaking, but Geoffrey was wearing the paper crown and leaning over her.

He mouthed the words Charlie spoke, "And I kiss your lips, my beauteous Snow White, knowing you will never know how much I wish to worship you with every breath."

She fought to keep her hands from slipping along his arms as he bent toward her. Not moving, she searched his face. Was this another of his jests?

As his lips lowered toward hers, she knew all her attempts to convince herself that she did not love him were futile. She closed her eyes and softened against the rugged planes of his body.

His hands framed her face, and he brought her mouth to his. Slowly he explored her lips, setting them afire with his heat. As his kiss deepened, she raised her hands along his strong arms to curve around his shoulders. His muscles contracted beneath her touch as his tongue grazed hers.

She quivered in his arms as he drew her to her feet and against him. His broad hands climbed her back. She gasped into his mouth as the motion pressed her even more tightly to his hard body.

A throat cleared from the wings. When Geoffrey raised his head, Joyce saw Charlie's grin. Had the two of them conspired about this from the beginning?

Geoffrey released her, stepped back and bowed. "My princess, you are alive," he said, winking at Charlie, "and I wish you to be mine."

"I am yours forever, my prince," she replied as she had dozens of times before. As she gazed up into Geoffrey's eyes, she wondered where the line blurred between what was real and what was only a part of the play.

He swept her up into his arms and carried her off the stage. Enthusiastic applause followed them. As the others gathered to take their bows, he carried her to an antechamber of the ballroom. Napoleon's squawk greeted them, but she paid the bird no mind as Geoffrey set her on her feet, but kept his hands locked around her waist.

"We should go back," she said, although she did not want to budge from his embrace. "The rest—"

He silenced her with a swift kiss. "Let them applaud as much as they wish. They should applaud, for you were the perfect Snow White. Once you were as cold as snow, but now your lips are white-hot against mine." He brushed a lock of hair back from her forehead. "I want you to share this adventure only with me."

"Adventure?" She started to step back. "Geoffrey—"

Once more, he interrupted her. "Sweetheart, you are mistaking my intentions again."

She ran her finger along his lips. "I think I understand your intentions all too well."

"I think not." He took her hand and pressed it over the ruffled shirt of his costume. "I can never give up the search for adventure."

"I know." She curled her fingers over his. "You love traveling off to Africa and other distant places while you seek adventure."

"True, but not all adventures need to be grand or silly or dangerous." His frown would have daunted her if she had thought it was aimed at her. "I learned that last night. Forgive me for endangering you when all I wanted was for you to learn how wondrous even a simple adventure can be. I was a widgeon."

She smiled. "That also is true."

"Adventures can be as glorious as finding my way along a river through the jungle or . . ." He tipped her mouth beneath his, searing her lips with a slow, deep kiss that left his voice ragged as he whispered, "Or an adventure can be as splendid as finding a way to free your heart from its cold prison, so I could offer it love." His hands edged her face. "This is an adventure I would like to experience for a lifetime, if you would agree, Snow White."

"Are you asking me to marry you?"

"If you will have this replacement for Prince Charming, for, to own the truth, I can think of no one I would as lief share this adventure with than you."

Laughing, for she could no longer silence her joy, she said, "Nor I."

"Bamboozled addle coves," grumbled Napoleon.

"He is right, you know." Geoffrey curled his fingers through her hair.

"I know." Her laughter faded into the heated kiss that would ensure her heart never grew cold again.

About the Author

Jo Ann Ferguson lives with her family in West Chester, Pennsylvania. She is the author of over five Zebra regency romances, including MISS CHARITY'S CASE and THE WOLFE WAGER. She is currently working on her next Zebra regency romance, THE COUNTERFEIT COUNT, to be published in June 1997. Jo Ann loves hearing from readers and you may write to her c/o Zebra Books. Please include a self-addressed stamped envelope if you wish a response.

The Winter Wager

Isobel Linton

One

It was only the matter of a certain spider having run clear across the club-room ceiling into its web before its prey, a confused moth, was able to escape, but on this chill January night Sir Philip Lansdowne's luck was not in; anyone could see that the spider was already dining upon its victim, and that Sir Philip had well and truly lost the wager to Lord Adrian Hensley.

It only remained to settle the matter. Their rash agreement had been for "Favor or fifty," a style of wager which, to the denizens of the Raffles Club, meant that the loser of such a bet must either give the winner fifty thousand pounds, or else must pledge his solemn word of honor to perform whatever favor the winner asked of him, no matter what the favor might be.

"Favor or fifty" was rarely a real wager. It was used mainly as a rhetorical ornament, a comment made to underscore instances of sheer certainty. For instance, a gentleman in his cups might say sarcastically to a friend, "I wager that Prinny will not sleep with Princess Caroline tonight. Take me on, man, favor or fifty!" No one would take him on, of course, since it was clearly a one-sided bet that could not really be won.

In fact, the porter at the Raffles Club could not recall the last time that a genuine "favor or fifty" had been placed.

For this reason, when Lord Adrian Hensley began to urge Sir Philip Lansdowne to accept a bet on such terms, the gentlemen members were completely nonplused. They were so taken by surprise that no one uttered a word against it, but only watched in awe while the drama unfolded. Once the thing was done and sealed, the Raffles Club members began to whisper to one another, trying to puzzle things out. Why should Lord Adrian have offered the bet? Whyever should Sir Philip Lansdowne have accepted it?

As to the first question, good guesses were easily made. Lord Adrian Hensley was the youngest son of the Duke of Malden, a short, husky, unprepossessing young man with an irrepressibly high opinion of himself combined with the very devil of a temper. His hair was dark blond and perpetually unkempt, his eyes an almost evil shade of blue. Perhaps due to his own high birth and small personal fortune, he had a chip on his shoulder and a talent for giving offense wherever he went.

Lately, he was, to his everlasting chagrin, known about London town as a man with a broken heart. His offer of marriage to the Lady Davina Hampton had been refused, and the inner devastation that followed upon that, it was thought, could have been the force responsible for making such a rash wager as he did that January night.

Whyever should Sir Philip Lansdowne have accepted the bet? That, most observers felt, was the most intriguing question. Sir Philip was fully one and thirty, and known for being the very most astute of gentlemen, awake upon every suit. He was a tall and elegant gentleman: his hair was black as soot; his complexion pale yet perfectly manly. His cheekbones were pronounced, his nose high and aristocratic. His lips were full, his chin strong, firm, and de-

THE WINTER WAGER

cided. His eyes were slightly hooded, like a hawk's—he gave one the impression of being constantly on the alert, ready to strike should need be.

Why indeed, the members wondered, would such a sharp character agree to such terms as "favor or fifty?" Much less to wager such a grand sum on an insect's progress!

What *was* clear, however, was that by the time that small brown spider reached its web, Sir Philip had lost. When the outcome of the wager was known, a low murmur passed around the company at the club; Sir Philip himself showed no response at all, taking his loss in characteristic stride.

A moment passed, then Lord Adrian, a weird smile on his face, said in a too-conciliatory tone, "Well, Sir Philip? Luck seems to have favored me this evening. What is your pleasure? Favor or fifty?"

Sir Philip's face darkened, and he gestured toward a green baize door.

"I think, Lord Adrian, that since we have some personal business, it should be conducted in a more secluded setting."

"Certainly, Sir Philip. Let us retire together at once."

Lord Adrian gestured to Sir Philip Lansdowne to follow him into a side-room where they might be private together and discuss the particulars in depth. He ordered a bottle of fine claret and two glasses, and the two went within, disappearing from general sight.

"What in the name of Heaven was that all about?" inquired Colonel Lord Edward Crenshaw, as the door to the side-room closed behind the two men.

"I've no idea, I'm sure," replied Lord Butely, twirling

his quizzing-glass, "but I'd pay good money to be a fly on that wall and discover what they're saying."

"I'd find something else to spy at, if I were you, Butely," pointed out Harry Winslow. "After all, it were a fly on that wall that got Sir Philip into this mess, weren't it?"

"Indeed it was—oh, those hazardous insects, bringing on hazardous debts! Devoutly to be avoided! One really should *not* wager on insects. It's not sporting."

"Come, come, Butely! I disagree. It is the very essence of sport!" said the Colonel.

"How so?"

"If one wagers on a prime bit o' blood, a horse everyone knows to be excellent, then the horse is *bound* to win—unless it trips in a rabbit-hole, and that's just bad luck. The logical outcome is what it is to begin with. But—to place a bet on a race between two insects, or on how many times a certain turtle will circle a pole—that is *completely* up to chance! And *that's* sporting!"

"Oh, just as you wish, Crenshaw. At any rate, I, for one, am very suspicious of Lord Adrian's part in the whole affair. Did you notice?" asked Lord Butely rather unsteadily, taking a sip of fine *jerez*. "As the evening went on and Hensley became more deeply foxed, it seemed as if he was trying to find a way to draw Sir Philip in. They were drinking rather heavily, and Hensley was putting a great deal of energy into getting Sir Philip to bet with him, raising the stakes all the time. I thought it odd—do you not agree?"

"Yes. It was particular odd, in that they are not great friends, nor never were," said Harry Winslow. "Sir Philip, for a fact, has not been seen in London this twelve-month."

"Not at all the same kind of fellow, are they?" said Colonel Lord Edward. "Sir Philip is a mature, refined, reserved gentleman, whereas Maldens scion is a young pup who wears his heart on his sleeve and puts out all his emotions on public parade. Wants conduct, if you ask me."

"Something very unstable about the boy, to be sure," averred Lord Butely. "His father never noticed his existence, and I think that has made him sullen. Nor did her grace the Duchess of Malden pay him notice. I suppose at the time she was all too busy visiting with Lord Ardrey, wasn't she?"

"A beautiful thing Clarissa Malden was, though," said Colonel Crenshaw with a distinct sigh. "Too busy going out to balls, breaking the hearts of her cicisbeos. Sometimes the really pretty ones don't make good mothers."

"And as to fathers, old Malden *would* do nothing but hunt. Should as lief have been born a hound, and so he'd tell you if you'd asked 'im, the silly old man," replied Lord Butely with a yawn.

"Liked his eldest, though," said the Colonel. "Damned if he didn't love that boy!"

"Benedict? That's so, and in his turn, I have it on good account that the young duke won't even give Lord Adrian the time of day!" said Harry, wondering if they should call for cards or make it an early night. "Thinks his brother's feckless."

"He *is* feckless," said Crenshaw, trying to disguise a hiccup. "And why shouldn't he be? I was, at his age, in his position. He's a younger son—doesn't *have* enough blunt of his own to be good at anything, does he? Not really his fault, when you think on it."

"It would have been all right for the boy if he'd made

that match with Lady Davina Hampton," said Lord Butely with a knowing sneer. *"She's* got enough for the two of them."

"One imagines that's just what Lord Adrian thought," said Winslow. "Perfectly understandable consideration. Nothing to be ashamed of."

"He was in much love with her, though," commented Colonel Lord Edward. "Damnably so, I believe."

"Then why did the boy cry so much over spilt milk? Made a great cake of himself. The chit just wouldn't *have* him," pronounced Lord Butely. "Thought she was too good for him, one supposes."

"Lady Davina Hampton? You must be joking, Butely! She *is* too good for him, man," roared Crenshaw, laughing.

"*Much* too good!" agreed Mr. Winslow, as all enjoyed a good joke at Lord Adrian Hensley's expense.

In the side-room at the Raffles Club, Lord Adrian Hensley and Sir Philip Lansdowne had settled in for a little talk. The fire had been stoked up and refreshments brought in, poured out, and consumed.

Sir Philip Lansdowne said nothing, but merely looked intently at Lord Adrian, waiting patiently for him to speak. This intense scrutiny lasted until Lord Adrian became so uncomfortable under the weight of it that he blurted out, "So which shall it be, Sir Philip? Favor or fifty?"

"Which would you prefer, Lord Adrian?" replied Sir Philip coolly.

"It is entirely your choice, of course," sputtered Lord Adrian. "F-favor or fifty. Whichever you like."

Sir Philip once again said nothing for a period of time that Lord Adrian found impossibly long. At length Sir Philip drawled, "Why don't you explain to me what the favor might be about so I may choose more wisely?"

A complex look of mixed relief and agitation flooded Lord Adrian's face. He fought it back and replied, trying to keep all his emotions under wraps, "The favor concerns a young lady."

"I thought it might," said Sir Philip simply.

"The young lady is the Lady Davina Hampton. Have you made the pleasure of her acquaintance?"

"I have not."

"She is the most wonderful creature in the entire world!" cried Lord Adrian, running his fingers through his wild blond hair. "Yet she has played me for the fool, and I *must* be repaid for it!"

"Hardly a gentlemanly motivation, my friend," pointed out Sir Philip, twirling his wineglass in his languid, disinterested way.

Stung, Lord Adrian's complexion turned beet-red.

"You are correct, sir. My motive is revenge, and yet, by the terms of our wager, you must do me the favor I ask or break your word of honor."

Sir Philip's brow was in a slight frown as he considered this, saying, "I shall certainly honor the terms of our wager. What is it that you would wish me to do?"

Lord Adrian's lips tightened, his fists clenched, and his demeanor became almost fierce. He said in a savage tone, "I should like you to *break* the chit's heart! I should like you to break Lady Davina's heart utterly and ruthlessly, precisely as she has broken mine!"

"I see," said Sir Philip in a neutral tone, pouring himself another glass of wine. "And just how do you propose that I should do this deed?"

Lord Adrian gave a short, harsh laugh.

"Come, come, Sir Philip. I know all about your reputation as a ladies' man, as does all of London."

"I'm afraid you flatter me, sir," he said.

"By no means, Sir Philip. You must know that the list of your many conquests is no secret in London. Poor Cecily Braithwaite, gone into a severe decline from which she has only lately recovered. The lovely Lady Anne Siddons, sent by her family to their lands in Carolina to recover her health and her heart. Clementine Fellowes, Mary Burke-White, the names just go on, and on, Sir Philip, do they not? You can hardly deny it! What about poor Muriel Dalrymple, the very worst of them, throwing herself at your feet at Almack's till she had to be dragged out by her family and put away?"

"Don't speak of poor Muriel in that unfeeling tone. She couldn't help herself. It was a very sad business."

"To be sure it was. But see here, Sir Philip—if anyone can do the deed, I believe you can, sir. That is why I particularly wished to make myself known to you this evening and to engage you in a few games of chance, hoping against hope that my luck would, for once, be in, and that I would be able to enlist your aid in this matter, which is of such desperate importance to me."

"Tell me a little more about the girl. How old is she? In what circles does she move? Who are her friends and acquaintances? What are her interests?"

"Yes, of course, I had forgot—you have been away from town some time. Lady Davina is just eighteen, the only daughter of the late fourth Earl of Hampton. She grew up at Crolle Hall, the family estate in Hampshire, and has been living with her widowed mother and her young brother James, who now holds the title. She made her come-out this past season, and, of course, she took at once. In the time since her come-out, she has turned down numerous offers of marriage, not just my own, for she captured the hearts of all who beheld her."

"If that is so, perhaps the girl does not wish to marry."

"All girls wish to marry!" exclaimed Lord Adrian.

"Or else, forgive me, but perhaps she does not wish to marry *you*—or those others who asked her. I don't see why such a refusal requires vengeance. It's hardly uncommon. In fact, it happens all the time."

"It was the *manner* of it, man! It was the depth of it!" he cried out intemperately. "It was all her fault! She *made* me fall in love with her! She enticed me, she inveigled me, she made it clear that she desired my attentions! I would come up to speak to her at a ball, and then she would turn around, and then turn upon me those eyes of the *most* entrancing blue, speaking softly to me with that musical voice, the voice of a veritable angel! Her address, her carriage, her conversation—everything was always perfection itself!

"I remember, in particular, one night when I met her at Lady Keswick's—everything was set up for guests to perform impromptu readings from literary works. She chose a section from *A Midsummer Night's Dream* for me to read with her."

"Which bit?"

"She read Titania, and she had me read Bottom," he admitted.

Sir Philip's lips quivered very slightly.

"I wanted her to read from Childe Harold, but she refused to do so," Lord Adrian said disconsolately. "It was not well done of her."

"Why did she refuse?" asked Sir Philip, betraying a gleam of interest.

"Told me she thought Byron, and all things Byronic, were a great lot of rubbish!" cried Lord Adrian. "Said she'd never heard a man make so much nonsense out of nothing! Said that kind of intemperate emotional indulgence makes people turn into virtual Bedlamites, and to prove it, she talked about poor Caro Lamb in a most critical and unsympathetic tone. I was so disappointed!"

At this, Sir Philip's eyes gleamed in an unusual, appreciative way, but he made no outward comment.

Lord Adrian blurted on, "It hurt my feelings when she said that, I can tell you! I thought she was wrong, quite wrong! But it was no matter, I read whatever she wanted me to, and I bowed to her taste in everything. I was undone, undone. From her shockingly fair hair, to her ruby lips, her smooth complexion—she captivated me, just like Circe or some other evil Siren sent to lure men to their deaths!"

"Come, come, man! I have been about the world a bit, and I know quite well that no woman is such a paragon, nor indeed such a hazard!"

Lord Adrian Hensley's eyes grew preternaturally bright as he grasped Sir Philip's coat by the lapels, a grip Sir Philip removed at once, hiding his distaste with a small shudder, as Lord Adrian whispered, "You've not met her, sir. When you meet Davina, and I pray that you soon shall, you will understand everything I have said and shall have pity on me!"

"That I have already, believe me, sir," he said gently.

"Then tell me, Sir Philip," cried Lord Adrian with undisguised desperation, as if anticipating certain failure. "Which shall it be? Favor or fifty?"

"Why, favor, I should think," replied Sir Philip imperturbably, a slight smile playing on his lips.

"You are the very best of men!" Lord Adrian cried with relief, getting to his feet and trying to shake Sir Philip's hand. "Oh, it is a great thing when gentlemen can band together and strike a blow against all manner of dark things that do not belong on earth! I knew you should not fail me!"

"Sir! Get a grip on yourself!" said Sir Philip, his patience thinned to the breaking point. "You may be sure I shall not fail you in your endeavor. After all, as a gentleman, my word is my bond."

Two

Having agreed to carry out the favor on behalf of Lord Adrian, it only remained for Sir Philip Lansdowne to effect a meeting between himself and Lady Davina Hampton. He soon discovered that Lady Davina was in London with her family, who were friendly with the Earl and Countess of Keswick, mutual acquaintances. Sir Philip easily arranged to be invited to a musicale at Lord and Lady Keswick's residence on St. James' Square.

His first glimpse of her was no glimpse at all—rather he divined her presence by observing a crowd of young men encircling something, like ripples in water. Sir Philip assumed that the center of such enthusiastic worship must be Lady Davina, and so it was. Sir Philip was tall enough that, moving slowly through the crowd, he was at length able to set eyes upon the lady whose acquaintance he now sought.

It was immediately apparent that the Lady Davina Hampton was Venus herself—she was tall, very blond, blue-eyed, and statuesque. She wore a stunning ball-dress made in the latest French mode, a gown of thin silver gauze over a slip of celestial blue silk; there were many rows of blue silk ribbons at her neck, and row after row of ribbons lining the hem of her gown.

Her golden hair was swept up and set in ringlets that

framed her face, with a silver fillet carefully threaded through them. She had a small necklace of pearls, with matching pearl earrings and a pair of pearl bracelets over her long white gloves.

The moment Sir Philip first laid eyes upon her, her head was thrown back in gay laughter; it was a sight and sound he would never forget, for the Lady Davina Hampton turned out to be everything that Lord Adrian Hensley had described, and even more. Her great beauty was the very least of her charms, for it took no more than a few minutes of his attending to her conversation for Sir Philip to deduce that the girl had character and wit, as well as kindness. Though obviously the object of much male admiration, she appeared to have no pretensions to superiority; her manner was fresh, frank, and unspoilt.

Sir Philip noticed an immediate attraction toward her, which caught him rather by surprise. He was thinking of just how he should present himself to Lady Davina when Lord Adrian Hensley approached him, caught his arm, and drew him aside.

Annoyed, Sir Philip whispered, "What are you doing, Hensley? If she sees us together, your little game will be all over."

"There are too many people here and we are still too far away. She will not see us," Lord Adrian assured him. "I must speak to you!"

"What is it, then?" said Sir Philip, wishing him otherwhere.

"Is she not the most beautiful creature in the universe?" he sighed. "Is she not Heaven itself?"

"Lady Davina is certainly a very lovely young girl. I do not at all see why you wish her so ill," commented Sir Philip.

"I do not wish her ill! I adore her!" cried Lord Adrian. "I would throw myself at her feet in an instant!"

"You have already done so, I collect," replied Sir Philip wryly.

"I *did* throw myself at her feet! And she rejected me, cruelly. That is why I must have satisfaction—she must be made to feel *my* pain just as *I* feel it. When she understands the wrong she has done me, she will think better of it and be ashamed of herself—and accept my love at last!"

Sir Philip gave him an odd, quizzical look, but Lord Adrian was so caught up in this theatrical account that he paid no notice. Sir Philip shook his head, sighed, and took his leave, wondering why he had allowed himself to get caught up in this wretched matter in the first place.

He decided to find Sarah Keswick and ask her to perform the introduction of himself to Lady Davina Hampton. He looked around the large room and presently espied a pair of white plumes shaking vigorously above the heads of the crowd. From the spirited animation of their movement, he recognized that they must belong to his great friend, Sarah Keswick.

He made his way through the crush and tapped Lady Keswick on her shoulder.

"Philip!" she cried, turning around and teasing him playfully with her fan. "How nice that you could come! It is *such* a cold and dreary time of year that I just *had* to do something to enliven life in town, and see how wonderfully it has turned out! So many people, all in town, and all *dying* to divert themselves! To entice *you* to attend such a function, that is really a feather in my cap, my dear! Is there something in particular you wanted, or did you just come by to say hello?"

"My dearest Sarah," he said, bringing her hand up to his lips, "you know full well that you alone are the light of my life and the reason for my existence."

"Do stop bamming me, Philip. Your honeyed words will get nothing more out of me than a glass of ratafia, which I *know* you do not care for."

"Ah, Sarah, you know me too well, alas. Here is my purpose, besides paying you my deepest respects: I seek an introduction to that young lady over there, the one so deeply surrounded by admirers."

"Davina? Why do you wish to be presented to her? Nicest gal as ever was, Philip, but I should think she is a little too young, and a little too tall, and a little too—how shall I put it?—perhaps a little too needle-witted to suit you—is she not?"

"Not yet having had the pleasure of her acquaintance, I cannot say with precision what she is really like," said Sir Philip. "I have an intuition that I shall find her perfectly enchanting. Won't you indulge my whim and introduce me?"

"Oh, all right, if you must, but I think there is something very havey-cavey going on, for I know you are *not* in the petticoat line, and don't think you can pull the wool over *my* eyes. I've known you forever, and I'll find you out in the end, believe me."

Lady Keswick threaded her way through the crowd toward Lady Davina, Sir Philip Lansdowne following dutifully in her wake.

"Excuse me, Lord Brook. Excuse me, Robert. Excuse me, Sir Nelson. Excuse all of you, I'm sure—please, gentlemen, do back away from poor Davina, can't you give the poor girl some air for once?" exclaimed Lady Keswick. "I'm sure I would be put out of temper by having this horrible crush of gentlemen around me all the time. I can't think why you don't faint, Davina; I'm sure I should, in your shoes."

"How do you do, Lady Keswick?" said Lady Davina. "How kind of you to have invited my mother and me to your musicale."

"Where is your mama, Davina dear?"

"She is sitting just there, behind us." Lady Keswick found her, waved to her vigorously, and returned her attention to Lady Davina, asking after her mother's health.

"Mama is quite well, really, thank you, but I think she has tired of London a little and wishes we could return to the country."

"That's hardly surprising, is it? The weather has been *so* terrible of late, and town *so* very thin of company. I often say to Keswick that it would be better to flee to the countryside, and wait out the winter weather there—but alas! Poor Keswick still has business that keeps him in London. Perhaps we should *all* make a plan to flee London at a later date, not too far in the distant future. Her grace of Pyttwich has been talking about putting together something of the kind, I can tell you, if she can just get the duke to come round to it. The country really is the place to be, don't you think? Out at Belmont Court, our fireplaces are far superior and our chimneys in excellent shape, something I cannot say for *this* house, at least in its upper floors. And these London chimney sweeps are so small and filthy! Something should be done about them, as well! A smoky townhouse is really an intolerable thing!

"At any rate, my dear, Keswick and I are of course quite delighted to see you both tonight. Now, Davina, here I have brought someone who particularly wishes to be made known to you, if you have no objection. May I present Sir Philip Lansdowne?"

Sir Philip stepped forth and bowed slightly.

"How do you do, Lady Davina?"

She curtseyed, inclining her head toward Sir Philip, and she gave him a small, shy smile, all the time wondering why this tall, not-so-very-young, extremely good-looking gentleman had sought out an introduction to her.

"Davina, I shall not scruple to tell you that you must certainly watch your step with Sir Philip, for his reputation is that of a famous, nay, a *gazetted* flirt, whom no one has been able to bring up to scratch!"

"Surely you are much too harsh on me, Sarah," said Sir Philip, pressing Lady Davina's hand very briefly.

The young woman colored prettily, and, with what Sir Philip felt was a particularly provocative smile, declared, "I have heard of you, sir, from other lips than Lady Keswick's. When I was being tutored about the *ton,* you were described by the elderly gentlewoman responsible for educating me in these important respects, both as a confirmed bachelor and a flirt of the very first magnitude! That being the case, I fear that the dangerous pleasure of your acquaintance will be much too much for me, a green girl in her first season. Already I feel my knees turning to water, and my heart fluttering like a butterfly!"

Sir Philip smiled broadly and asked Lady Keswick, "The young lady appears to have a satirical disposition."

Lady Keswick threw up her hands, saying, "That is her besetting sin: she has a very great fondness for nonsense. I don't know *how* many times we have told her that being nonsensical is *not* the way to go about things among the *ton,* but as you see, she pays no heed to us. However, in all other respects, she is quite the darling that everyone in London must have already described to you."

Lady Davina answered this by throwing Sir Philip a challenging glance, saying, "Dear Lady Keswick, now I think you are being much to harsh on *me!* I am neither such a darling, nor so fond of fustian! Sir Philip, I fear that listening to Lady Keswick's opinion of me will lead you not to believe a word I say."

Enjoying her spirit, Sir Philip replied meaningfully, using his deepest tones, "To the contrary, ma'am, I believed every word you said—particularly that bit you mentioned about your knees turning to water in my presence, and so on."

Lady Davina felt herself blushing suddenly again. Looking into Sir Philip's laughing dark eyes, she gasped very slightly, for she now actually did feel a distinctive weakness in her knees and a sudden, uncontrollable trembling somewhere in the region of her heart. At once, she realized that she was in the presence of a dangerously attractive gentleman who was very clearly a master of the romantic arts.

Noticing her response and enjoying it, Sir Philip said to her in a soft whisper, "I am sorry that these highly exaggerated rumors about my reputation seem to have affected you so strongly, Lady Davina. Might I nourish the hope that your constitution may be strong enough to withstand a dance with me?"

"I am engaged, sir, for the next dance," she answered, glad of a chance to regroup and have some respite from Sir Philip's flattering attentions.

"I say, Lansdowne! Don't try to cut in on me, man," said Sir Nelson Benton, approaching quickly from one side to claim his partner. "Lady Davina's promised to me for this dance!"

"Certainly, Benton! If you think on it, however, you *do* owe me a favor—you know you do!"

"What? For that tip about the grey mare? Oh, go ahead, then," Sir Nelson said crossly. "Take the dance, if the lady will accept you as a desirable partner."

"Well, Lady Davina? Are you up to it?" Sir Philip asked. "Will you do me the honor of dancing with me?"

She first hid her face behind her fan in mock shyness, then extended her hand to him, ready again to take up the fight. "I am ready, indeed, to dance with you, sir. Why, my heart pounds like a mallet at the very prospect!"

"Like a *mallet?*" inquired Sir Philip gravely, only a slight twitching at the side of his lips betraying his amusement. "Dear me! Is that a constitutional weakness? *Dare* you to dance with me, or ought I rather to notify Dr. Knightley, letting him know that, overtaxed by my introduction to you, you find yourself unable to stand up with me?"

"There is no need, I assure you. Pray, be so kind as to lead me out on the floor, and I shall, on the way, nod soberly to dear Dr. Knightley, so he may keep me under *most* strict observation while we are dancing!"

"When I asked if you would give me the honor of this dance, Lady Davina," he said with solemnity, "I did not think I might be putting your life in actual danger! I am shocked, quite shocked at the thought!"

"No, Sir Philip, pray, do *not* be shocked, for I am so very sensitive that the very slightest shock may mean an end to me!"

"Indeed? What very subtle sensibility!" he declared as he led her through the fine movements of the set. "That being the case, would it shock your delicate nature very much if I were to compliment you on your truly exquisite grace in dancing?"

Lady Davina blushed prettily as they completed the figures.

When the couple came together again, to move down the line, she whispered, "Indeed, you must *not* shower me with such pretty words, sir! *Just* that sort of shock can be so very dangerous, you see, coming from a grown gentleman, and being so generously showered upon a girl in her first season! Already during our extremely short acquaintance, you have put me to the blush more times than I can count, and certainly more times than I can long endure. It is not fair of you, not fair at all. I pray you, Sir Philip, *please* pay me no more pretty compliments—not upon my truly exquisite grace in dancing, nor upon my many accomplishments, nor upon the lilt of my voice, nor upon the tilt of my upturned nose—"

"I don't think I should ever go *that* far, ma'am."

Lady Davina's eyes narrowed and she gave him a quizzical look, asking, "Whyever not? Other gentlemen compliment my nose excessively. Do you dislike my nose, then?"

"By no means, madam. My point was that, to the best of my belief, I have never rendered an aesthetic judgment of any kind upon *any* nose."

"I am quite relieved to hear that!" she said laughingly, flashing him a brilliant smile. "Now that my nose is well out of it, and the music is ending, perhaps you would be so kind as to procure for me a glass of refreshment? I really must sit down for a moment. I am all out of breath, both from our dance and from so much rigorous badinage."

THE WINTER WAGER

"I am your servant, Lady Davina," he murmured, backing away politely, and his words rang oddly true.

Sir Philip Lansdowne, a man of unerring experience amongst females, went over into the next room to fetch the girl the glass of negus she had requested of him; as he made his way through the crowd, it occurred to him to look back at her, and he did so. He saw the girl once again surrounded by many young and handsome admirers vying for her time and attention. He felt a quick pang of jealousy, and wished he had not agreed to leave her side.

Noticing this unaccustomed arising of jealousy, Sir Philip suddenly became conscious that it could only be explained by one circumstance: that he had himself begun to fall under the spell of the gaily enchanting Lady Davina Hampton.

Sir Philip turned back away from her to complete his task and turned his mind toward shaking off the fever of infatuation as best he could, remonstrating himself harshly. He had a task to carry out, unenviable as it was, and he could not allow himself to become vulnerable to the many obvious charms of this young girl. If he did *not* steel himself against her, he would fail to carry out his commission and then, among gentlemen, he would have no honor left at all—a state that, of course, was not to be endured.

One *had* to settle one's gaming debts.

Three

Sir Philip Lansdowne strongly believed in pugilism as a reliable source of solace during life's less happy moments, and therefore it was to Bond Street and Gentleman Jackson's Rooms that he repaired to contemplate his position more clearly the day after his introduction to Lady Davina. A few rounds with a notable fighter and several sharp blows to the head had always sufficed to clear out the cobwebs after a night's debauchery, or, on occasion, to lessen the pain of separation during the few days after Sir Philip gave one of his pricey ladybirds her *conge*.

He had walked alone to number 12 Bond Street all the way from his rooms at Belgrave Square, through Green Park, for the weather had cleared somewhat, and he liked to walk when his mind was strongly preoccupied.

It was cold and windy as Sir Philip turned from Piccadilly onto Bond Street; the omnipresent mud-puddles lining the busy, cobbled way had frozen into long, sepia-colored, slippery sheets. Sir Philip walked carefully yet briskly up the street, shouldering past his various London neighbors, both rich and poor, who for once were looking more or less the same for being so well bundled-up against the weather and wind.

All in all, Sir Philip mused as he walked, he preferred winter in London to the summer months, despite the cold

THE WINTER WAGER

and strong winds; the air was chilly, but so much cleaner and the smell was so much less strong. He looked up into the sky and noticed it was whitening, as if a hard snow was on the way.

It looked as if it would be a long winter. It certainly had begun to feel interminable to Sir Philip, who devoutly wished he could get this wretched matter with Lord Adrian Hensley settled conclusively and put out of the way. As the cold wind whipped past him, he adjusted his long scarf and wondered whether a trip to the Mediterranean would not be in order, in the end.

He went up the stairs at Jackson's and entered, nodding to his various acquaintances as he did so.

Gentleman Jackson himself gave his greetings to him; he set up a round of sparring for Sir Philip with one of his best men, and Sir Philip lost himself in sport for an hour or so. When they had done, his partner complimented Sir Philip on his good science, for he was talented with his hands and always in rare fighting shape.

Though onlookers told him they thought he had done well, Sir Philip felt rather melancholy, as if the exercise had not served its real purpose. Though he had jabbed, punched, and dodged Ted Walsh's blows in prime style, fighting on relentlessly until his strong body poured with sweat, his mind was not put at ease, nor were his problems put at any distance by having indulged in his favorite pastime. He felt just as bedeviled at the end of the bout as he had when he had arrived at first.

He thanked his partner and his teacher and had just gotten himself washed up and dressed again when Harry Winslow, an enthusiastic fighter himself, hailed him.

"Saw you with Walsh! Looking very good, very good

indeed, Lansdowne. I heard even the Gentleman say so—but don't let it go to your head!"

The two friends exchanged various gentleman-like pleasantries concerning dogs, fights, and horses until Winslow took him aside, whispering, "Now, Lansdowne, do tell me—why did you take on that young puppy's bet the other night? Silliest thing I ever heard of, betting on spiders and moths. Whatever came over you?"

"I hardly know myself," admitted Sir Philip somewhat sheepishly. "I do have my reputation as a gamester to keep up, of course, but placing that particular bet was a bit of an error. I didn't think I was so far in my cups, but I must have been!"

"Oddest wager since the one with Prinny and Charles James Fox and those cats out on the street. Remember that? Capital!"

"*That* wasn't an odd bet—it was just more easy money for Fox! Of course, there *would* be more cats on the sunny side of a street, wouldn't there?"

"Just so. Poor Prinny. Never thought of it that way," admitted Winslow. "Say, old man, you wouldn't be willing to tell me which you took, would you? Favor or fifty?"

"Why? Is there so much speculation about it?" asked Sir Philip, rather amused.

"There is, rather. I bet that you took on the favor, while Butely bet you'd pay the fifty thousand just to be done with it and get Lord Adrian out of your hair."

Sir Philip laughed out loud at this, saying, "Butely knows my nature all too well."

"Look out, here comes Hensley! What's he doing here?" said his friend. "Tell me, won't you, if you're not sworn to secrecy? Mean a lot to me."

"Would if I could, but I'm not at liberty to say, I'm afraid."

"I understand. Very well, then. Best of good fellows," he said, shaking his hand and wishing him well.

As Winslow went into the changing parlor and Sir Philip emerged, he encountered Lord Adrian Hensley, who was not a usual sight at Jackson's rooms. Lord Adrian hailed him with a loud and intimate friendliness that Sir Philip found nauseating, but he could hardly give Lord Adrian the cut he might otherwise have done. He did raise his eyebrows and quizzing-glass toward him, and replied, with some hauteur, "How do you do?"

"I need to have speech with you, Sir Philip."

"Have we not already settled our affairs with one another?"

"No, sir. We have not."

"Must we then conduct our affairs in public, on these stairs?"

"Certainly not. I have brought a carriage. We may be private there."

With great reluctance, Sir Philip followed Lord Adrian downstairs, out to the street, and entered into the carriage bearing the crest of the Duke of Malden. Lord Adrian gave the coachman orders to drive on and the carriage took off, threading its way through the busy, noisy traffic of Bond Street.

"You live in Belgrave, do you not? Let me convey you home!"

"Thank you, that would be most kind. I take it your brother doesn't mind your using his coach?" inquired Sir Philip.

Lord Adrian reddened guiltily and sputtered, "My brother is out of t-town. He doesn't mind my using the coach when he's not in London. Family coach. M-my own father's coach. Nothing wrong with my using it. Quite the thing."

"What is it you wished to discuss?" asked Sir Philip wearily.

"Ah, yes! You almost made me forget why I came all that way to find you! How foolish of me. The thing is, Sir Philip, I know that you have seen her at last!" cried Lord Adrian. "Is she not a wonder of the world?"

"A veritable Venus," replied Sir Philip dryly.

"What did she say to you? What did you say to her? I must know!" said Lord Adrian with great excitement.

"We exchanged the usual ballroom pleasantries. I liked her very well. Lady Davina has a delicious, teasing, playful manner and was really quite a charming partner. It was easy to see why she is the object of so much admiration among the young men in town."

"Did she like you? Did she show you any partiality?" Lord Adrian demanded. "Is the plan working? When will the thing be done?"

"You must be mad, Hensley. Matters of love are very delicate; they require time. How should I, or any man, expect a woman to fall in love with me at first sight?" he asked, incredulous that such a conversation was even taking place.

"How long will it take, then?" Lord Adrian demanded again.

"How can I *possibly* say such a thing with any precision?" Sir Philip said scornfully. "You didn't ask me to seduce the chit, did you? Of course, if it's seduction you want, *that's* done easily enough of an evening, if you're in such a raging hurry. *Are* you in such a hurry? I thought you wanted me to pay my addresses to her and make her love me in return. You must make your wishes upon this point very clear, man. Do you really wish me merely to *have* her, then?"

Lord Adrian's eyes began to burn with a sudden, perilous jealousy, and he snapped back, *"Have* her? What do you mean, *seduce her?* I do not wish that you seduce her! If you ever dared to do so, I should call you out—at once!"

"Don't try to threaten me, Lord Adrian," replied Sir Philip grimly. "It just won't fadge. We both of us know between us who's the better shot, do we not? I will keep my word of honor and repay the foolish debt I undertook at Raffles to the last miserable letter, but once that's gone and done with, I intend to wash my hands of it, and of you, and of that poor, wretched girl—once and for all! Do I make myself perfectly clear? Our business being at an end, I shall alight here, I think. Good day, Lord Adrian."

He signaled the coachman to stop and got down from the Duke of Malden's carriage, finding himself in the foulest of tempers. The carriage had only just reached Green Park, and there was some way to go before he was home. In this very black mood, he strode on toward Belgrave, trying to clear a suffocating sense of entrapment from his head, but neither the walk nor the fresh air sufficed to do so. He thought himself a stupid, wretched fool.

When he reached his rooms, he went upstairs at once. He went into his study and called for his man, Stevens, to bring up a bottle of sherry and some biscuits while he continued to meditate upon his difficulties.

That was the last anyone saw of Sir Philip Lansdowne that day. He remained closeted in his study, shut up in his room for so many unbroken hours that his valet, near to dying of boredom, began to grumble that if Sir Philip insisted upon keeping up such disgracefully monkish behavior, he would just have to find himself another master!

Four

The most immediate result of the conversation in Lord Adrian's carriage was that Sir Philip Lansdowne's attentions to Lady Davina Hampton became very much more marked over the next fortnight. He began to put in regular appearances amongst her circle of admirers who accompanied her wherever she went, and his address was such that he very naturally attracted a great deal of attention, not the least of which was Lady Davina's.

What young lady, after all, could fail to admire such a fine figure of a man, whose dress and demeanor were so particularly excellent? To see Sir Philip's broad, powerful shoulders well-turned out in a close-cut coat by Weston of teal superfine, with biscuit pantaloons and shining, tasseled Hessians, was to see the very idea of a gentleman perfected. There was nothing of the dandy about him—there was only quiet elegance, from his high white cravat to his boots.

If at first his figure and address attracted her notice, it was not long before he attracted her admiration as well. He made her laugh in a way that no other man had, and it was that attribute, beyond his manners, his handsome countenance, and his polish, which soon gave him a distinct edge over the rest of her suitors.

Sir Philip was persistent where others were diffident,

and he was bold where others were merely soft and flattering.

Sir Philip Lansdowne went after her like a general storming a citadel, never letting up and never retreating. At Lady Barcroft's rout, Lady Davina and Sir Philip were seen to dance together twice, and their mutual animation set many *ton* tongues to wagging, and convinced onlookers of the deep pleasure they took in one another's company. Dowagers exchanged knowing glances as they saw a brilliance to Lady Davina's blushing complexion that had never appeared so before.

The night that Lady Davina and the Dowager Lady Hampton attended the Royal Opera House at Covent Garden for a performance of Shakespeare's *Macbeth,* it was discovered that, by fortunate chance, the large subscription-box directly opposite them was occupied by Lord and Lady Keswick. Again, by fortunate chance, Sir Philip Lansdowne just happened to make part of their party and was able to take full advantage of this auspicious coincidence.

When, simultaneously peering through their respective opera-glasses, Lady Davina and Sir Philip discovered one another, salutes between the parties were made, and at the intermission Sir Philip was able to occupy the greater part of Lady Davina's time and attention. Lady Davina was looking particularly charming that night, dressed in a pure white, *gros de Naples* gown, a white satin sash around her tiny waist, and a hem of three white satin *rouleaux* wreathed in pearls. Her hair had been charmingly arranged in damask roses and ringlets; she wore long white gloves and small white satin slippers.

With her blue eyes and blond hair, Lady Davina looked a veritable angel, but no one save Sir Philip could keep that angel so happily occupied; though many young bucks tried to interrupt the couple to attract Lady Davina's attention to themselves, no one succeeding in parting them during any of the three intermissions, so rapt was the young pair in conversation—about the Bard, about the theater, about music, about the *haut ton,* and about life in general. Lady Davina's circle of admirers was much put out.

Some nights later, at the very fashionable winter ball given by Lady Stevenson, Lady Davina allowed Sir Philip Lansdowne to dance thrice with her and to take her down to supper, and she did not scruple to give other gentlemen even the most perfunctory attention.

This was found a helpful circumstance by other young ladies who had come out that season, and who had been regularly cast into the shade by Lady Davina. That same evening Sir Nelson Benton, annoyed at being cut out again by Sir Philip, began to pay his addresses to the eldest Miss Stoughton, and Lord Brook was noted to ask twice for the honor of a dance with young, merry Lady Jane Darcher. Miss Stone said she was ready to send Sir Philip a posy of thanks, for his attentions to Lady Davina had been wondrous good at improving all the other girls' chances on the Marriage Mart.

It seemed as if the universe itself recognized that there had been a final shift in the balance of relationships, and as a result, Lady Davina and Sir Philip were a pair. When they danced together that evening, they were remarked upon as an exceedingly handsome and well-matched couple, which was nothing more than the truth.

On the night of Lady Stevenson's ball, Lady Davina, always lovely, had chosen to wear a pale blue gown ornamented by lace and pretty flounces; there was a simple golden cross around her neck, and a small bunch of flowers Sir Philip had given her at her waist. The effect of the presence of her companion seemed to be that she looked not only beautiful, as she normally did, but beautiful and content, which gave a kind of luster to her complexion and brightness to her eyes, as was unsurpassably lovely. Sir Philip, on his part, looked very much the gay beau, dressed in a perfectly cut black coat by Weston, immaculate white shirt and waistcoat, and a cravat that, it was agreed, must have taken hours to tie to that perfection of simplicity. His own demeanor seemed brightened by his new lady; no one had ever seen him looking so well.

It was supposed to pass as sheer chance when Lady Davina went to the Royal Italian Opera House, the King's Theater, to see Handel's *Semele* as a guest of her godmother, Lady Overton, and found the ubiquitous Sir Philip seated in a box precisely across from her party. Sir Philip greeted her warmly, and then, at intermission, proceeded to preoccupy Lady Davina's time much as he had become used to doing, with the addition of the exchange of several meaningful personal glances. There was also a significant pressing of the lady's hand by the gentleman and the acceptance by the lady of a proffered bouquet of fragrant hothouse violets that were, of course, normally unobtainable in that winter month, and must have cost Sir Philip a small fortune.

It was clear to all onlookers who were neither blind nor slow that Sir Philip Lansdowne was plunging headlong on a campaign to win Lady Davina Hampton's heart.

But, to what purpose?

Did he wish to make her Lady Lansdowne? Or was there some other motive behind his action?

There were some serious particulars to be considered. While Sir Philip was always most attentive to Lady Davina, sending her posies, lovely ivory fans, ribands and laces, books, and many other small tokens of regard, it was widely remarked upon about town that it was odd he did not call upon her at her home—not even once—nor did he invite her out for a winter's drive through the park in his carriage.

Sir Philip as well did not make himself known to Lady Davina's mother, nor did he seek out the acquaintance of the lady's brother, the young Earl of Hampton. This omission in particular caused comment, and indeed, it was the source of some concern to both Lady Hampton and her son. Although Sir Philip was a perfectly eligible bachelor, whose fortune and breeding were of the very best, her relatives wondered why he had so obviously ignored directly approaching Lady Davina's family? If his intentions were honorable, if his heart were seriously involved, would he not have done so? Was his studied neglect of her family not proof enough that he was merely trifling with her?

During these weeks, the sacred hallways of the Raffles Club were as filled with wagering activity as ever. Sir Philip had spent little time there of late, and if he had, he would have had the unhappiness to discover that his own marital intentions were the subject of frantic betting. The odds were running three to two against his offering marriage to Lady Davina Hampton within the next month; the odds were even as to his offering her marriage before the end of the year.

Further, this was not the only aspect of Sir Philip's life

that had been scrutinized, contemplated, and wagered upon by his compatriots. The Raffles Club was rife with suspicion that the famous 'favor or fifty' bet between Lord Adrian and Sir Philip had *not* been settled by payment of monies owed, but by the much more delicious setting of a favor by Lord Adrian for Sir Philip. What everyone and his valet were betting on now was, what was the favor?

It had been noticed that Lord Adrian and Sir Philip met frequently, and the only other difference in behavior was that Sir Philip was attending *ton* parties with more regularity than before, and that he was paying his attentions to Lady Davina Hampton in particular.

Some facts of the case were clear and undisputed. Everyone knew that Lady Davina had rejected Lord Adrian's suit; everyone knew Lord Adrian to be a poor loser and an intemperate fellow. Everyone knew Sir Philip for a consummate ladies' man. Everyone knew he had recently lost a large wager. What was the connection between all these things, if any? It was a most intriguing puzzle.

Lord Butely thought that the favor Lord Adrian had demanded must be for Sir Philip to ask Lady Davina to marry him, the favor being considered here more in the light of a dare. Butely, of course, as part of the other bet, had money on Sir Philip's offering for Lady Davina before the end of the month, and so was no objective commentator.

"It can't be that he's hanging around her for no purpose, can it?" Lord Butely reasoned. "Lord Adrian must have dared Sir Philip to ask her, knowing that if she rejected Philip as well, his own rejection would look somewhat less stupid. Did the thing to keep up his own reputation, don't you know?"

"But—if Sir Philip asked for her hand, and she'd said yes, they'd have to marry. No one would take a favor *that* far."

"Quite right," agreed Harry Winslow, who also had laid money on their swift engagement. "Besides, the two of them look perfectly well in love, do they not? That cannot be a manufactured thing."

"It could be something quite other, you know," said Colonel Lord Crenshaw. "The business with Lady Davina could be quite on the side, something personal that happened to the both of them quite suddenly. The favor or fifty is more likely to lie in another area of life entirely. For example, Lord Adrian Hensley more likely would have made a favor of getting Sir Philip to lend him some blunt, or give him a tip on his horses, or sign off against one of those loans of his to the cents-per-cent. It really must be a favor *worth* fifty thousand pounds, you know, otherwise it doesn't make any sense, does it?"

"Whole thing makes no sense, if you ask me," said Lord Butely. "I always thought Lansdowne had some very particular reasons for remaining a bachelor and not getting leg-shackled. I just can't remember what they were."

"I remember perfectly well—it was Muriel Dalrymple, that fubsy-faced Bedlamite. You know, the girl somehow related to the Duchess of Pyttwich? The season before last, she developed such a crush on Sir Philip that she made a complete cake of herself in public. Very embarrassing for her family, and very embarrassing for poor Sir Philip, too. Had to ship her off to some medicinal convent on the continent to recover from it, and she near to died. Philip took himself away from town as well," explained the colonel. "Didn't come back till just now."

"So what?" asked Winslow.

"The Duchess of Pyttwich, Sir Philip's godmother, had been fond of Muriel since she was in leading-strings. Quite blind to the girl's defects, she thought it was high time Philip married and wanted the two of them to make a match of it," said the colonel. "Pressured him something fierce to marry her."

Lord Butely shuddered and delicately took a pinch of snuff. "Ugh! Imagine having Muriel Dalrymple to bed at night!"

"I'd sooner die!" said Harry Winslow, letting loose a loud hiccup as punctuation and motioning to a servant to refill the glasses all around.

"No doubt that's what Lansdowne thought. At any rate, the way Philip could keep the girl at arm's length and get himself out of such a neatly arranged marriage without offending his godmother, whom he loved, was to keep up his reputation as a gamester. Which was and is about the only thing about him that Muriel Dalrymple could not abide," pronounced Lord Butely with certainty.

"Why couldn't he just have given her the cut direct? It's a lot simpler," pointed out Harry Winslow as he stuffed a bit of beef in his mouth.

"Sir Philip has a very kind heart. I think he really felt sorry for her and wanted to get rid of her in the kindest possible way. As long as he's a confirmed gamester, she don't mind so much that he don't love her, you see," averred Lord Butely.

"I see. And the sillier the things he bets on, the worse he looks to her. Very good. I like that. Good plan, good plan. Wish I'd thought of that myself," said Colonel Lord Edward.

"So, if she's still on the continent, what's all this about?" asked Harry.

"Maybe she isn't anymore. Maybe she's back in town."

"Good God, no!" cried the other two.

All these denizens of the Raffles Club then drained their glasses, passed round the port again, drank one toast to the survival of the human race, and a last toast to the survival of the male species in particular.

Five

A great part of mothering a daughter of marriageable age is to develop a strong sense of where one's daughter's heart lies, just in case it should happen to lie in a place where it really ought *not* to. As part of this exercise in judgment, Lady Hampton had noticed some signs in her daughter's demeanor that led her to believe she had begun to prefer Sir Philip Lansdowne to her other suitors. For one thing, Lady Hampton had found a posy of violets he had sent her—it had been carefully hidden in the rear of the top drawer of her daughter's bureau. Violets, of all things! Where had he obtained them, she wondered? At what price had he done so? What did it all mean?

The violets had been dried and lovingly wrapped in tissue paper and hidden behind some lace, as if they had been saved as a special memento. Finding this relic caused her ladyship to retire to her sitting-room and re-evaluate the entire affair of her daughter's relations with Sir Philip Lansdowne, from beginning to end.

When she put her mind to it, it was obvious, must have been obvious to anyone for some time, that Davina was showing a marked preference for the man. A vast number of times she had seen the couple talking together, the young lady blushing and Sir Philip whispering words that could only be interpreted as being words of love and affection.

She recalled her daughter's demeanor throughout all the rest of the previous year and realized that something entirely different was now going on. She cursed herself for having been so blind—it had been right there, in front of her eyes, and it had taken her all this time to figure it out! Davina was deeply in love with Sir Philip Lansdowne!

In itself, this was not a problem. In fact, it was a very good thing the girl had made her choice at last. Lady Hampton had been afraid the girl would never make her mind up—now, she had shown a clear preference, and that was all to the good.

So much for Davina's choice, but—had Sir Philip really chosen Davina? That was the crux of the thing! It was Lansdowne that was the problem, with his charming, careless bachelor ways, for London and the continent were littered with the corpses of Sir Philip Lansdowne's lost loves.

Now, had Sir Philip made the slightest attempt to contact Lady Davina's family and seek *permission* to pay his addresses to her, those little signs of true affection and admiration would have been the source of joy. His fortune and breeding were excellent, his character above reproach. The odds were, however, that the man was merely engaging in another of his delicious flirtations. He had not paid court in a manner that would suggest any seriousness to his intentions.

Under the circumstances, Lady Hampton feared that the best outcome of the affair would be that the man would break her daughter's heart—the worst outcome would be that he might ruin her. Sir Philip, it must be said, had not the reputation of such a rake, so her fears

THE WINTER WAGER

here, she thought, were most probably unfounded, but what was to be done about the affair?

The Dowager Countess of Hampton carefully re-wrapped the violets in their tissue paper and concealed them among her daughter's lace. She would have to see Davina and tell her of her fears. This was something she could hardly look forward to, since her daughter had a mind of her own and a firm willingness to express her opinions.

Lady Hampton steeled herself for the confrontation; she rang for a maid and asked that her daughter be brought to meet her in the blue parlor. She found her work-bag, pulled out some fringe she had been making, and settled down to wait for her child to come.

Lady Davina answered the summons at once. She entered the parlor, gave her mother a kiss, and took a seat on a small gilt sofa.

"Are you well, Mama?"

"Yes, thank you. I have something very particular to discuss with you, Davina. My dear, it was remiss of me not to have spoken to you sooner. I should very much like to know upon what terms you stand with Sir Philip Lansdowne."

Lady Davina blushed to the very roots of her fair hair.

"I-I have a great deal of respect and affection for Sir Philip," she ventured bravely. "He has lately shown me the most distinguishing attentions, and he has done so on a very consistent basis. I-I have the very warmest feelings towards him."

"You do, do you? Well, I think all of London must be aware of that, Davina," her mother said pointedly as her daughter began blushing again. "Tell me this: has Sir Philip asked you to marry him?"

"N-no, not in s-so many words. But I believe he will."

"Why do you believe that?" her mother said, rather coldly. "Whyever should you believe that, Davina?"

Lady Davina looked at her mother in blank astonishment and cried, "Mama, I feel he harbors the same warm feelings toward me as I have toward him. H-he has said as much. Upon more than one occasion."

"But you have *not* spoken of marriage."

"No, not in so many words—but that is what I believe is his intention."

"Although he has not spoken of it?" cried her mother.

"One does not, when one first falls in love, immediately speak of ceremonies and settlements, and financial arrangements, Mama!" replied Lady Davina fervently. "First, there are only the arrangements of the heart to be considered."

"That is complete, utter, romantical nonsense, Davina, and I am most surprised at your being so stupid about this whole business."

"How can you say such a thing?"

"How can you, an intelligent girl, have been so blind? It's unconscionable, it's amazing, it's appalling!"

"What is?"

"The way you have conducted yourself with this man! You seem not to have noticed that Sir Philip Lansdowne has not approached your brother to ask permission to pay his addresses to you!"

"I had not noticed," she said limply.

"Everyone else in London has!" pointed out Lady Hampton. "How can this be? How can you not have noticed that he has made no mention of marriage to you?"

"That I had noticed, but I thought nothing of it!"

"You have fallen headlong into the love-trap of a man

whose pleasure is to entice young ladies of quality into losing their hearts to him. Are you quite deaf to Sir Philip's reputation?"

"No, I am not," Lady Davina said stiffly.

"What makes you think you are different from Cecily Braithwaite?"

"I am different because he really, truly loves me," she insisted, tears beginning to well up at the corners of her eyes.

"Oh, poppycock! You must break it off at once! You must break off the acquaintance at once before you, too, become the laughingstock of all London!" said her mother warningly, putting down her fringe for a moment. "You must give this man up, Davina! He can give you no more than he has done already. I am sorry to have to say it, but you have entirely mistaken his intentions."

"Mama! I cannot believe I am hearing such words from you!" said Lady Davina, outraged. "Do you think I am so green, and so stupid, that I would so far delude myself? I know when a man loves me, and when he does not! I know that Sir Philip Lansdowne means to marry me! I would wager my life on it!"

"Famous, Davina! You may go right ahead and wager your life on it, with my blessing," said Lady Hampton crossly. "Go to your room at once, child, and think very carefully upon what I have said to you. I am very seriously displeased."

Lady Hampton put down her fringe-work and retired up to her bed-chamber. She pulled the bell for her abigail, who drew the drapes closed and fetched her mistress her vinaigrette and her hartshorn. Lady Hampton remained there, resting, for the remainder of the afternoon, mulling over this very dangerous and unfortunate situation.

When, late in the day, she arose again, Lady Hampton called for ink and paper. Writing in a feverish haste, she dashed off a letter to her son, the Earl of Hampton, and sent it by express to Crolle Hall.

Lady Hampton demanded that her son, in his role as head of the family, come to London at once to take up the reins, for his silly, heedless sister was flinging herself headlong into danger! He was to come directly to town and do something about it—at once! There was no more time to be lost!

Six

The Earl of Hampton folded up the letter, put it away on his writing desk, and sighed with irritation and impatience. Being abruptly summoned to town by his mother, and on such a trivial matter, was not at all to the liking of young Lord Hampton. It so happened that, when in the country, he had been engaged in serious matters of business concerning Crolle Hall, and the last thing he wanted to do was to interrupt his labors and go running off to London to rein in his obstinate elder sister.

He tried to temporize, and to this end there soon followed a flurried exchange of letters between Crolle Hall and the Hampton townhouse in London. He wrote to his mother, asking as politely as he could that Lady Hampton please try again to handle the matter herself. She replied that she had tried and that it was high time her son showed a little more strength of will.

He wrote again, ordering his sister to come out to Crolle Hall to speak with him; his sister politely declined. At this juncture, Lord Hampton gave in and quickly made the necessary arrangements to drive himself to town in his curricle and four and settle the matter himself.

The moment he arrived at the house on St. James' Square, he handed over to Buxton his tall beaver hat, his silver-tipped ebony cane, his immaculate gloves, his many-caped driving coat, and sent for his sister to see him in his book-room, not even waiting to change his clothes after his journey as he would normally have done.

The scowl on the handsome face of the Earl of Hampton should have told Lady Davina the whole story. The earl was very tall and blond like his sister, but with a touch of impatience and petulance about the mouth. He had been somewhat over-indulged as a child, and had inherited wealth and title at an age early enough for him to consider his own desires as paramount, since he had always had means at his disposal for fulfilling whatever desires he had. That being the case, he found dealing with other people's desires, such as his sister's, little more than an annoyance.

When his sister arrived to his summons, Lord Hampton motioned to Lady Davina to take a seat, taking no time at all for the formalities, and began at once to read her the riot act. "I am sorry to see you in all my dirt, but I will settle this with you at once. There is to be an end to all this business with Sir Philip Lansdowne, Davina!" said the Earl of Hampton while he motioned a waiting footman to pull the bell for refreshments. "You must do as our mother asks and break off with that man. You shall go by carriage tomorrow to Crolle Hall and I wish to hear no more about it! Have I made myself perfectly clear?"

Davina, although she was fond of her brother, disliked it particularly when he put on that head-of-the-family tone, even more so when he took it upon himself to order her about so thoughtlessly.

"I will not go, James!" said Lady Davina defiantly. "This is all fustian! I can't think why you should have troubled yourself to drive all the way to town to make me do something I do not wish to, and will not, do! I will not break off with Sir Philip just because you order me to. Do you think because you have inherited our father's dignities that you have inherited the right to dispose of me just as you wish?

"Am I your chattel, like one of your Sheraton chairs? Must my heart obey your orders? Why should it?

"No, James, you should have saved yourself the trouble you have taken in coming here. I will not retire, craven, to the country and nurse my wounds. I will remain in London and we may all see what comes of this."

"Very well, Davina. Go ahead—stay in London if you wish. Find yourself a decent home, find retainers to serve you, find funds with which to sustain yourself—*if* you can. Anyone like you, who cares so little about what is owed to her family, can do as ever she likes. Why should I trouble myself about such an arrogant, heedless person? If you make that choice, Davina, know that you are on your own, and that I wish good luck to you!" snapped the young earl, showing a steeliness his sister had not realized that he possessed.

"You wouldn't dare to cut me off like that, James!" cried Lady Davina.

"Wouldn't I just?" replied Lord Hampton, drumming his long fingers on the side-table. "Try me."

"But only think of the scandal!" she cried, shocked.

"That, my dear Davina, has been my entire point throughout this little discussion of ours. I wish that you might have attended more closely. If you persist in this attachment, you will lose the resources of this family which you have been accustomed to, and don't think that I can't do it or I won't do it, for I will do just as I see fit. Choose, Davina: you are either with this family or against it.

"The scandal of disowning you can mean nothing next to the scandal you are just now beginning to bring upon yourself. It is *your* behavior that has started tongues wagging in London, and it is this behavior that must stop at once, do you hear?

"I won't have you running around, behaving in this care-for-nothing way, Davina. You are not to encourage the attentions of Sir Philip Lansdowne any more. He has made it obvious to everyone in town, except yourself apparently, that he is only enjoying a pleasurable flirtation with you, and nothing more.

"Davina, however much you may dislike it, the fact remains that finding a husband upon the Marriage Mart is deadly serious business, and you must regard it in that light. It does you no good amongst society for other eligible, interested gentlemen to watch you, night after night, frittering away your time, receiving the attentions of a gazetted flirt who intends to remain a bachelor."

"He loves me, James!" she blurted out. "He has told me so!"

"He may very well love you. But—has he offered for you?" said her brother in a soft, smooth voice.

"No. I already explained this to Mama. Why do I have to go over it again?" she replied pettishly.

"Has he even hinted that he might offer for you?" said the earl in a softer voice.

"No, he has not. At least, not in so many words," Lady Davina admitted, much against her will.

"Well, he certainly has said nothing about it to me, for if he had, I assure you, I would regard the whole matter in an entirely different light. I have nothing at all against the man personally. Sir Philip Lansdowne is a very respectable and most eligible man. If he were thought to be at all in the petticoat line, I would be the first to wish you two joy.

"However, your mother and I do not believe his intentions to be serious, no matter what your opinion is. Nor does most of the rest of London. You are nothing more than a green girl who has unfortunately been taken in by a more experienced man who means nothing serious by his attentions to you."

"How can you talk to me like that?" she cried, stamping her feet. "James, I am older than you are by two years!"

"Precise age is not the point, Davina. I am the head of this family, and I am responsible for decisions affecting it!" he said threateningly. "You must give up this man, and the polite world must know that you have done so!"

"Rubbish!" she replied, sulking.

"As long as Sir Philip continues to preoccupy your attentions, he frightens away other, more serious admirers. It provides all the town biddies with something to talk of, and that is what I particularly dislike. Why should all the town be speculating about whether my sister's heart will be broken, or why she encourages Sir Philip's attentions, or anything of the sort? The name of a lady of quality should not be bandied about thus, Davina. Can't you see the impropriety?"

"Oh, I suppose so, James," admitted his sister unwillingly.

The earl rose, crossed the room, and took his sister by the hands, pressing them fondly.

"I fear you have fallen in love with him, Davina," he said in a sympathetic tone.

"I have," she replied, brushing away a single tear.

He gave his sister a strong, brotherly hug and tipped her chin up to his. "Then we must get you away from this place, Davina, and take you back home, where you may recover from your unfortunate attachment just as quickly as may be."

"Must I really give him up, James?"

"Of course you must. You will understand that it's all for the best once you've had a chance to think on it. Retire to the country, my dear, and let your heart recover from the shock of it all. Then, later on, when you are quite yourself again, you must come back to town. It will be the height of the Season, and once again you will be the belle of the ball. You will then be in a position to find yourself a real and reliable husband. If we let this affair drag on weeks or months longer, your recovery will take just that much longer as well. Cut your losses, Davina. The man's a great charmer, but he's not the marrying kind. There's nothing to be done about it. With some men, that's just their nature."

"Very well, James," she replied with a terrible reluctance. "I shall do just as you say and leave London on the morrow."

"Good girl, Davina."

"But what if he *does* speak to you about me? What will you tell him then?"

"If he asks me for permission to pay his addresses to you, Davina, I will give him not only my permission, but my blessing. I promise you that much."

"Very well, then. Very well. I will do just as you say."

Seven

Sir Philip received another irritating visit from Lord Adrian Hensley just as soon as word had gotten around London of Lady Davina Hampton's strategic retreat to Crolle Hall in Hampshire. Sir Philip received him at his lodgings in Belgrave Square, more than a little annoyed at the man for harrying him so needlessly.

His man showed Lord Adrian in and attempted to take his hat and gloves, which Lord Adrian fairly tossed at him. Hensley, not sitting down, instead took a whole three turns around the room in great agitation, running his fingers through his hair nervously, making it all the more disordered and Byronesque.

Sir Philip remained in his chair, unamused, tapping his fingers against one another, waiting impatiently for this seemingly endless Cheltenham tragedy to end.

"What will you do now?" Lord Adrian cried finally, throwing his arms up in a gesture of despair.

"What do you mean, what will I do?" answered Sir Philip with his customary coolness. "What will I do about what?"

"It's obvious the girl has broken off with you. She doesn't want to see you. My plan is at an end!"

"Why should you think so?"

"Because she's gone, man. She's gone!" Hensley cried.

"Lady Davina's leaving town means nothing of the kind, Lord Adrian. As the girl is not entirely without protectors, her abrupt departure means merely that her family has begun putting pressure on her to break off with me. It is a perfectly proper, and a very logical, step to take. Any other family would do just the same, for I have, naturally, been unable to provide the girl or her family with any assurances as to my honorable intentions. Her leaving says nothing as to her own feelings, which, I assure you, are of the very warmest kind toward me."

A pang of jealousy crept across Lord Adrian's face.

"Are they so?" he hissed, giving Sir Philip a black look.

"Indeed they are. But you mustn't find that objectionable, old man. It's just what you told me to do, is it not?" pointed out Sir Philip.

"I suppose so," Lord Adrian confessed darkly. "I can't say I like it."

"I assure you, Lord Adrian, I am carrying out your wishes to the very letter," drawled Sir Philip in a bored tone, wishing his visitor at Jericho and the interview at an end.

Lord Adrian made as if to rise to leave, but seemed to think better of it and sat down once more. He ran his fingers nervously through his hair once again.

"But if, as you say, her family is interfering, what happens now?" he asked with a small, nervous laugh.

"Lady Davina Hampton will spend time out in the country and a little absence will make her heart grow fonder towards me, I would surmise. While staying at Crolle Hall, she will think of me at night, every night, before she falls asleep. Women are like that; it has always been thus. I will invade all her thoughts and dreams.

"I, on my part, will contrive to write her secret and highly romantical letters, and, on a more practical level, I shall begin to work to arrange events such that we two will meet again just as soon as possible," said Sir Philip. "I am working on such arrangements even as we speak. I intend to seek the help of my godmother, who may be able to bring us together once again."

"Then will I have my revenge, man?" cried Lord Adrian, smashing his fist on the table and overturning some bric-a-brac in the process.

"Yes, of course you will," said Sir Philip rather coldly, picking up the detritus. "I will keep my word, just as I said. I always do. It is a matter of taste, and a matter of honor."

"Sorry, old man. So sorry," said Lord Adrian in an agitated manner. "Yes, of course. I should never have questioned your motives. You are a gentleman of honor and are just paying off your debts. Forgive me—I should never have suspected you of having any other motives."

"Other motives?" inquired Sir Philip silkily, leaning back in his leather chair.

"You know—personal motives. Romantic ones," Lord Adrian hinted rashly, looking around for the hat and gloves the servant had taken from him. "It was foolish of me, I know, but that is what I was most desperately afraid of."

"You're not making sense, man," said Sir Philip with some irritation. "Spit it out plainly, won't you?"

"You see, Sir Philip, it came to me last night in a terrible dream. I awoke from it covered in sweat and trembling with the most horrible fear."

"What fear?"

"The fear that—in the dream I was afraid that you'd

fall in love with Lady Davina just as I did!" cried Lord Adrian in a wild tone of voice.

"Indeed so?" said Sir Philip smoothly.

"I couldn't stand that, you know. I couldn't live with that, not at all. If I can't have her, no one else shall, that's for certain," said Lord Adrian. "When I awoke, I had to come to see you. I know you told me not to, but I had to come to find that the dream was not real. I just had to make sure you were going along with my plan and keeping your word."

"I shall certainly keep my word. You may depend upon it."

"As to the rest, you must swear that you have no other motives toward Lady Davina. Have you?"

"I? Sir Philip Lansdowne, confirmed bachelor and notorious breaker of female hearts?" asked he, yawning very slightly. "What other motives *should* I have? I assure you, Lord Adrian, I cannot think what you mean. Everyone in London knows I'm not in the petticoat line."

Eight

Not more than a fortnight later, fifty or so fortunate souls belonging to the Upper Ten Thousand received beautifully inscribed invitations written on the elegant, hot-pressed crested paper of the Duke and Duchess of Pyttwich, requesting the honor of their presence at a grand country house-party to be held at Pyttwich Castle in Hertfordshire.

Certainly this would be considered *the* party of the winter season; it was to be as grand as it was wholly unexpected. To shake off the doldrums of a dreary February, her grace of Pyttwich had finally persuaded her husband to loosen the purse-strings and hold a grand entertainment which would last for a week at least and would be the talk of the town—or, at least, it would be until the hostess with the next grand scheme came along.

It is amazing the lengths to which people will journey, lured by the prospect of a grand ball in winter, especially at such a splendid place as Pyttwich Castle. Invitations were received and accepted by virtually all who had been invited, for who could turn the Duchess down? Who would reject the idea of forming part of such a grand occasion? There were several high Ministers and numerous Members of Parliament coming. A Royal Duke or two would most certainly attend, or would put in a brief appearance at the very least.

The Duke and Duchess of Berwick were coming. The Duchess of Underhill was coming. The Duke of Malden was coming, along with his younger brother Lord Adrian Hensley and their still-lovely mother, Clarissa, Duchess of Malden. Lord and Lady Keswick were driving out from London for the event.

Invitations had been sent over to Crolle Hall, and as a result, the supremely eligible Earl of Hampton was going to attend, bringing Lady Davina Hampton along with his mother.

Sir Nelson Benton, Baron Brook, and Robert Tiverton were coming, as was Sir Philip Lansdowne, for the Duchess of Pyttwich was that gentleman's godmother. Some said it was actually Sir Philip who had been the driving force in succeeding in getting the Duke to open his doors to society, but that was uncertain. Whoever had done the deed, society was grateful.

Lord Hampton had written to Edward, Lord Brook, perhaps the most wealthy of Lady Davina's admirers, suggesting that should Lord Brook wish to offer for Lady Davina, coming to Pyttwich Castle might be just the thing to see it through. With such a large party, and everyone being thrown together for a week in the middle of winter, there would be many opportunities for Lord Brook to spend time with Lady Davina and win her favor. In fact, such large country house parties were notorious occasions for engineering political maneuverings, carrying on romantic affairs, and manipulating marriages. In London, with everyone spread out so, it was a much harder thing; in a country house, even in one as grand and vast as Pyttwich Castle, one could arrange for "chance" encounters in a music room, strolls through the galleries, or secret meetings in the conservatory. Notes could much more easily be passed and assignations more easily made. Besides these, there would be dinners and balls and breakfasts and musical events, each offering increased possibilities for intermingling.

These opportunities were precisely what Sir Philip Lansdowne had in mind when he left London and traveled to Hertfordshire to visit his godparents at Pyttwich Castle. He had then used his extensive charm and undisputed powers of persuasion to coax his godmother into giving the grand house-party in the first place. Sir Philip had even offered to finance a certain portion of the party's outrageous expenses, though the Duke turned down his offer. Sir Philip let his godparents know that he had a very particular and urgent reason for wishing this party to occur, but, though he loved them well, he would not reveal his reasons, no matter how hard they pressed him.

The household of Pyttwich Castle had been in a bustle for days beforehand, for as soon as the decision to hold the party had finally been made, there was endless work to be done as the servants aired out and readied wing after wing of guest bedrooms. Menus had to be planned, and venison and pheasants and sides of beef and hams bought and brought to the Castle. There were eggs to be collected, breads and cakes to be baked. Tradesmen were called to offer various kinds of cheese and whatever fresh vegetables were to be found at such a time of the year. Fish, from both the frozen rivers and the sea, were not difficult to procure, and as to wine, the depth and breadth of the Duke's cellars were legendary.

The best linens and china were set out and cleaned; enough wood and coal for the many bedrooms had to be acquired. The ballroom floor had to be polished, and all the rooms, from the most private to the most public, had to be readied to receive the *crème de la crème* of society.

The expense of feeding and housing and looking after so many notables would, of course, be enormous, but the Duke of Pyttwich had deep pockets—and his wife a love of extravagance that only a country house party on such a scale could exercise to the fullest.

It was on a Thursday afternoon that the first carriages began arriving. Many more came and went as bandboxes and trunks were handed down and taken to their rooms. Valets and ladies' maids arrived and took charge of their masters' and mistresses' belongings, brushing down coats, shaking out wrinkles from ball gowns. They carefully set out the belongings of which they had charge with pride and precision, for their own consequence depended entirely upon just how well-turned-out were the persons by whom they were employed. The house-servants, though burdened with much extra work, were happy as well, looking forward to the extensive vails they would be able to collect from every guest at the end of their house-party.

Dinner on the first evening was vast and very grand; to Lady Davina Hampton, it was nearly interminable. She was already overtired from the long journey, and more so from the long series of scolds she had received from her mother and her brother, seemingly all the way from Crolle Hall to Pyttwich Castle. They had extracted repeated promises from her not to spend any time with Sir Philip should he attend the house-party, and she had promised to turn her mind toward more interested suitors, such as Lord Brook.

THE WINTER WAGER

She soon learned that Sir Philip was indeed staying with his godparents at the Castle, but, quite naturally, there had thus far been no opportunity to meet with him privately. The Dowager Lady Hampton and the Earl of Hampton were most displeased at Sir Philip's attending the party at all. There had been some talk between them of refusing the invitation on the strength of Sir Philip's probable presence, but in the end they had decided that the possibility of arranging a marriage between Lord Brook and Davina was more significant than the possibility of the two lovers renewing their acquaintance.

Lady Davina, whatever fictive assurances she had given her relations, wanted nothing more than the chance to encounter Sir Philip, a man she felt she loved, at the earliest opportunity. She, too, like her family, wished to question him as to his intentions toward her, although she felt instinctively that he would never betray her love and trust. She undressed from the journey with some impatience, anxious to speak with Sir Philip; she took a nap, bathed, and allowed her abigail to dress her in a lovely gown of pale yellow silk, which made her hair look like a golden diadem.

Lady Davina looked all around the parlor where the dinner guests had assembled in all their finery, but she could not see Sir Philip Lansdowne. It was hardly surprising to her when she found herself going in to dinner on the arm of Lord Brook, a pleasant enough fellow, but, compared to a man like Sir Philip, really a bit of a bore.

When she was finally seated at the long table, she finally saw that Sir Philip, indeed, was there. However, he was so far down at the end of the table that, from where she sat, she was unable either to converse with him or to catch his eye.

She felt as if her cheeks were in an eternal blush, so much was she filled with desire to see him and to talk to him after so long an absence, but it could not be done. As she studied her turbot, she conversed with Sir Nelson to her right and Lord Brook to her left about the long winter and about the long journey out to Pyttwich Castle. They also discussed England's muddy roads, and muddy shoes, and muddy clothing, waiting all the while for the endless dinner to end. She could not wait until she could meet with Sir Philip alone and learn the answer to her only question: *if you* do *love me, when will you offer for me?*

From his end of the long table, Lord Adrian Hensley watched the face of his beloved Lady Davina very carefully as well. Every perfect word that issued from that perfect face, every perfect smile she gave to her dinner partners, every time she touched her hand lightly to Lord Brook's arm, every silvery laugh, was a torture to him.

She had dressed with the greatest of care, he noticed, but she always did so. She looked beautiful in her jonquil gown, its satin slip covered in net, its sleeves decorated with knots of white satin ribands in the latest French style. The high waist of her gown was ornamented with small frills of blond lace, matching the deep flounces that trimmed the bottom edge.

The dress was cut extremely low around Lady Davina's ample bosom, and it was upon that and upon a circlet of diamonds which ornamented it, that Lord Adrian's eye naturally fell and remained.

As he watched her, her beauty as fresh as ever it had been, the crushing pain of her rejection arose within Lord

Adrian's heart, as strong as it had been on the night she had dismissed his suit.

God help him, he had loved her so! His love had been so real, and so pure, and so unselfish! It had been a far cry from his relations with his many London high-fliers, ladies he had taken and discarded with no involvement of his heart. Davina, dear Lady Davina—she was the one who had turned the world round for him!

Yet, with all this great love that he had placed at her feet, she had had the audacity to reject him!

She was a heartless, unfeeling jade! She would never know the wretchedness, the agony she had caused him, and yet she *must* know!

Soon enough, he swore to himself, she would know! His love for her, the great love of his life, would not be in vain! She would not be permitted to cast him off thoughtlessly and get away with it, going on to lead her life, perfectly unconcerned, while his own lay in ruins at his feet. No, everything was going to change for Davina Hampton—nothing would ever be the same for her.

They would soon become equals. She would soon understand his anguish, very precisely.

It only remained for him to strike back at her, using the tool that fate had placed in his hands: Sir Philip Lansdowne.

Nine

There were mostly ladies in attendance at the breakfast room at Pyttwich Castle the next morning. A sideboard filled with food was laid out between ten and noon, and the various guests could come down at their leisure to choose their repast. There were eggs of every description, sausages, bacon, and various kinds of breads; there was ham and kippers and fresh butter and jellies and jams. There was hot chocolate and various kinds of tea. Everything one might wish for had kindly been supplied by the Duchess of Pyttwich and her staff.

Lady Davina Hampton had been lingering after she had finished her meal, still hoping to catch a glimpse of Sir Philip Lansdowne, but she could not. Besides, her mother seemed to know just what was on her mind, for she was careful never to leave her daughter's side for a moment.

Sir Philip, Lady Davina began to think, seemed to be purposely avoiding her. Whyever should he do that? It was worrisome, very worrisome.

Mother and daughter had been chatting with Lady Keswick for a few minutes, discussing the weather, which was expected to turn much colder; word had come up to the Castle from the surrounding farms that there would be snow coming, and that if it did, it would be sudden and heavy—or so the country prognosticators thought.

"I shouldn't mind being snowed in at Pyttwich Castle, I'll tell you very plainly. Only what would we all do once all this lovely food runs out?" asked Lady Keswick.

Lady Davina smiled politely and turned her head toward the door, still looking for Sir Philip Lansdowne. A young lady older than herself entered the room accompanied by the Duchess of Pyttwich.

"Who is that girl? I don't think I know her," Lady Davina asked.

"That, my dear, is Muriel Dalrymple, a great favorite of the Duchess' whom she hoped to marry off to Sir Philip Lansdowne. Unfortunately, it didn't take, and Miss Dalrymple's heart was sadly broken. It was quite the talk of the town when it happened, which was a while ago now. You're not still thinking of that man, are you, Davina?"

Lady Davina said nothing but blushed angrily and referred the question to her mother, who said, "I believe Davina is quite over that attachment now, thank you, Sarah."

"I certainly hope so," said Lady Keswick. "As you know, I was the one who introduced them, but as I told Davina at the time, I had no expectations of Philip's ever coming up to scratch, because who would? Look around you, just in this room—the casualties of Sir Philip's charm are everywhere around you.

"See, Davina? Over there? The Duchess of Berwick is related by marriage to dear sweet Cecily Braithwaite, who fell so desperately in love with Sir Philip that she tried to starve herself in a misguided attempt to gain his sympathy. Now, at the other table is Lady Siddons, the mother of poor Lady Anne—*she* actually had to be sent away from England in order to recover from her passion for Sir Philip! Can you credit it? One must be so very careful with one's heart, mustn't one? Really, if you think on it, Davina, you have escaped from his toils with relatively little damage to your feelings or your sanity, you know. You should be very thankful that your family extricated you so soon."

During this speech, Lady Davina paid close attention to every word that Lady Keswick said, and as she did so, she became aware of a strong feeling of fear that arose in her as she laid eyes on this or that victim of Sir Philip, or upon a victim's relative. Had she herself been taken in? Was she another of Sir Philip's victims?

Had *she* been mistaken, just as all those other girls had?

It was a truly daunting thought. Had she been mistaken in her perception of his attachment? Were all those sweet words insubstantial, coming to nothing? Had her deep love been in vain?

Sarah, Lady Keswick, nattered on heedlessly. "There was also Clementine Fellowes and the Burke-White girl—need I say more? He's a lovely man, a wonderful man. His ways of making a girl feel at the top of the world are most enjoyable—but that's all there is to it.

"Davina, dear—what is wrong? Why do you look so? Look, Jane, there is something quite wrong with Davina. She is pale-white and trembling like a leaf in the wind! You must take her upstairs at once!"

In that manner and in that mood, Lady Davina Hampton was quickly spirited back upstairs to her bedchamber, where she stayed for the whole remainder of the day, nursing an overpowering headache.

Ten

Lady Davina Hampton recovered sufficiently to come down to dinner, although her appetite had deserted her entirely. A glance at a platter of pheasant or a joint of beef was enough to unsettle her, and so she spent the greater part of dinner gazing at her lead-crystal glassware.

After dinner, there were card tables set up in the green salon for those inclined to play, and in the large music room, there were opportunities for the many accomplished young ladies to show off their musical talents by playing on the pianoforte and singing.

Other guests were admiring the Duke of Pyttwich's vast, double-storied book room, and in this setting, in which people could mingle freely and wander from place to place, Sir Philip and Lady Davina Hampton's paths crossed at last. Her brother, Lord Hampton, happened at that time to be engaged in another room, discussing matters of his estate with his neighbor, Lord Brook, whom he hoped to induce to offer for Lady Davina. Lady Hampton happened at that time to be still in the drawing room, enjoying a comfortable coze with the Duchess of Pyttwich and Sarah, Lady Keswick.

Lady Davina had been inspecting an old copy of Shakespeare's sonnets when Sir Philip came up behind her and whispered in her ear, "Davina, my dear! I have been looking for you these ages. Kindly step behind that bookcase to your left and we shall be able to converse unobserved."

Lady Davina blushed so hard she thought she would never recover. The nearness of the man she loved so absolutely was enough to make her tremble; her breath caught in her throat. This interview would prove the case, she thought. Did he love her? Or did he not?

She moved silently into the alcove he had indicated. She allowed him to take her hand, which he pressed against his heart.

"I have been trying to get in touch with you, Philip," she told him urgently.

"I was out of town. Forgive me—it was quite unavoidable."

"My family has forbidden me to see you. Did you not know? My brother made me leave London and repair to Crolle Hall. I have been immured there these two weeks. He is trying very hard to make a match for me with Lord Brook."

"I had heard that you had gone to the country," Sir Philip admitted. "I did not know the terms, though I must say I am hardly surprised. I'm sure that if I were in your brother's shoes, I would do just the same for my sister. One really cannot blame him."

"You must talk to my brother tonight, Philip."

"Tonight—is not a good time."

"Philip, I beg you, go to him now before it is too late. Or, is what all London says true—have you no feelings toward me?" she demanded.

"Davina, my dearest love, I have the very warmest feelings toward you. You must believe me. This is neither the time nor the place, however, to reveal them. You must promise me you will have faith in me no matter how things appear on the surface. Will you promise me that, Davina?" he said.

"Yes, yes, of course I will. But when will you settle things? It must be done at once."

"Tomorrow night, during the ball, everyone will be preoccupied. You must slip away and meet me in the conservatory, and then I will explain everything."

"Oh, Lord! I see my mother approaching. She must not see me speaking to you. Tomorrow, then, I will come to the conservatory."

"Until tomorrow. I love you, Davina. Remember that—be constant to me and pay no attention to whatever gossips may say."

He kissed her hand and left her. She emerged into the main part of the library and was immediately accosted by her mother.

"Davina, I told you to stay away from him. Whatever will Lord Brook think?" Lady Hampton demanded.

"He only asked after my health, Mama," said her daughter guiltily.

"If you think I believe *that* piece of nonsense, you're quite wrong. I saw that look on your face and I know perfectly well what it means. If you can't break your attachment to that man and conduct yourself with more dignity in public, we shall all go back to Crolle Hall."

"Mother! You wouldn't!" she cried, shocked.

"Of course I would. Now, promise me you'll stay away from him, Davina. Or do you prefer to have your unrequited attachment become known to all the *ton,* your heart worn on your sleeve, and become a laughingstock like Muriel Dalrymple?"

"No, of course I do not!" she replied fiercely.

"Then, do not be seen talking with him in such a private way. Do you promise me that you will not single him out again?"

"Yes, Mama," she said, hating herself for her lies. "I promise."

Eleven

The next morning in the breakfast room, she saw Sir Philip again, but her mother was with her and she was able only to acknowledge him with a polite nod. Her brother, the earl, was not in the habit of coming down, but his friend, Lord Brook, was there and invited Lady Hampton and Lady Davina to have their food at his table.

"Will you do me the honor of dancing with me this evening?" Lord Brook asked.

"Certainly," she replied.

"Davina is a very accomplished dancer, Lord Brook," said her mother proudly. "But of course, you must know that already."

"I have had the honor of dancing with your lovely daughter many times in town. I hope Lady Davina knows me as a very faithful and enthusiastic friend—and a sincere and genuine admirer," said Lord Brook so feelingly that Lady Davina had to blush. Really! Such sweet words at breakfast-time. It would be only a matter of time before the man proposed to her—she could feel him in pursuit of her already. When would she be able to settle things with Sir Philip? The delay was putting her in a terrible position: her brother would not like it a bit if she mishandled Lord Brook.

Lady Davina smiled sweetly and said nothing. She

pushed the food around her plate, still unable to eat very much due to all the pressure and excitement. Her mother was still chatting away happily with Lord Brook, who had not only wealth but great estates in Hampshire and Hertfordshire, when she rose and excused herself.

On the way to the door, her exit was interrupted by the sudden appearance of Lord Adrian Hensley, whose existence Lady Davina had almost entirely forgotten. They collided with one another, which sent Lord Adrian into a fluster of blushing apologies. He gave her a look that made her think the man had lost his wits. He stammered and repeated himself, then asked breathlessly if he might have the honor of a dance with her this evening at the ball. Although she had no wish to dance with a rejected suitor, she had to oblige him.

She fairly ran upstairs to her bedchamber, nursing the oddest premonition that something was very wrong. She tried to soothe her spirits by reading a romantic novel by Mrs. Edgeworth, but it only made her fall into a deep sleep.

She woke up terrified, having had a nightmare. Lady Davina had dreamed she walked into Almack's and threw herself at Sir Philip's feet. He laughed at her and ran off with another, as she lay there weeping. All around the room she saw elderly ladies laughing at her disgrace and young ladies pointing and sneering. Gentlemen had their heads together, whispering and nodding towards her. Sir Philip had rejected her utterly and completely, in full view of the *ton,* and she was sent off to a recuperative farm in the country, populated by Sir Philip's cast-offs—Cecily Braithwaite, Lady Anne, and Muriel Dalrymple.

* * *

Lady Davina splashed cold water on her face, trying to rid her mind of all her dark, uncertain thoughts. Her dream had left her with a residue of terror which she could not shake entirely. It would be wonderful if it were already time for the ball and she could slip off to the conservatory and settle things once and for all with Sir Philip. Much as her heart trusted all he had told her, her intellect was subject to attacks of reason, stemming from all she had heard about Sir Philip and the many women who had worn the willow for him.

She put the dream out of her mind; she put her fears out of her mind.

Lady Davina called for her abigail to come and dress her for the ball. She did not bother to go down for dinner, but spent the time instead upon perfecting her toilette: she wanted to look particularly good this evening.

She had brought with her a creation of Madame Fanchon's—it was perhaps the most exquisite, and certainly the most expensive, ball gown she had ever worn. Her mother, now set on working out terms with Lord Brook, had insisted that she purchase it. No one, said Lady Hampton, who saw Davina in that dress could resist being completely captivated.

As she regarded herself in the looking-glass, she could not help but think it suited her very well, all things considered.

Lady Davina's dress had been fashioned of French blue satin with an overslip of pure white lace. The lower half was ornamented with pearls sewn in plume-shapes; the lace slip was decorated with pearls and roses and was cut high on the left side, revealing the satin gown beneath. Its sleeves had been slashed, Spanish-style, so that both the blue satin and white lace alternated. Its bosom was cut very low and ornamented with lace and satin. She wore her mother's pearls and matching droplet earrings. Her headdress was her mother's small pearl tiara, which made her look even taller and more elegant.

The ball was well under way when the Earl of Hampton was announced, along with his mother, the Dowager Countess of Hampton, and Lady Davina Hampton.

A murmur passed round the crowd when Lady Davina could be seen, standing regally at the top of the few stairs that marked the entrance to the ballroom. She glanced around, hoping to see Sir Philip, but caught the eye of Lord Brook instead. He smiled and made his way through the crowd to greet her.

"You look marvelous tonight, Lady Davina. You have promised me the honor of a dance. Would you care to do so at once?"

She nodded her assent and he led her out onto the floor. The musicians had just started up a waltz, and so Lady Davina allowed herself to be taken in Lord Brook's arms and led through the circular steps of her favorite dance. Lord Brook kept up a sequence of social small talk, to which she responded in polite, distant monosyllables. He was going out of his way to make himself agreeable, but Lady Davina just wished he would stop talking. She was concerned with nothing more than finding Sir Philip Lansdowne and straightening out this whole sorry business.

Her attention returned to her partner when he spoke her name twice.

"Lady Davina? I beg you will listen to me. Surely you are not unaware of my high regard for you. I have seen your brother, Lord Hampton, just today, and as a result,

I have something extremely important to discuss with you. May I have a word in private?"

Please God, she thought to herself, *don't let Lord Brook offer for me now!*

"In private? Why, Lord Brook, certainly there can be no need of that!" she said. "Really, I am wanted otherwhere just now."

Lord Brook attempted to lead her from the dance floor, but she resisted, saying that her next dance was promised to Lord Adrian Hensley, which it was.

Lord Adrian came to claim her, and she went out onto the floor on his arm, relieved to have escaped Lord Brook for the moment. The meeting with Sir Philip could not come too soon! If she were to offend Lord Brook, it would look very bad.

The dance with Lord Adrian happened to be a *contradanse,* one that Lady Davina knew well and Lord Adrian did not. That would perhaps explain his odd behavior: he said barely a word, but fixed her with rather a fierce expression she could not make out at all. Odd fellow! Why had he wanted to dance with her, if it only meant glowering at her throughout the set?

During this dance she finally located Sir Philip, who smiled at her from across the room and came toward her, waiting until the set was over to approach. She saw her brother not far away and indicated with her eyes and a shake of her head Sir Philip must not approach her within sight of Lord Hampton.

Sir Philip passed her as if by chance as he threaded his way through the crowd, whispering, "Meet me at eleven o'clock in the conservatory, at the far end, near the Japanese orange tree." She nodded in return.

When Lord Adrian overheard this exchange, the expression on his face turned almost beatific. His expression became filled with delighted anticipation.

Noticing this odd reaction, Lady Davina wondered what was ailing the man—his behavior had become more peculiar than ever. She shrugged the matter off and tried to contain her anticipation. Eleven o'clock would come and everything would be settled for the best.

Twelve

Lady Davina knew not how she passed the hours between nine and eleven. Afterwards, she only remembered things as a blur, filled with dances with various gentlemen and her contrived conversation with them. She partook of refreshments, Lord Brook tried to ask her to marry him again, and she parried him again. It was a mélange of candles and chandeliers and crowds.

At last, the tall French clock struck eleven, and, her breath catching in her throat, she tried to slip away to her meeting with the man she loved. She checked on her mother's whereabouts—Lady Hampton was deep in conversation with Lady Brook, Lord Brook's mother. Lady Davina thought, sarcastically, that they must be planning the marriage settlements. She checked on her brother—Lord Hampton was rapt in conversation with an entrancing Cecily Braithwaite. Good for Cecily, she thought to herself.

There was no one to stop her. She glided toward the far end of the ballroom and disappeared from view. She walked swiftly down the main corridor, turned through the music room and library and through another hallway. She turned the knob on the conservatory door and walked in.

She was greeted immediately by a heavy tropical atmosphere. The room was kept very warm and humid, for the Duke of Pyttwich was a great collector of orchids and other heat-and-humidity-loving plants. Exotic perfumes wafted toward her; she felt she had entered another world.

What an excellent place for an assignation! Even in his choice of a meeting place, Lady Davina could feel the romantic genius of Sir Philip Lansdowne.

She walked to the southern end of the conservatory and there, at last, in a darkened corner near a fragrant orange tree, she beheld the face of the man she loved.

Somehow, in the dim light, his handsome countenance had become even more so; his kind, clear eyes drew her in to himself. His strong chin and brow looked as if there were no other woman for him in the universe. The intensity of his adoring gaze was such that she blushed despite herself.

Sir Philip moved out from the shadows; he took her hand and used it to draw her into a strong and passionate embrace, saying nothing at all, not even a word. Never before had they been utterly alone; thus far their love-play had had to be confined to a few stolen kisses and the holding of hands.

She had never been kissed before, not in this strong, possessive, intimate way, and it fairly took the breath away from her. Lady Davina felt as though she were melting from within, she felt as though she could laugh and cry at once, so deep were the primal emotions that possessed her.

The two remained locked within each other's arms for what seemed an eternity until at last, Sir Philip whispered, "I have missed you so much, my darling. We must never be apart this long again."

"No, Philip. Never again," she said. "I cannot bear any

separation from you. It is too painful. Pray tell me that this will not happen again."

Sir Philip said nothing, but took her wrist and turned it upward, and covered that delicate skin with soft, tender kisses that made her mind whirl and her senses reel.

Her voice hardened and she said to him, anxiously, "Philip, if we are never again to be apart, you must speak to my brother about your intentions."

"I cannot speak to your brother, Davina," Sir Philip admitted. "He will call me out. You know he will."

"Are you afraid, then?" she said in a challenging tone.

"Why should I be? If we met in a duel, I would kill him, you know," said Sir Philip forthrightly. "You wouldn't want that, would you? I certainly should not. Devil of a way to make oneself known to a girl's family."

"Don't speak such rubbish, my dearest. If you ask James for his permission to pay your addresses to me and he knows you wish to offer for me, he will not call you out. They have no objection to you as a person—they are only upset because you have not made clear your honorable intentions—and have not offered for me."

"Ah, my sweet and lovely Davina," he said in dulcet tones, running his fingers through her golden curls. "I'm afraid there are reasons for that which I cannot now explain."

"Reasons?" she cried, becoming angry with him. "You said nothing of this to me before! Why? Are you promised to another?"

"Are you doubting me now?" said Sir Philip, tipping her chin up toward him with one hand and kissing her lightly just above the brow.

"I just don't understand all this mystery," she said, turning away unhappily. "You have done nothing but make love to me since the day we met. I have never been so seriously, so calculatedly pursued. You have won my heart, long ago. Is this the end of it? Is your conquest sufficient to your ends? Do you not wish to have me for your own, forever?"

As if in answer to her questions, he took her in his arms again, embracing her, kissing her again and again until her breath began to come in short, passionate gasps.

"Oh, Philip, you must stop," she cried.

"Is this a mystery, my love?" he whispered, not heeding her plea.

"No, Philip," Lady Davina said, pushing him away. "Why can you not speak to my brother and ask to pay your addresses to me? It is all perfectly straightforward."

"At this time, I cannot," said Sir Philip, rather stiffly. "I am prevented from doing so."

"By what?"

"By circumstances which are beyond my control," he admitted, taking her two hands in his one and pressing them strongly. "Please, Davina, you must try to trust me."

"I don't understand, Philip, not at all. If you are not promised to another, and if you love me, why do you hesitate?"

"There is a grave matter of honor I must settle first. Davina, please, you must try very hard to trust me, my dear, even though your family and your friends—and your own heart and all the world—tell you not to."

"You know, that is true—they all *have* told me not to trust you! All evening, everyone has been telling me that you will never be faithful to me, that I will become just another of your many cast-offs."

"Things are not always what they seem. There will be times to come, soon, when you will mistrust me even more. Things are not what they seem. Swear you will remember it—it is our only hope," he said. "So very much depends upon it."

"I swear, my dearest."

They clung to one another tightly, as if the strength of their embrace itself would serve as a barrier against all threatening outside forces. Lady Davina sighed, wanting to believe every word her lover said to her, and yet afraid to do so. Sir Philip began another long series of expert kisses, along the back of her shoulder, along the soft skin of the nape of her neck; Lady Davina was nearly in tears as he whispered in his low, soft voice, "Davina. Do you love me, Davina?"

"God help me, I do, Philip," she said, beside herself with passion. "I do love you. I love you more than my name and more than my reputation. God help me, I love you more than life itself."

The loud, invasive sound of applause was heard coming from behind a ficus; at once, the couple sprang apart, angry and embarrassed.

"Well played, Sir Philip!" Lord Adrian sneered, emerging from the corner in which he had hidden himself. "Well played, my lady. 'I love you more than life itself!' Dear me, what a charming couple you two make. The depths of your happiness are so profound as to be almost unbearably nauseating to an innocent onlooker such as myself.

"Pray tell me, Lady Davina and Sir Philip—just when *am* I to wish you joy?" he asked sarcastically.

"Lord Adrian, what do you mean by spying upon us in this sordid manner?" cried Lady Davina, her eyes flashing with anger. "Leave us in peace, I pray you. You are being entirely ungentleman-like."

"If I was ungentleman-like in my occult observations, what about *your* conduct, pretty Lady Davina?" he said nastily. "Is it lady-like to kiss a man behind a bush in a country house, a man to whom one is not even betrothed? I think not, my dear."

"This is not your concern, Lord Adrian. Leave us, please," ordered Lady Davina abruptly.

"I don't think I shall, my dear," he drawled unctuously. "I have some extremely important matters to settle, here and now. I take it you still reject my offer of marriage, Davina?"

"Your self-importance is beyond comprehension, sir. You find me in the arms of another man and you try to renew your suit?" she cried, shocked. "You must be mad!"

"Perhaps I am mad, but we shall see, my dear," Lord Adrian said in a hard tone, looking like an animal circling for the kill. "Tell me this, Sir Philip. I love the Lady Davina Hampton and have loved her for some time. I even tried to take her as my wife, but the silly chit refused to have me. Now, this evening, I discover you here with Lady Davina, enjoying a passionate embrace. But tell me, do *you* love her?"

There was no putting it off any longer—the time had come at last. Sir Philip's face paled to a terrible whiteness, then it reddened for a while, then it became dark and dusky. His lips tightened, his brows drew together; he grew unspeakably angry. Still, he made no audible reply.

Lord Adrian's voice rose and took on a vicious, taunting tone as he cried out, "I challenge you, Sir Philip Lansdowne—upon your honour—do you love her?"

Sir Philip's face paled again; he looked like a man ready to kill.

"No," he shouted in a loud, clipped voice. "I do *not* love her!"

"Philip!" cried Lady Davina, unable to believe what she had heard. "What can you mean? Can you thus betray me?"

Sir Philip Lansdowne turned to face Lord Adrian and hissed at him, "That's the end of it, Hensley. The deed is done; the terms are met. Now, I am a free man! Are you perfectly satisfied?"

"Oh, I am quite satisfied, thank you, Sir Philip," said Lord Adrian in a cheerily vengeful tone as he watched the woman he desperately loved and had wanted to marry break down completely into long, uncontrollable tears. "I am quite satisfied with your work, Sir Philip. Thank you so very much. Exquisite, exquisite. One really could *not* have asked for more!"

Sir Philip Lansdowne turned toward Lady Davina and said, "Davina, listen to me. I can explain everything. This is not as it appears—you must believe me. Remember what I just said to you?"

He reached for her hand as if to take it in his own, but she yanked it out of his grasp, pulled herself away, and then leaned back in and struck him, full in the face, hard.

"Remember? I remember that you said you loved me!" she shouted, furious to be so completely betrayed and humiliated. "I remember that you then said, in front of this, this perfect *insect* of a man, that you do *not* love me! I remember everything—everything I have been told about Cecily Braithwaite, and Muriel Dalrymple, and

Lady Anne, and all the rest of them, and I cannot *believe* I was such a fool as to disregard your wretched reputation and fall so hopelessly in love with you!

"Don't try to talk to me, Philip! I hate you! I hate you! I never want to see your face again, not as long as I live!"

Weeping with outrage, Lady Davina Hampton picked up the skirts of her beautiful ball gown, and ran from the conservatory, letting the connecting glass door slam dangerously as she did so.

"My, my! What a little hellion!" said Lord Adrian smoothly. "She'll never believe you now, will she? I tried to warn you not to fall in love with her, you know, and you assured me there were no personal motives involved. What a pity for you that you were dissembling! I'm afraid your heart must be broke as well, what? You have my deepest sympathies, I'm sure."

Sir Philip said nothing in return, but removed his Weston-cut coat of ebony superfine, folded it carefully, and hung it on a rhododendron. Then he walked up to Lord Adrian, looked him straight in the eye, and planted him a facer, straight to the jaw, saying, "I've been waiting to do this since you told me of the iniquitous favor you desired. You are a cur!"

He struck Lord Adrian again, and drew his cork. Lord Adrian tried to hit back at him, but his arms were too short, and he had no science at all. Sir Philip hit him again, and again, until Hensley was lying on the floor in a pool of his own blood, whimpering.

"I should kill you for what you have done, Hensley. Perhaps I shall, someday," he said with disgust. "I have other concerns at the moment."

"What concerns?" sneered Lord Adrian as he removed his cravat and used it to try to stem the flow from his nose. "You'll never win her back, you know. I intend to tell her everything about the terms of our little wager, and I shall do so in the greatest detail. I assure you, once she is apprised of all the particulars and realizes she has become the subject of ridicule and gossip of the most calamitous sort, you will never, ever be forgiven."

"As to that," Sir Philip said chillingly as he left the conservatory, "as to that, Lord Adrian, we shall see."

Thirteen

Lady Davina Hampton could not reach her bedchamber fast enough. Thankfully, between the conservatory of Pyttwich Castle and her room in the east wing, she came across few other guests, so she hadn't had to endure the additional humiliation of watching people exclaim as they saw her running through the long galleries, her nose and eyes red from weeping.

When she reached her room, she shut the door tight behind her and rang for her abigail. Breaking down completely now that she was in a private place, she wretched sobs of grief and fury. Her abigail arrived moments later, bobbed a curtsey, and was told to pack all her ladyship's things at once. The maid, if she felt any surprise, showed none and went quickly about her task.

Lady Davina fairly threw off her gorgeous ball dress; she vowed to herself to give it away at the earliest opportunity, for it held nothing but base memories. Letting her maid pack her things, she dressed in a fur-trimmed red velvet pelisse, matching muff, and high boots.

She hastily scratched out two notes: one to Lord Hampton, asking that his carriage be put at her disposal this very night, and the other to her mother, telling her it was imperative that she return to town at once. She assured her mother that she would be traveling safely in her brother's carriage accompanied by her maid, so that all the proprieties were observed. She wrote that she was leaving for personal reasons which she could not, at this juncture, disclose, and begged her mother to make her excuses to kind Lord Brook and let him know she would be pleased to receive him in London.

She folded up the writing paper, rang for a footman, and directed him to take the messages. She told her maid to pack her own things as well.

She planned to leave before anyone was the wiser, and, if her abrupt departure should cause comment—sobeit! Lady Davina could not endure being in the presence of either of those two wretched men, not for a moment longer! She sat down, blew her nose into her handkerchief, took some hartshorne, and waited for news that her carriage was ready and waiting.

It took no more than three quarters of an hour for a footman to bring word to Lady Davina from her brother that his personal carriage had sprung a wheel, but that he had made arrangements for another to be available to her at once. Lord Hampton said he was entirely at her disposal and hoped to see her in town at her earliest convenience.

Lady Davina was extremely relieved at this news; everything, even her sanity, depended upon leaving Pyttwich Castle at once. The footman brought down her valises as she covered her face with a muffler, and she and her abigail went down the stairs, through a side door, and were helped up into a well-appointed carriage pulled by four fresh greys.

The carriage had started to pull away when there was a knock at the carriage door. A footman told Lady Davina that a jewel box had been left behind—could her ladyship's maid kindly retrieve it? Lady Davina was annoyed, but she let the girl return to fetch it. She could understand how the Duke's servants might be less than anxious to touch a guest's jewel box, lest something go missing and they bear the blame.

Lady Davina waited a minute or two for the girl to return when she heard an odd sound at the latch of the door. She peered out the isinglass window, and was dismayed to see that it had started to snow, not just a light flurry, but in earnest. Nonetheless, she was determined to escape Pyttwich Castle; if, on the road to London, the way became impassable, she would just have to spend the night at an inn.

She waited impatiently a few more minutes and then slid back the little door that communicated with the driver. "Where is my maid? I said I must leave at once!"

"Leave at once?" the coachman repeated. "Yes, your ladyship!"

He whipped the horses into a sound canter and took off, leaving Lady Davina to lurch back dreadfully against the squabs.

"Stop! Stop! Coachman!" she cried. "Go back! I didn't mean for you to leave! We must wait for my maid, do you hear? Stop this carriage at once!"

However, Lady Davina Hampton soon discovered two things: the door communicating with the driver had been shut securely from the coachman's side, and her own doors, belonging to the carriage box, had somehow been locked as well.

The carriage had swung out past the gates of Pyttwich Castle and was traveling at breakneck speed down a country lane—she could not quite make out the direction. She kept screaming at the coachman, banging on the inside panels, wriggling the door handles, but it was all to no avail.

The countryside flashed past her, obscured by the ever-increasing snow. It had begun to fall in large, thick flakes, coming so fast that nearby paths and trees and fences already bore an inch or two of white.

She pulled out her handkerchief, already wet with tears, and applied it to her nose once again and dabbed at her eyes. Events had escalated far beyond her control and she was at her wit's end. So much had happened, so quickly—and yet there was no respite.

Lady Davina Hampton realized with horror that she had become nothing more than an abducted prisoner—*but whose prisoner was she?*

Bad dreams pursued Lady Davina as the coach tore on through the night. She tried to sleep, but the motion of the carriage was so sharp that she could sleep only fitfully and she began to feel rather ill.

In another hour, her headache had only worsened from the bouncing and swaying of the coach. Lady Davina began to rant at the coachman once again and even began to try to hammer the small door open, but it was useless.

Looking out the window again, the snowstorm had turned into a full blizzard. How the fellow on the box could see his way to drive she had no idea. Every once in a while, as they came round a corner she could feel the wheels skidding sidewise on the snow and she began to be frightened, not merely for her honor and reputation, but for her physical safety. She had heard of all too many people who had lost their lives in carriage accidents, particularly in such horrid weather as this.

Was that to be her fate?

"Slow down! Slow down, for the love of God, won't you?" she cried out to the coachman in despair, but he did not heed her request.

She let her head fall back against the velvet squabs as she tried to put the pieces of this puzzle together. Who had done this to her? Why?

A series of disjointed thoughts ran through her head.

If the man responsible for this was Lord Adrian Hensley, she would probably find herself dragged all the way to Gretna. The stupid, vicious man! She swore that if he was the culprit, Lord Adrian would soon learn that she was *not* the sort of girl to be carried off and married in such a fashion! She would kill him before she married him!

Fourteen

Lady Davina Hampton was hanging onto the leather carriage straps for dear life when the carriage rounded a tight corner, the horses going neck or nothing. She felt the wheels skid off to the left, and with a straining, sickening lurch, the whole carriage toppled over onto its right side and crashed to a halt.

Lady Davina's breath was knocked out of her; she fell against the inner door latch and hit her head hard against the wooden panel. She let out a sharp cry and, as she lost consciousness, became dimly aware of the snow, beaten by a cold wind, coming through the broken windows. Groggily, she tried to rouse herself and escape, but she could not. Swooning again, she fell to the side of the carriage.

When, slowly, consciousness once again came upon her, she felt herself being carried in the strong arms of a man. Her feet were freezing cold; she had lost her boots, and was being carried over drifts of snow with some difficulty. She tried to talk, but had not enough energy. She let herself sink down into blessed sleep once again.

When Lady Davina awoke, she found herself lying in front of a blazing fire, wrapped in a blanket. Her wet clothes had been pulled off and replaced with some sort of fine, soft woolen cloak. She had a splitting headache, which she attributed to both the arduous carriage ride, and the blow from the accident. When she felt her head, there was a sore, swollen spot the size of an orange.

She inspected her surroundings; she was in a small but well-constructed and well-furnished country house. It might well be a hunting box, she thought, from the masculine decorations—nothing flowery, only polished leather and polished wood. Whose house was this, and was she alone?

She tried to get up to find out, but she fell back upon her feet at once as a sharp, shooting pain collapsed her ankle. *Sprained it,* she thought, *but it must not be! I must get out of here at once—I'm in deadly danger.*

Reason stopped her from trying again. *I have no shoes. I have no clothing. I cannot walk. If I am to survive this, it must be done by using my wits, not by walking off into a storm. Where is the coach driver? Did he die when the carriage went over? Where is Lord Adrian Hensley?*

Lady Davina pulled herself up onto a sofa and looked around for something that might serve as a cane. As she did so, she heard a rustling sound coming from another room. She dove back to the floor, covered herself in the blanket, and pretended she was asleep.

She could hear someone entering the room, gaily humming a country air. The nerve of that Hensley man, singing songs now that he has me in his power! What limitless gall! She swore that Lord Adrian would feel the sting of her open hand before long.

Someone came over to her and shook her gently, trying to see whether she was awake or no. Lady Davina let her eyes spring open suddenly and when she saw her target, struck out at him just as she had promised herself she would.

When she opened her eyes, she saw Sir Philip Lansdowne!

"There, there," he said gently, looking vastly amused and holding her hands so she could not hit him again. "There's really no need for that, my dear."

"Don't you dare speak to me in that familiar way, liar! What do you mean by taking me in this way?" she stormed at him.

"I'm afraid I had a few very important things to say to you. When I learned you planned to leave for London last night, I had to seize the opportunity to arrange matters so we might enjoy a few private moments."

"What?" she asked angrily. "You do not love me, but you want to make love to me, is that it? Very well—you've gone to such a lot of trouble to have me—go ahead, quench your passions then, and be done with it. I'm sure I couldn't care less what you do, you heartless swine."

Sir Philip Lansdowne chuckled and shook his head.

"You do have a devil of a temper, Davina. I'll say that much for you. Do you wish to hit me again or can I let loose your wrists?"

"Let me go! I'll strike you whenever I wish."

"Davina, my dear, dear Davina."

"Stop speaking to me in that nauseating tone of voice, will you? You are a despicable, odious, unworthy, untrustworthy man. I thought it was Lord Adrian who had abducted me—but it's you! You're worse than he is!

"What scheme did you share with Lord Adrian? How dared you treat me as you did? Did you only wish to make me your mistress? Is that why you trifled with me, but were so craven that you would not make an honest woman of me?

"You'll never know how much I despise you, Philip. As much as I loved you once, just so much do I despise you, from the very bottom of my heart, hiding here in this little love nest!"

"A hunting box, actually," he pointed out. "It's a hunting box."

"Famous!" she said with a harsh laugh. "A notorious place for assignations, is it not? Here I find myself in your charming little hunting box, and now, I presume, your lusts come to the forefront and you wish to take from me by force what you did not wish to take by marriage?"

"Oh, no, my dear. You quite misunderstand things."

"How so?" she asked, not trusting him. "Nothing can ever reverse the feelings of hatred I harbor toward you. Nothing will assuage my humiliation!"

He continued, unfazed. "I want to ask you to do me the honor of consenting to be my wife."

"Fiend!" she screamed, throwing the nearest available object at him, which happened to be a candlestick. "Stop these lies at once!"

"It's true," he said, ducking the missile neatly. "I wanted to take you to wife the first moment I laid eyes upon you, at Sarah Keswick's party."

She shrieked some other unintelligible phrases and struck out at him again. Taking a strong hold of her wrists, Sir Philip replied softly, "All right, Davina, I have had quite enough of that. Stop behaving like a spiteful cat and a fool. Be quiet and listen to me."

"I won't!" she cried, and he transferred her two wrists to one of his hands and with his free hand, he put a piece of blanket up to her mouth, effectively silencing her. All of a sudden, Lady Davina began to laugh. At this, he removed the blanket, and put a warning finger to his lips.

"Hold your tongue, my dear. There are extenuating circumstances that fully explain my behavior. Have the goodness to listen to what they are.

"Listen to me, Davina. I love you now. I loved you then. I have always loved you, since that very first moment. I indeed wish to marry you."

"Never! Never in this world!" she retorted. "Don't be ridiculous!"

"You *shall* hear me out, cat. Some time ago, there was a wager between myself and Lord Adrian Hensley at the Raffles Club. The result of this wager was that I lost, and that, as a result, I owed Lord Adrian, upon my word as a gentleman, whatever favor he desired of me."

"Rubbish! Don't try to gammon me! I may be a green girl, but even *I* know that favor or fifty is never played out!" she said decisively.

"It was that night. There were and are witnesses to the wager who will back up what I say, some of whom are known to you as honorable gentlemen: Colonel Lord Edward Crenshaw, Harry Winslow, Lord Butely. Any of them can back up my story—they merely do not know the precise terms of the favor that was asked of me."

"Oh, really? And just what was the favor?" she asked contemptuously. "Did Lord Adrian ask you to make love to me and win my heart and then deny it?"

"It was so," he admitted softly, taking her hand in his. "It was just so."

"You men and your disgusting honor!" she cried, shocked. "Whyever would you so debase yourself as to accede to those terms? I never would have believed it of you! What kind of a man *are* you?"

Sir Philip Lansdowne looked rather rueful and replied, "I am a man of honor, to the very core. As a man of honor and a man of his word, I was required to discharge my gaming debts at once and in full.

"The favor that Lord Adrian demanded of me was dishonorable, stemming from an execrable desire to wreak vengeance upon you. I am not proud of the part I played in it, and I despised it from the first."

"As well you might," she said, somewhat mollified.

"Can you deny that I tried to prepare you for it? Did I not beg you to trust me and to remember to trust me even when all outward things pointed against it!"

"But it was wrong of you!" she said with some acerbity.

"Wrong, yes—but it had no real meaning. I spoke a false phrase, once, to satisfy a debt: they were words, only words. It was a denial of a moment, one isolated moment of farce. I could deny I loved you, say the words I had to say, and then, after I had played my part, the spell was broken and I was free again.

"I never felt anything but love for you—that I was forced to deny you once, for a single moment, must not be allowed to wipe out everything else.

"You must know that I love you, Davina. Somewhere, deep in your heart, you must know."

Sir Philip took her into his arms and swept her into his strong embrace, kissing her first gently, and increasingly with a deep physical passion he barely held in check. Feeling an overwhelming surge of emotion well up in her, Lady Davina gave in at last to her profound love and forgave him from the depths of her heart.

* * *

THE WINTER WAGER 315

The crisp winter morning found the two lovers wrapped securely in many thick, soft woolen blankets, lying lazily in front of the embers of a fire which was nearly out. Sir Philip woke first and planted a kiss on the cheek of his still-sleepy love. Then, with great competence, he laid out a new fire and soon had it blazing.

Lady Davina yawned delicately as she awoke; she rubbed her eyes and, like magic, Sir Philip's face appeared, leaning over her solicitously. At this, she gave him the most delicious smile he had ever seen, making him desire very much to take his love into his arms again, but there were other, more prosaic, things to be seen to first.

"How is your ankle, my dear?" he inquired, patting it lightly.

"Passing good, I think. Not so bad as yesterday, but I still don't think it will bear my weight."

"Let me get you something to walk with."

He found a walking stick, and gave it to Lady Davina, who soon found she could hobble about quite well. She began to explore various nooks and crannies, found a very nice, small book room, and curled up in a chair with a leather bound volume of poetry.

"I'll make us something warm to drink, shall I?" asked Sir Philip, interrupting her briefly.

"Oh. Can you cook?" Lady Davina asked in a tone of surprise.

"I, happily, can do all manner of interesting things. As you come to know me better," he said with a meaningful tone, "you shall learn what those things are."

She blushed a little and made no reply, but closed her book and hobbled out into the kitchen, looking for eggs and bread and cheese, which she presently found.

"There is even some milk here, Philip!" Lady Davina

said with some awe. "Why is this hunting box supplied with food when it's not in season? How can a house be so well stocked when there are no servants to be found?"

"Ah, well, you see, I gave the servants the day off. My man will come by to see to our needs a little later on in the morning," he admitted.

Lady Davina found this intelligence annoying in the extreme, and she snapped, "This is *your* hunting box? You *planned* on all this happening, did you? It wasn't just a matter of intercepting my message to my brother yesterday night and abducting me on the spur of the moment—you had it all planned out beforehand!"

"Ah, well, yes—of course I planned it, my dear," he said carefully. "Why should I not have? Had I not planned all the details, the affair might have been most imprudent. Taking such risks as that is not in my character. It was perfectly logical to assume that once you witnessed me renouncing my love for you in front of someone else, you might become a tad out of sorts, angry with me just a bit, and I might have to spirit you away in *just* the sort of fashion in which I ultimately *did*. Hence, I had to allow for the possibility."

"Indeed?" she cried, crossly. "I could kill you, Philip!"

"I'm sure you could, my dearest, although I really don't see why," he replied smoothly.

"Because—you have used me abominably."

"I have not, my dearest Davina," he pointed out without rancor. "I did *only* what I had to do—I met the terms of the wager. By means of that unfortunate favor, I was fortunate enough to meet the love of my life. Realizing that early on, I did all that I could, under the circumstances, to see to it that our mutual happiness might be achieved. It was perfectly logical, really."

"If I hadn't already forgiven you, I'd never forgive you," she said with a dangerous look.

"You must admit it has all worked out quite well. I recognized at once that you were a female with a strong taste for drama. What could be more romantic? A flight through a snowstorm, nay, a blizzard . . . an overturned coach, a romantic hideaway . . ." Sir Philip's voice trailed off theatrically.

"The coach overturned because you are ham-handed," she snapped.

"It did not! I am not! That's gross slander, Davina, and I won't have it! I know that road as well as I know my own face—every rut and bend and rabbit-hole. When I was younger, I made quite a hobby of overturning vehicles of every kind at that precise point. Curricles, phaetons, barouches—I can overturn any one of them on cue."

"Rubbish. Do you really expect me to believe that?"

"Not necessarily," he said. "Though it's quite true, I assure you. I can point to the fact that I am a member of the Four-in-Hand Club, where just such driving follies of one's youth can be pursued by entirely grown men."

"Is that so? I suppose it must be. But, by the way, how came you to put your hands on a travelling coach that could be locked from the outside?" she asked suspiciously.

"Oh, *that!* It's very special to us—an heirloom. It's the old family abduction coach. Every old family has one. Doesn't yours?"

"I'm sure I wouldn't know," she said haughtily. "What I object to in all of this is that you, Philip, *expected* that a night spent with you in this hunting box would restore my good opinion of you."

"I wouldn't say that I *expected* it, precisely. I certainly *hoped* so. I took a calculated risk. Either you would forgive me, in which case my life would have meaning, or you would not, in which case my life would be at an end."

"Nonsense," she declared. "You'd never go into a decline on my behalf!"

"I certainly would have," he replied firmly. "If I had lost you. But let us be serious for once. Come here, Davina. You must look at me right now and tell me that you love me."

She dropped her bantering tone immediately and looked anew at the man she loved, searching his face long and hard to find in it the answer to his question.

When Sir Philip looked at Lady Davina, he was looking beyond her mere golden beauty: he was seeing the woman he wanted to be with till the end of his days, the woman whom he would protect with his own life. Every plane of her face, every curl, every movement was inexpressibly dear to him. He could only wait with impatience till they could wed and he could claim her as his own, for all time.

He lowered his tone, and spoke to her in a voice meant for her ears alone. "Davina, you must know how much I love you. Do you return my regard? If you do, you must say these words to me: *I love you Philip, and I will marry you.*"

She allowed Sir Philip Lansdowne to take her small hands in his large ones and bring them to his lips. Seeing upon his face all the love and tenderness a woman could ever wish for, she smiled her divine smile once again.

"Well, Davina?" he asked her, "will you or won't you have me?"

Happier than she ever knew a person could be, Lady Davina whispered, "Yes, of course, I will. I do love you, my dearest Philip, and I will marry you!"

About the Author

Isobel Linton lives with her family on Cape Cod. Her many Zebra regency romances include FALSE PRETENSES and AN IMPROMPTU CHARADE. She is currently working on her next Zebra regency romance, THE COUNTERFEIT HEIRESS, to be published in July 1997. She loves hearing from readers and you may write to her c/o Zebra Books. Please include a self-addressed, stamped envelope if you wish a response.

ROMANCE FROM FERN MICHAELS

DEAR EMILY   (0-8217-4952-8, $5.99)

WISH LIST   (0-8217-5228-6, $6.99)

AND IN HARDCOVER:

VEGAS RICH   (1-57566-057-1, $25.00)

Available wherever paperbacks are sold, or order direct from the Publisher. Send cover price plus 50¢ per copy for mailing and handling Penguin USA, P.O. Box 999, c/o Dept. 17109, Bergenfield, NJ 07621. Residents of New York and Tennessee must include sales tax. DO NOT SEND CASH.